The Argon Factor

Heather Harlow

Sojourn Publishing, LLC, PO Box 1234, Sedona, AZ 12345

Cover design by Heather Harlow;
cover photograph by Maxim Pasko.
www.TheRealHeatherHarlow.com
www.HeatherHarlow.net

This is a work of fiction. Names, characters, places, and
incidents either are the product of the author's imagination or
are used fictitiously. Any resemblance to actual persons,
living or dead, events, or locales is entirely coincidental
and not intended by the author.

PUBLISHING HISTORY

Sojourn Publishing, LLC / September 2015

ISBN: 978-1-62747-171-8
eISBN: 978-1-62747-172-5

Library of Congress Cataloguing-in-Publication Data
Printed in the United States of America

Acknowledgments

Thank you to all of my friends and family who made writing this book possible.

Special thanks to Beth Burklin, who without you, I'm not sure I would have ever have gotten this book out of my head and onto paper. You introduced me to a program that gave me the inspiration to make this happen. You were there for me to help me with words and especially with the final editing, when I was so stressed.

Thanks to Kari Smith who was there with me every step of the way. You provided me with invaluable technical editing and have been my consummate sounding board throughout.

My deepest gratitude to Cheryle Boyle, my fellow author, who cried with me and was there to help me through the most difficult time in my life. Your friendship and support is priceless. Being able to collaborate with you on our book releases and promotions has been invaluable and encouraging.

Thanks to the Tom Bird publishing program, Sojourn Publishing, RamaJon, and the authors in the program who showed me the way to publishing my first book and provided insight and guidance.

Thanks to my sister, Melanie Sloan, who's last minute editing was essential to showing me what was needed to make this book flow and read with ease. You really have a hidden talent for editing.

Prologue

Susan is pacing in front of picture windows that depict the most gorgeous Caribbean beach scene. If she didn't know better, she would think that she was actually at the beach. Unfortunately, she wasn't at the beach – or anywhere tropical. Far from it. She was hiding in a secret, underground, alien complex beneath the city of Boston. 'Of all places, of all things, how did I end up *here?*' she thought to herself. She reached up to rub her temples, feeling a migraine coming on.

Susan woke up all alone about an hour or so ago. It was *his* apartment; extremely spacious and luxurious, with the most ultramodern flair she'd ever seen. She was glad that she was alone; she didn't think she could deal with *him* right now. 'He's an *alien,* for God's sake!' her mind screamed at her.

She didn't think that she could process all this right now. She'd grown close to him and was finally beginning to trust him. Hell, just to trust again, period, is a major milestone for her, especially when it came to men and relationships. What the hell is she going to do?

'Escape, escape,' kept coming into her mind. "If only I could escape to where everything is right in the world, as normal as normal is these days," she said out loud. She wanted desperately to escape. She had a terrible headache. She decided to take the pills *he* left for her. She hoped by taking them she could escape, if only for a little while. She wanted sleep, and to get rid of this headache, forgetting.... forgetting all about him and his touch.

Chapter 1

She's uncontrollably trembling when she wakes from the dream. The sheets on her bed are tangled and wet from her sweat.

Still trembling and cold, Susan grabs her duvet and pulls it up over herself for warmth. Stunned, she lies there and falls back asleep. The dream continues —-

She's struggling and trying to move. He's touching her bare breasts. Her arms won't move and she can't stop him from taking off her bathing suit top. He pinches her nipples and she tries to cry out, but it just comes out as a bare whimper. He bends his head over and sucks on each nipple in turn. She tries to move her body back and forth, but she can't budge.

He pulls up and starts kissing her, by forcing her mouth to open and sticking his tongue in. She tries to move her head from side to side. She can't move. She doesn't want to kiss him. He is so disgusting! She just wishes it would stop.

Again, she tries to move her head from side to side to get him to stop sliming his tongue in her mouth, but her head just won't move. She might as well have been trussed up in a BDSM dungeon for all that she could do to stop him from mauling her body. She wants it to stop, so she closes her eyes – at least she won't have to watch.

'Can she ignore it if it's not violent?' Her self-conscious reasoned, 'Don't look; you can ignore it. Pretend you're somewhere else. It can't be violent if you're not conscious. No resistance is non-violent, isn't it?'

The fear permeates throughout her body, causing her to sweat and thrash about; once again, kicking off her duvet. In her dream, she can only lie there, unable to move, although she continues to try.

The scenes are vague. There's so much sudden movement that the details evade her, but the emotions and fear are clear.

He leaves her for a moment and then comes back, spreading her legs wide. Try as she might, she can't stop him.

He is towering over her, pinching her nipples as he slides inside her in one quick, hard movement. Every time he thrusts into her, it is hard and rough. He grabs her hips and holds her up to him, and pounds her hard.

Her shoulders and back are in terrible pain, rubbing against the knots in the roped canopy. Over and over again he pounds into her. It isn't hard to keep her eyes closed. She just wishes it would stop and be over. He is hurting her back. Tears are leaking out of her eyes as she keeps trying to move, to no avail. She gives up; she's beaten and can't take anymore when he finishes. 'Oh God, I hope he used a condom,' she thinks.

Her subconscious wonders 'what will people think of her?' If she doesn't tell anyone, she can bury it and forget. Nobody will need to know. After all, she wasn't harmed physically. She was just given no choice. It's revolting to have to be intimate when you don't want it. Having sex with somebody you'd rather not have touch your body...

'Slut,' her self-conscious called her. 'You're a stupid slut for getting yourself into this situation,' it claimed.

She wakes herself up, yelling, "Shut up! I am NOT!" Freezing, she gropes for the duvet and pulls it up again. Her heart is racing as she just lies there trying to get warm. She can't believe she dreamed it again so soon. The entire dream was so disturbing, it was absolutely awful. Her perpetrator seemed to get more revolting in every dream.

It's the same dream, every time, but only occurs when she's stressed. Trying to land her job was excruciatingly painful, with numerous interviews and tests. She had been so nervous that she'd dreamed the awful dream several times a week. When finally she started the new job, she was no longer stressed and the dream stopped.

At last, she was in Boston with the job she wanted. She should be okay now, so why did she dream it again? She'd have to think about that, but for now, it was time to shake it off and get up.

She looked over at the clock. 4:58 a.m., still a half hour before she has to get up to go to work. 'Ugghhh, no sense in going back to sleep,' she thinks to herself. She grabs her cell phone to thumb through her personal email and world news before she has to get out of bed.

An email from Boston Fertility Clinic was at the top of her inbox. She immediately opened it. She'd been on the waiting list for sperm only one year and anticipated another two years before it was her turn. It was so difficult to get sperm from reliable and reputable sources these days. There were so many sketchy sperm banks out there. And she needed a specialty clinic like this one in Boston.

Her fertility problem was the major reason she chose this clinic. Her doctor is a specialist whose treatments have been proven to overcome the uterine acidity issue she has. It's the only program in the world for her specific problem. But just as important, their sperm bank has the most sought-after sperm on Earth. Their criteria for acceptance were extremely high, and their screening procedures were second to none. Seeing an email from them immediately made Susan's heart race with excitement. She quickly opened it to read:

Dear Ms. Caldwell,

Due to recent changes to our waitlist, you have been moved up to the twentieth position on our list for sperm fertilization treatments.

Dr. Kalhoun would like for you to schedule an appointment for two weeks from now. You will need to begin reception procedures as soon as possible. It is estimated that you will have your insemination procedure in less than three months.

Please contact us at (email address)…

Susan's heart was now racing faster, but this time for joy instead of fear. She read the email several times. She couldn't believe it! She banged her feet in the bed and even thought of jumping on the bed like a little kid, she was so excited. But common sense took over and she decided to get out of bed. All she could do was pace, back and forth, thinking, 'in less than three months I'll be pregnant!! Wow!!' She'd only been on the wait list one year. It must be her special condition that bumped her up because they needed more case studies. Susan was honored to have been chosen for the particular study. This is amazing! 'A_MAZ_ING!!' Her excitement was fueling her daydreams and plans for the future.

Susan always wanted a family of her own. She had started putting her plans in motion, just the way most women these days. All you have to do is decide when you want to have a child, and then you sign up at a sperm bank with enough advance notice that by the time your number is up, it is the time you chose and planned for. All the noteworthy sperm banks had waitlists. They regularly published their standard waiting periods, so it was easy for women to plan. Rarely did men and women marry and have children the way they did in her great-grandparents' day and earlier. Women took it upon themselves to plan and make a family if they desired. But, not every woman did.

While Susan was making the arrangements to plan a family, she had to face a unique situation because of her special fertility problem. It had been difficult to find a stateside physician who specialized in acidic uterine linings. Susan's planning had been more tiresome and challenging due to needing a specialist, so the feeling of excitement and underlying anticipation was more rewarding to her and shot her adrenaline through the roof. She was so happy. It was easy to forget the dream. She didn't give it a second thought as she turned on the water for the shower.

Susan steps into the shower and feels the hot water run down her body, soaking her. She puts her head directly under the water and lets the water run all down her face, rinsing the night away. Feeling the pure exhilaration, she shakes the water from her face and begins washing her hair, when she remembers the project at work.

The potential code breach at work has her worried. She frowns into the wall as she rinses her hair.

Susan gets out of the shower and gently rubs her hair with a towel. She's anxious, her stomach is turning over and the butterflies are out of control. She's going to have a baby! But she has to deal with the code breach first. Her job is of ultimate importance if she is to support herself and her new family.

She needs to get to the office early today. The stress of a code breach is likely what is disturbing her. It is time to get to the bottom of it and exorcise it from her mind, so she can concentrate on planning for her child.

She hears her cell phone ringing as she is drying herself with her large bath towel. She races to the phone. When she manages to get across the bedroom and answer it, she is out of breath. "Hello," she pants into the phone, catching her breath quickly.

"Susan, this is Luis Perez, part of your Boston security team," he began.

"Yes, I'm glad you called. What did you find?" she says easily, as she automatically slips into her professional mode. She doesn't have to tell him that she is standing naked, dripping water all over her hardwood floors. Despite her attempts, she can't wrap the towel around herself with one hand, so she puts it on the floor and stands on it.

"Sorry to bother you so early, but I had to tell you that I found the code. It's on the Apache development server. I was afraid to tell anyone but you," he explained. "I'm just finishing up the night shift. I had to come downtown to the office to log onto the server. That's the key. Whoever put this on the server had to have been in this office. It's the only way you can log in to the server, as its part of the Security 1 group of high-priority, high-availability servers, even though it's a development server. It's connected to the production servers and has to follow the same login protocols."

"Did you figure out who it is?" Susan asked anxiously.

"No, I haven't had enough time. It has taken me over a week to uncover all the anomalies and tie the sequence of events together that had to have occurred for a breach of this magnitude. The intruder's methodology is extremely sophisticated, and unlike anything I've ever seen or even heard of before. That's why it has taken me so long," Luis provided.

"Okay, well, have you been able to verify that it is compromising the production systems?" she asked.

"I'm not sure. I haven't been able to dig to that level yet because I don't have permissions. I submitted a user-access request that I'd need you to approve for me to access the production boxes. If you can approve it this morning when you get to the office, it will be ready when I come back in this afternoon, after I've had some sleep," Luis said.

"Okay, yes, of course. I'll make sure that is the first thing I do. As a matter of fact, I think I can do it while I'm driving in to work. Is there anything else I should know?" she asked.

Luis let out a loud sigh, "I'm exhausted, and I'm leaving as soon as we hang up. I'm just ending a twelve-hour shift of OT, but I've sent you a status update with links and examples to your email. I also left a few voicemails on your office line." Changing his tone, low and urgent, he continued, "You need to be cautious. This is the most sophisticated intrusion I've ever seen. Be very careful who you talk to and tell about this. It has me worried."

"Of course. Please go home and get some rest. I'll review everything and approve your access. Let's talk again when your shift starts tonight," she requested before hanging up.

The criticality of this potential data breach was alarming to Susan. She wondered if it was even safe for her to have a conversation with her boss about this. Mr. Jones is a nincompoop and would probably turn it around and get both her and Luis in trouble. She had to have proof first and be able to explain it. But time was of the essence, especially due to the way wealth is controlled in these times, now that gangs were eradicated.

The world economy, recovering from the worst financial downfall in history due to worldwide gang control, was in its initial stages of recovery and re-digitizing of monetary assets, including money. Physically, cities are showing progress in repairing storefronts, and refurbishing buildings. But the monetary infrastructure has almost completely recovered due to technology advancements and GTS's ability to secure the data stores.

If it hadn't been for GTS and their alien abilities, rampant crime and gangs would have continued to be prevalent across the globe. Once GTS stepped in to take back the cities for the world's governments, they efficiently and with little bloodshed eradicated all of the gangs, reducing crime to pre-Civil War levels. But the damage done was catastrophic.

The cities were trashed. Storefronts were practically nonexistent after the ravaging. Slowly the cities were beginning to recover and clean themselves up, but it had been less than two years since GTS had wiped out the gangs. While they brought violent, physical crime to an all-time low for the modern era, there still existed rampant computer crime.

Because computerized crime is at an all-time high, it was even more important that it be under the alien protection, in the guise of GTS. Given that most wealth is controlled by computers nowadays and is simply a value in a database, it only makes sense for crime to be aimed where the wealth is located. The governments try to add to it in underhanded ways, plus it's an obvious target for criminals. The world needed a data protection solution and only GTS had one.

GTS Security, again stepped in to guide the humans, and manage the funds as an outside third party. Because no countries used cash anymore, data breaches were now of the highest priority. GTS's alien code was impenetrable by humans. They knew they could keep the fragile world financial recovery safe and growing. Keeping it safe was another way to prove to the leaders of the world they could be trusted.

Their strategy for keeping the growing economy safe, involved opening three branches across the globe. They set up an office in Boston, responsible for protecting all the monetary data in the United States/North-South America and European markets. Its two sister companies divided responsibility for the rest of the world: one for Africa/India/Middle East in New Delhi and one for Asia/Australia/New Zealand in Perth. If there ever was a breach in any branch, the entire world's financial markets could be in jeopardy. The massive impact and reach that this current breach in the Boston office could have on the world is what stunned Susan as she contemplated the task ahead of her.

Susan tried not let the magnanimity of the potential situation crowd her mind too much as she quickly dressed and fed the dog before heading out. She couldn't let it bother her or else it would paralyze her, she knew it. 'Don't worry and don't stress,' she told herself as she got in the car.

While driving to work, she listened to all of Luis's voicemails and went through all of his emails. After reviewing them all, she was certain Luis had found a viable and active security data breach. Embittered by the thought of such an intrusion, Susan was growing impatient to log on to the main server and verify his findings once she was onsite. If only she could get to work faster.

She couldn't make her car go any faster in this traffic, but at least she was able to work during the commute. She was lucky: she had made enough money from her last job to invest in a self-driving car.

Engaging the autopilot when on the freeway allowed cars to drive themselves. All cars had bumper sensors, Wi-Fi and a data-transmitter program which enabled them to move seamlessly down the interstate without stoppages. Most people had cars with autopilot, thus there was only one lane for manual cars on the interstates. It helped manage the flow of traffic immensely. There may be some slowdowns every now and again, but traffic was never the way it used to be with human-driven cars. For her, the best part was being able to work while she commuted the forty-five minutes to work every day. But today, her urgency to get to work fast was making her very impatient and frustrated with her autopilot.

As she arrived at work, there were emergency vehicles, fire trucks, police cars and even an ambulance parked in the covered drop-off area of the building. The company parking garage entrance was blocked from incoming traffic. Police directed her across the street to a lot they'd secured for the day for GTS employees.

She made her way back across the street and had to walk through all the emergency personnel and past their vehicles to get to the entrance of her building. She had had to show her ID badge a few times in order to pass. She couldn't imagine what was going on, but she finally decided to ask somebody what had happened.

She approached an officer who had just helped load the ambulance with a covered body. "Excuse me sir, what happened?"

After waving the ambulance to take off, the office looked at Susan, noted her ID badge was from GTS and said, "A bomb exploded in the car garage." He didn't seem too keen on providing her with any more information.

Susan thought of Luis. Before the officer had time to turn to leave, she asked quickly, "Was anybody hurt? Here's my badge, I have security three clearance." she said hoping it would get the police officer to give her more details.

The police officer examined her badge and after a minute of consideration replied, "Yes ma'am, but I don't know many details. We could only make out the last name on the driver's license: Perez. We have investigators working on identifying the car make and model. We couldn't even make out what color the car was because it was so badly damaged. It could be days before forensics can confirm and cross-reference it to the company. Everything was so badly burned in the explosion that it will take some time to figure out."

'Perez... Luis Perez, could it be?' she thought to herself. The police officer left Susan standing there in shock. Poor Luis. It might not be him, but it was too close to what she knew for it not to be him.

She herself, like her car, was on autopilot as she walked to the elevator and started to enter it as soon as the doors opened. She was in such a daze, she didn't even think to watch to see if anyone was coming out. In the mornings, it was unusual for anyone to get off in the lobby, as everyone was going in to the office; but still, the standard common courtesy for a seasoned professional working in a downtown building was to wait.

Susan didn't wait this morning. The elevator doors opened and she walked right into a wet, sweaty, smelly, solid wall. Surprised to run into anything at all, she said, "Oh, I'm so sorry." It was a man, and she quickly tried to step out of his way. 'OMG, he really reeked!' she thought. But damn, he was handsome and had a nice hard body. It was odd, but she felt immediately attracted to him.

The man, wearing running clothes and running shoes, seemed to hardly notice her as he gently steadied her shoulders, saying "No problem." He left the elevator and walked toward the building exit.

'Peeyu,' she thought. It didn't matter if he was interested or not, he really *did* stink, even after he left the elevator. Susan covered her hand over her mouth and nose, thinking, 'On second thought I'll pass on that guy!' The smell was awful, she really should get off and take another elevator, but too late – it was already on the way to her office on the forty-first floor.

She loved her office with a window high up in the sky. It was another perk that she loved about her new job, besides having finally gotten the job... Her enthusiasm impacted her work and every day she excelled at managing her department. She would go to work for the day, and come home to her dog and an otherwise empty, but meticulously clean house.

She had a lovely, quiet life with the house, the dog, the car, and soon a baby!! She'd lived her life very independently.

She'd had no choice, since her parents had passed on long ago and her one sister, Myrtle, lived so far away that it was difficult to even go see her.

And why would she want to visit her anyway? It was always so trying and emotionally taxing. Myrtle was always telling her what to do. And to give *men* a chance! Myrtle seemed to live in the dark ages. Her sister was living in a time of their great-great grandparents' day, back at the beginning of the second millennium. Those were the days when women thought they had to have a man or a partner.

Why would she want a man in her life anyway? It'd just complicate her life and add more drama. These days, men didn't want a relationship any more than most women did. The world had changed. It was all about one-night stands and hookups.

Most women in the modern world were completely independent and lived without men. She had several friends from college who were single parents, on purpose. Going to the fertility clinic to purchase sperm to have a baby was the new norm among the human females. So much had changed since her ancestors' day and the old-fashioned fairy-tales. Just because her sister chose to have a husband, it definitely wasn't the normal thing to do. But she admired Myrtle for being different.

Susan had never met any man that was good enough to even attempt what Myrtle had chosen. Besides, dating had become so tiresome, and the quality of men she was meeting never matched up. They were good enough for a toss, but even then one had to be so careful of diseases, it wasn't worth it.

Because of the numerous pitfalls, Susan had given up on dating years ago but she was living an otherwise normal life. She had all the expected amenities that a young professional should have and she was very satisfied with her accomplishments. But as she thought of the future, her stomach butterflies fluttered again as she thought of having a baby – and a family of her own.

More and more, Susan had contemplated having a child. She'd been on the sperm-donor waitlist for only one year, but had a three wait time expectancy which was normal for the high-quality sperm banks. Even though she had a special fertility condition, her doctors were confident that with the proper supplements, she could conceive. It was expensive to try. Thankfully, her girlfriends said it was totally worth the cost. They'd had babies by sperm banks and were extremely pleased and happy as could be with the outcome. Plus, Susan was able to control the timeframe, at least she had thought she could. Now, she was going to change her plans, but she could do that. Moving her plans up was something she could still control.

Susan had to stay within the confines of what she herself could control. She had to be the one in control of her life. She couldn't trust the things that she couldn't control, simply because she couldn't control them.

The elevator doors opened on her floor startling her out of her thoughts. She was anxious to get to work on verifying the code breach. Her work was something she definitely could control, and it was very rewarding for her. Time to get to work.

As soon as the doors opened on the lobby level, Christoph tried to get off the elevator, but he bumped into a lovely, wonderful-smelling woman. Clearly, he'd startled her. She quickly apologized. He replied with a curt "No problem," as he grasped her arms to steady her while he sidestepped out of her way. She was shorter than he was by about a foot, so he was able to steady her easily. He was sweaty and grimy from his workout in his private gym in the basement of the GTS building.

Christoph looked into her startled green eyes as he released his hold on her. She had the most beautiful green eyes he'd ever seen. He was fascinated by green eyes, since none of his people had green eyes. Only the Earth humans had green eyes. She was beautiful, but she had a frown on her face from bumping into his sweaty body. And she seemed troubled by more than just running into him. As he walked away, the doors closed.

He didn't have time to linger; he needed to get his run in so he'd have enough time to shower and change before the first round of all-day board meetings started. Until then, he needed to consider the bomb that had gone off in his company's parking garage and figure out possible culprits.

As he walked onto the sidewalk and left the property, he turned the corner to run down the city's main street. He timed his run for this hour every morning, because very few business people were headed into the office this early. As he picked his way around the few early birds, he wondered why the beautiful woman on the elevator was coming in to the GTS office so early. His company hired many humans, as it was necessary to keep up their front. But, he never saw any of his human employees this early. His mind wandered back to the explosion in the company garage that had killed one of his third-shift human employees. His personal security team was reviewing the security footage to see if they could find any leads, and confirm who had been killed. It was disturbing to him that this had happened on his watch.

His phone rang, "Yes," he answered.

It was his private alien security team lead. "We've found the footage of the employee leaving his workstation, entering and exiting the elevator. We confirmed it was Luis Perez, a third-shift security team member. But we can't pinpoint when his car was tampered with. There seems to be footage missing from the parking garage," the security expert revealed.

"Okay, I want to see the footage you have. Send a secure link to my tablet so that I can view it when I get back to the building," Christoph requested. "Once I look it over, I'll send a copy to the human police task force to help them confirm his identity faster."

"Yes, Commander," the security expert confirmed.

Christoph disconnected the call, and turned to double back and make his way to the building with haste. As he jogged down the street, he thought of what a huge difference his jog here is in Boston this morning compared to two days ago in Africa.

He'd just returned from a three-month business trip in Africa. The GTS security forces had finally gained control of the area, eliminating the last of the global gangs that threatened the peace there. The infrastructure in Africa was a total nightmare, and it would take over twenty months for them to repair enough of the damage to give the Africans a working telecommunications and electrical grid. He had had to stay long enough to make sure the plan was laid out and timed in a reasonable way. Thankfully, most Africans still lived off the land and were accustomed to not having cell phones or electricity. But still, he felt better for making sure their lives were no longer threatened. He'd left one of his trusted staffers there to oversee the execution and implementation of the plan.

While Christoph was a natural-born protector, he had an ability to gather strong supporters and delegate efficiently to those he trusted. It increased his ability to protect because it widened his reach. He was a protector not only of his own people, but of all humans on Earth. He wanted to see the planet advance to a state where peace was present for all, and where everyone lived in harmony – just the same as on his home planet, Argon. Christoph was ready to pave a new road, one that nobody had ever traveled before. It was his destiny to do so for his people. His father had given him that responsibility. Luckily for Christoph, they found a universe, and planets, that would sustain Argon life and provide them with the planet they needed. As they observed the planet, they couldn't turn a blind eye to the massive troubles the gangs had caused.

His people had watched the downfall of Earth's global society and the emergence of gangs around the world. The gangs had destroyed the inner cities and had begun ravaging the suburbs. It had come to a point where there wasn't anywhere on Earth that was safe. The human governments hadn't been able to enforce law and order due to political corruption. It had taken Christoph two years to convince a global coalition to let his company take control of the cities to give them back to the governments.

They initially granted him an opportunity to prove himself by restoring order to the northeastern corridor of North America. Once he'd shown what he could do, the coalition had given him free rein to restore order everywhere. With the advanced technology available to him and his special teams of alien security experts, it had been a steady and sure advancement. Although the human coalitions had no idea he and his team were aliens.

Of course, his GTS security teams were made up of Argon warriors – but it still hadn't been easy, by any means. Their success would never have been possible if they hadn't been aliens, with extremely advanced technology and surveillance systems in place. Human gangs were no match for theirs. It had come to a point that any gang member caught would be eliminated, until finally, gangs around the world started dissolving, and finally losing their power completely.

Eventually, each city that Christoph's team entered took less time to clean up than the one before. The gang threats took only two years to eradicate on the entire planet. Now, after two years of peace, and slow government re-integration with the people, the humans were beginning to rebuild. It was a perfect opportunity for his species to help them.

He, personally, took on the responsibility for insuring that the Earth humans were protected – and also educated, in order to bring them more quickly along their evolution timeline. It was his wish to focus on Earth's advancement so his people could integrate more easily.

Chapter 2

Susan had been working for two hours, reviewing Luis's emails and the links he'd provided, when the phone rang. "Ms. Caldwell, this is Nurse Adkins at the Boston Fertility Clinic."

"Yes, hello. I received the email this morning to schedule my appointment for two weeks from now," Susan replied.

"Yes, ma'am. However, I think we can skip that appointment if I can confirm your pharmacy. Do you still the use the Walgreens on Barton Street?" the nurse asked.

"Yes, that's still my pharmacy, and my insurance is current with them," Susan answered.

"Okay, I'll be calling in a prescription for you this morning. We need you to pick it up as soon as possible and begin taking it in order to prepare you. Given your special circumstances, you'll need to be taking this prescription in order to ensure conception through the procedures," the nurse explained.

"Okay, I can do that. But don't you also have to provide me with special supplements by injection?" Susan asked.

"Yes, either your partner has to be taking the supplement or we will administer it when we fertilize you through artificial insemination," the nurse explained.

"Okay, great, that's what I thought. I'll start taking the pills today. Should I schedule an appointment two weeks from today?" she asked.

"We will need to schedule it two weeks after you begin your next cycle. Please call us when that starts so that we can get you on the schedule," Nurse Adkins said.

"Oh? I thought the email said to schedule my appointment two weeks from now," she said.

"Yes, ma'am, that's standard in our emails. That appointment was for your examination to get these supplements, but since your records are already in order," the nurse explained easily, "we can skip that appointment for you – and I'm able to call in this prescription."

"Okay, terrific," Susan said. "Thank you so much for calling. I'll call you just as soon as my cycle starts," she confirmed.

"Have a good day," the nurse said, before hanging up.

Susan sat at her desk, contemplating what was to come. She was going to have a baby! For a few minutes she couldn't actually believe that this was going to be happening. She was so excited that the butterflies came back again. She'd been waiting for such a long time. For a moment, she let her mind wander into the future and fantasize about what her life will be like with a little family... her child, her dog and herself.

It was difficult to pull herself away from her fantasy and back to her work, back to the monumental task at hand and the code breach. She'd much rather fantasize about having a baby – but through sheer perseverance, she set her mind back to the task at hand: finding where the code breach occurred.

She still hadn't been able to confirm where Luis had found the code breach. Though she wasn't an expert at it, she was certain that she knew the code well enough to read it and figure it out. The stress was starting to overwhelm her, combined with her excitement over the baby. She needed to get up from her workstation and take a short break.

As she walked about on her floor, it seemed as if everyone in the building was in a tizzy. Her floor alone had an unnatural buzz of people talking here and there, which had grown quite a bit over the past hour as people arrived at work. Arriving in the break room, she saw groups of people gathered by the windows, gossiping, as they looked at the scene below. Susan didn't have time to socialize; she needed to figure out what Luis had found and why he might have been murdered. But first, she needed a fresh cup of coffee.

Thankfully, there was a fresh pot that had just finished brewing. She poured herself a cup and headed back to her desk. She kept thinking that it had to be Luis who was in the blown-up car. There were too many coincidences – and she had never believed in coincidences.

Back at her desk, Susan goes through Luis's emails another time. As she goes through them this time, she makes notes on a notepad to serve as her checklist. After her coffee is gone, in the sixth email, she notices a line she didn't notice before. He says he left projector equipment in the main boardroom. Susan doesn't even understand why he would be using the equipment, but it's best if she picks it up before those board meetings start today.

Susan heads to the elevator and punches the button to go down. She arrives in the boardroom, and it looks deserted except for the bulky equipment on the main table. Thinking the room empty, she waltzes right in.

She starts to gather up the equipment and wrap up the power cords when she sees the sweaty runner sitting on a couch at a corner table. Although she was in shock from the news of Luis's death when she bumped into the man, she couldn't forget his handsome face. He had been wearing running clothes earlier, but now he was dressed in a three-piece designer suit. He looked absolutely delectable, but her mind wasn't able to process that for more than a brief moment.

They nod to each other, and she says, "Hello."

He replies with a "Good morning," before going back to studying the financial spreadsheets he had sprawled out in front of him.

Susan is in a hurry to get this equipment before the meetings start, and doesn't give the man much more thought. The man in the suit seems oblivious to her, as he continues to study the papers in front of him and type on his tablet while she collects what she came for.

As Susan finished gathering the equipment, she finds a handwritten note with the equipment, which read, "*Danger, be careful. I think I'm being watched.*" Susan audibly gasps when she reads the note. An unexpected fear creeps up her spine.

The man looks up from his papers and asks, "Is everything okay?"

"Yes, yes, I just nicked my finger," she lies easily, as she thinks to put her finger in her mouth. The note unexpectedly raises her senses, and the hairs on the back of her neck. She has to figure out what the hell is going on with this code!

Quickly, she tucks the note in her pants pocket and awkwardly collects the bulky equipment. When she arrives at the boardroom door, the man is suddenly there to open the door for her. Shyly she smiles up at him before she walks through and says, "Thank you."

"My pleasure," he says, in his deep and sexy voice.

Susan walked as fast as she could to get to the elevator. For some reason her heart was racing a million miles a minute, just because he opened the door and spoke to her like that. He certainly smelled divine now, more like vanilla and spice.

As she approached the elevator banks, nobody was about, and she wondered how she would push the button, as the equipment was starting to get heavy. 'I should have brought a cart,' she thought, as an elevator door slid open. She didn't care if it was going up or down; there was already somebody in there who could press a button for her, so she took her opportunity, dashing in, just in time.

She then easily made her way to the media room and checked in and stored the equipment properly before returning to her desk. As she left the media room, she heard two personal assistants whispering about the "handsome CEO" being back from Africa. She thought about what the girls said and the stranger she'd seen twice. The runner/man in the boardroom must be the CEO they are talking about.

Susan made her way back to her desk with thoughts of the handsome stranger in her mind. She knew it had to be him because she'd been here long enough to at least see all the managers who worked at this location. Susan once again sat at her desk and proceeded to re-read several more emails and make notes before she had a complete list of checkpoints.

"Damn," she said, as she finished reviewing yet another program. Susan was starting to doubt her ability because she barely knew this code language. So far, though, she'd been able to read all the references Luis left her. She'd only been working at GTS for a little over a month, and she'd been hired as a development manager, which meant she didn't need to write code. She'd done so in the past and knew some other languages, but not this particular one.

Susan was learning bits and pieces of the code as various issues had come up for her team, which needed to be fleshed out and resolved. She was really good at it too. Since she didn't actually know the language well, she had a lot of questions and a fresh perspective, which had led to fast resolutions on numerous occasions.

Her team loved her. She always took the time to listen, and let them finish, before she tried talking or asking questions. They were very comfortable bringing their issues to her because she was always supportive, and she protected them from any political machinations that might develop. Her team management style and her meticulous organization skills made her a great manager.

Her organization skills were currently taking over as she continued to work through her checklist, reviewing the code again for the third time. However, this time, she decided to add some depth and draw a diagram of how each module interacted with the others, along with the apparent links between the sections of code. She spent all morning analyzing it and laying it out until finally, just before lunch, she found the breach Luis had found.

Luis was right: it was extremely sophisticated. If she hadn't drawn a diagram, she'd never have figured it out by just looking at one single program at a time. It didn't even follow normal human thought patterns.

The humans have lived on the Earth for thousands of years, but the species' reasoning and thought patterns have basically remained the same. It is clear that humans have been evolving over time, but their evolution became stagnant as gangs destroyed communities large and small throughout the world.

Today, while physical violence and gang crime were a thing of the past, there was still computer crime. It was harder to control. GTS had made immense strides in educating the world. They had developed specific security protocols in case of breaches, which had been outlined and approved by the world coalition. Everyone who worked for GTS knew which exact protocols applied to their particular role.

Susan knew she had to initiate the breach protocol for her department. The code breach Luis found, which she confirmed, was scary at best. She still wasn't sure exactly what it was and what it did, but it seemed to have a monitoring element and a copy command. Where it was coming from and how it was being planted was beyond her abilities. She needed her team to examine it. Before she could do that, she had to initiate the breach protocol; then her boss was to tell her the next steps. It was a very serious matter and she was scared, because she was sure Luis was murdered over it.

Her boss, and her boss's boss, are in the conference room in a meeting. Susan decides it's urgent enough, so she texts them both:

"**URGENT!** *A breach has been found in the Apache development systems.*
We need to implement the breach protocol."

Two minutes go by before she receives a reply text from her boss,
"*Hold off until 2 pm when the breakout sessions are done.*"

Her boss tells her to hold off for over two hours. 'What the fuck?!' she wants to text back. She told her boss there was a security breach and he told her to wait?! 'He really is an idiot' she thought to herself. But she'd included both of her bosses on the text. 'Could they *both* be so obtuse?' Her boss was an idiot, but he must have talked his boss, the assistant vice-president, into relaxing until he checked it out. Perhaps he used the argument that it was "just" a development server.

Susan had definitely found what Luis had discovered on the development server, but she really needed one of her senior team members to verify the evidence to make her comfortable. She couldn't make a move without approval and direction from upper management. It was the process required of the data breach protocol.

Still, she thought her boss's delaying the inevitable was crazy, but there wasn't anything she could do, short of walking into the boardroom in front of all the company brass and demanding an audience. 'No. Hell, no! That *is not* going to happen,' she confirmed to herself. She didn't know what to do with herself while she waited.

She got up and went to the break room. Back at her desk, she was too anxious to just sit there. She went to the bathroom. When she returned, it looked as if somebody had been in her cubicle. Thank goodness she had screen-locked her computer. But she couldn't just sit there and wait two and a half hours. She'd been there since 6:30 a.m., and it was now lunchtime. Plus, she was anxious to run by the drugstore and pick up her fertility prescription.

Both the pharmacy and deli were around the corner, and they would just be starting to fill up with people. It would be a good use of her time, plus she needed the distraction. She would be close enough that she could return quickly if her boss changed his mind and decided to implement the protocol sooner.

———————

The CEO of GTS, Christoph Baldric, is walking down the sidewalk towards the deli. As a fluke, he found extra time on his hands while the board was having some last-minute breakout sessions. He opens the deli door for two ladies coming out and his phone silently buzzes in his right pocket. He immediately pulls the phone out of his pocket and looks down to read it, as he makes his way inside and to the end of the ordering line.

Standing in line, he looks up from the email on his phone and notices the same attractive woman he bumped into in the elevator this morning, and then saw gathering equipment from the conference room. She was extremely attractive, with a figure that just wouldn't quit. The entire time she spent in the conference room, he couldn't focus on anything in front of him. All he could do was smell her. She had the sweetest smell about her, like sugar baking in the oven. He'd looked up immediately when she'd gasped. He knew she'd lied to him when she said it was her finger. He saw her reading the note as she gasped. But when she put her finger in her mouth, all he could think about was kissing her lips – and what else he could put in her mouth. He was still wondering, though, what had put that frightened look on her face. For some reason, his instinct had kicked in and he had an urge to protect her.

Christoph had strong basic protective instincts. He had a great responsibility for protecting his people, and in turn protecting humans. The humans were a prehistoric version of his race. His people were sure – through the various testing they'd done since finding this solar system – that these humans, as they were called, are very similar to themselves.

Their integration tests alone had been successful, surprisingly so. Therefore, his people had decided that they needed to fight for the humans.

It will be good to continue integration with the humans, as adding these new genes was making his own people stronger. The Earth's unique atmosphere does not bother the new offspring as much as it does the pure Argon race, and the offspring's metaphysical skills were enhanced twofold. Christoph made the commitment to secure the humans, and to ensure their education and technological advancements. Even though Christoph had a duty to protect her, he also was drawn to this woman in an unusual way. He wanted to protect her for much more personal reasons.

Christoph liked the human women. They were simple in an elegant way, yet they were complex in a way he had never known, given their propensity for emotion. There was a certain femininity that he enjoyed about the human women that was combined with an innocence they had in not realizing their own power. He was fascinated by them and wanted to learn more. Ever since his cousin had integrated with a human on the island, he tried to learn as much from his cousin's wife as possible. Integration with them did not bother him; he was not at all opposed to the idea and in fact, very much supported it. From what his cousin told him, human women were well worth the effort. Christoph very much wanted to get to know this human woman standing in line in front of him... intimately... in every way: mind, body and soul. Her eyes drew him as no other ever had.

She was about five foot five, with blonde hair, a small waist, reasonable hips, athletic legs, and a robust chest. Her face – and especially her green eyes – were the prettiest thing about her. She looked like an angel, and her eyes were a rare shade of green; one he hadn't ever had the pleasure of seeing before. Blue, brown, hazel, those were more common, especially in his race. It was the rare green eyes, which only two percent of the human race had, that drew him. He was extremely attracted to her and could feel the chemistry between them, even if she had no clue.

He feels a spike in their electrical chemistry when they make brief eye contact. But his other back pocket buzzes, and he hears his security guard say into his earpiece: 'DBS! Down! NOW!' His sixth sense draws his attention outside, where he notices a car about to drive by with guns hanging out the window. Acting on instinct, he lunges at the attractive woman and another woman in line, directly in front of him. He drags them both to the ground while yelling at everyone in the deli to "Get down! Get down!"

The guns shattered the front window of the deli. It was lunchtime, and every table was occupied. There was blood everywhere and people were screaming. Hardly anyone had time to register Christoph's warning in time to move, so many people were hurt. Blood and spilled coffee mixed all over the floor. Christoph still had his arms around the two women, but somehow his face had ended up right next to the face of the beautiful woman with green eyes.

Chapter 3

Christoph's instincts to protect were driven by his responsibilities, drilled into him from an early age by his parents, the current Crown Prince and Princess of Argon. His parents reside on the colony ship, just inside the Earth's atmosphere, while he assumes the responsibilities of command on Earth.

As the Commander, he has his own private security team that follows him and protects him. It is a difficult feat to avoid being noticed by the humans, but with the advanced Argon technology, it has been easy for them for centuries now. Even though Argons are not immune to bullets and bombs, they did have advanced lasers and healing technologies to give them a better survival rate than humans.

Luckily, in the drive-by shooting, he was only grazed by a bullet on his jacket, alerting him to the close call. While he wasn't harmed, he couldn't say the same for many of the humans in the deli. There wasn't much he could do for all of them at once.

Right now, he was staring into the most striking green eyes. And they were filled with horror and fear. His instincts to protect and comfort were kicked into overdrive.

In the immediate aftermath of the drive-by, Susan looks over at her rescuer. His face is inches from hers, so close he hears her whisper solemnly, "It's me they're after. I know it's me."

She is so sincere, and her fear is so transparent, Christoph can't help but believe her. He asks her, "Don't you work at GTS Security?"

Susan nods her head yes, without saying a word. Her frightened gaze never leaves his eyes.

At her acknowledgment, amongst the chaos, he abruptly tugs her from the floor and around the counter into the back of the deli. Without a word, he maneuvers her quickly out the back entrance into the alley.

"Come. Can you run?" he asks.

Susan again just nods her head, unable to trust herself to speak.

"Let's go. Follow me," he says, before tugging her behind him as he jogs out the back door of the deli across the alley and down about four buildings to another alley.

Through his earpiece, his security team told him the best way to exit the deli, just as Green Eyes was telling him they were after her. His instinct to protect kicked in and he took her with him. He would take her no further than his private gym. She was a human, and wasn't allowed to know about anything else.

Susan recognizes him as the CEO as they approach the GTS building. She hadn't officially met the CEO, but she is sure he is. Amazingly, she finds herself being dragged by the hand into a basement door of her office building. She can't believe this is happening to her.

Susan doesn't know what to think. Her mind is all in a jumble after the scare of machine guns pelting the deli. The CEO is so incredibly handsome, how can she not be affected by him? What she wouldn't give for a tumble with him! Perfectly acceptable in this day and age – although her great-great-grandparents would disapprove.

Christoph approaches the steps to the basement entrance and starts down them, pulling her with him. He needs to get them inside before they are seen.

He is about six foot two and solid muscle. She'd accidentally bumped into him this morning, so she knows that under his three-piece suit, he is solid muscle. He has blue eyes, but they are a pale blue, almost gray. He has light-blonde hair, cut military short, and very sexy if you like military hairstyles, which she does.

For a minute she let herself imagine touching his head and feeling the brush of his short hair against her hands. 'Ah, touching him would feel so good,' she thought. She felt a magnetic force pulling them together – either that, or she was horny. 'It's been a *really* long time,' her subconscious screamed at her. '*Any* hot guy would turn you on right now.'

She didn't know much about him, only that he'd recently arrived back stateside. During water-cooler gossip, she had heard he was working on telecom deals in Africa after GTS eliminated the last of the gangs there. The company's victories there were big news in the office. Up until his arrival, everyone had been discussing it, especially the women. Now she has followed him to this basement entrance and is watching as he is opening keypad panels.

Christoph punches another code on a keypad and does a retina scan, then opens the outer door and leads her into a medium sized room. The room is outfitted with exercise equipment and TVs. It isn't part of the normal company access, so clearly it is his own personal workout space. No wonder he was coming up the elevator dressed in running clothes when she was trying to board it this morning.

"We will be safe here," Christoph reassures her. He leads her to a workout bench and says, "Here, sit down; I'll get us some water."

He walks to a nearby bar area that looks like it has everything to cook a meal, plus a rather tall and skinny refrigerator. He opens the fridge and pulls out two unlabeled glass bottles of water.

Opening hers before handing it to her, he asks her, "What's your name and what department do you work in?"

"Thank you," she says, when he hands her the water. She takes several sips before answering his question. She still isn't sure how she can talk. "Susan. My name is Susan Caldwell." She stops, takes another drink, and looks around the room.

Christoph watches her give off all the signs of being in shock; her hands are shaking, and he doesn't even think she realizes it. "Take your time. You're safe here, I promise. So, how long have you worked at GTS?" he asks, thinking it might be easier to answer.

"Uh, only one month," she says meekly. Susan now notices that her hands are shaking. She takes another sip of water and looks for a place to set it down so it won't spill.

After setting the water on the floor, she takes a deep breath and tries to finish her explanation, "I work in the security development and production support department. My team handles security production issues, and we design and implement stronger security controls. I'm a development manager," she provided. Susan closed her eyes and took another deep breath. 'It's okay, you're okay,' she kept telling herself. 'You're safe now.'

"Why do you think those gunmen were targeting you?" Christoph punches out the question. Might as well get her answer while she's talking, before any other shock symptoms set in, like crying or fainting. He's seen it all.

Susan looks at him and contemplates quickly in her mind: 'He can't be the villain because he too was almost shot in the deli, so I should be good there... He is the CEO; it's his right to know.' She decides to trust him. "There's been a code breach on the Apache development servers. One of my third-shift team members found it. I think he was the one who was killed this morning." She practically blurted it out, all in one breath. 'Breathe deep, relax,' she told herself. She closed her eyes again.

Christoph could tell she was having a hard time with this, but Green Eyes – Susan – was in shock, and he needed to help her. "Easy, that's good. Take your time, and take deep breaths. Everything is going to be okay; we'll get it all taken care of," he said soothingly as he handed her water again. "Take a few more sips," he said. He knew it was laced with a special Argon supplement that helped one relax and deal with emotions quickly. In Argon, they'd found it improved their physical exercise benefits too, so he always had his gym stocked.

"Good. We had quite a run, so the water will do you good," he reassured her. "So, about this breach on a development server. Have you verified it?" There was so much more he wanted to know, like why hadn't she initiated data breach protocol? How many people knew about it? But she was in shock, and he needed to go slowly and keep her calm.

"My third-shift team member, Luis, the one I told you that I think was blown up? Well, he called me this morning before he left the office to tell me he'd confirmed it. He said to be careful who I told. Even this morning, when I picked up the equipment from the boardroom, I saw he'd left me a note saying he thought he was being watched," she said.

Christoph is listening to her when he sees blood on her right arm. Changing the subject, he asks, "Are you okay? That looks like blood." He leans in and touches her arm to get a closer look. As soon as he touches her, he gives her an electric shock. She jumps slightly, more from being startled than from pain.

"It does throb a little, but I didn't notice it until you asked," she explains.

Christoph touches something in his left ear and says, "Andre, send down a medic to the private gym." He releases her arm and says to her, "It looks like a scratch, but I'll have a medic here in a moment to confirm, and make sure you don't need stitches."

"Thank you," she murmurs as she tries to get a look at her cut, but it's on the back of her arm and she can hardly see it. All she sees is blood.

"When you found the note with the equipment, that's when you gasped?" he asked, pulling her back to his questions. He needed to get this information.

"Yes, it scared me. I wasn't expecting to find a note at all. He left me several voice mails and sent multiple emails with information," she said. "I worked all morning to figure it out," she added. "It's complex."

"How are we impacted?" he asked, pointedly. "Is it touching the data stores or the production system?"

"Well, that's part of the problem. I'm cannot find the link to production. I'm not an expert at this code language, but I can read it. It took me all morning, but I found what he was talking about and he was adamant production data was compromised. I need my team, who are the code experts, to figure it out and investigate," she explained.

"Why didn't you implement the data breach protocol once you confirmed it?" he asked, puzzled.

A little defensively, she replied, "I tried to. I notified my Director and AVP, but they told me to hold off until after 2 p.m. I just figured it was because it was on a development server."

Christoph accepted her explanation. She did follow what she was supposed to do by notifying two management levels at one time. He'd have to have a talk with both of them later. But for now, he still had questions for Green Eyes. "And you know it was your worker involved in the car bomb?" he asked.

"Well, I don't know for sure, but the officer I talked to this morning said they could only make out the last name, Perez. That's Luis's last name. When I talked to him this morning, he said he was in the office because it's the only way to access the system. He told me he would leave after he talked to me. I arrived at the office a little more than an hour and a half later, and the bomb had already gone off."

Without a word to her, he pulls his cell phone out of his pocket, keys in his password and selects a number from his call list. "George, I need you to put together a private team to watch over Susan Caldwell. She's in my private gym with me right now. I need somebody to watch her house twenty-four/seven, and she needs a private escort and protection around the clock," he says before pausing to listen briefly; then he says, "Thank you," and hangs up.

"Here, let me have a look at that." He sits down on the workout bench next to her. "It looks like it's still bleeding." He gets up and retrieves a clean towel from the bar area. When he sits back down, he takes her arm in one hand and places the towel on her wound with the other and holds it tightly.

'Holy shit, was I shot?' she thinks to herself. She only felt a dull throbbing, but she was becoming a little lightheaded. She wasn't sure if it was from his nearness or from the wound. Then again, 'Holy Cow – he is assigning a security team to watch over *me!* Seriously?' But she'd heard him order it.

Suddenly her heart accelerates and her knees become weak. She knows that if she weren't already sitting down, she would have fallen. The seriousness of what is happening is finally hitting her.

"It looks like a flesh wound, but it will still need to be cleaned and dressed," Christoph says, as two medics open the door and enter the room. "You're in shock right now, so try to relax."

The medic quickly gets to work to examine her wound, "Hello, ma'am, my name is Tony. Do you mind if I push your sleeve up past the wound?"

"No, of course not. Please go ahead," she says, as Christoph backs away to let the medics have space. She has never been so thankful for a short-sleeved shirt in her life. At least she doesn't have to take her shirt off for this. "Ouch," she says, as the medic applies something to the wound.

"Sorry. I forgot to tell you that there might be a sting with this ointment, but it'll counteract any biochemical that the bullets might have been laced with. You are lucky the bullet just grazed your arm. You won't need stitches," the medic explained, "but you'll need to keep these butterfly bandages on it at all times to keep the skin together, so that it'll heal properly and won't scar." He gave a knowing glance over her head to Christoph. The medic placed a pad over the bandages, and wrapped her arm in gauze.

Christoph nodded in agreement. He knew the chemical didn't burn Argons, only humans. It was critical to make sure she didn't develop any biochemical reaction that bullets from Grogan guns often cause if untreated. He didn't want to get into these explanations with her at this time.

Interrupting Christoph's thoughts, the medic says to her, "Here, take this pill. It will help with the shock," and hands her a small white pill and her bottle of water.

Dutifully, Susan takes the pill, but asks, "This won't put me to sleep, will it? I need to get back to work."

The medic explains, "You might feel a little lethargic, but if you feel you need to sleep, you should. Trauma such as this normally requires twelve to eighteen hours of sleep for the body to recover, so it might take you several days."

Christoph was becoming impatient. He needed to get her talking more about the data breach. "What else can you tell me about the data breach? What are the next steps?"

She looks at him questioningly, and then looks at the medics. She is afraid to say anything in front of them. It is obvious by the sudden fear in her eyes.

"It's okay, sir; we're just leaving," Tony says, as he gathers up the last of his supplies and leaves the room.

Susan looks down at her arm again, amazed that a bullet grazed her, but didn't hit her. But she needs to answer his question. Her brain is becoming fuzzier and fuzzier.

"Are you okay, Susan? Here, take another drink," he says, as he hands her her almost empty water bottle. Susan turns up the bottle and finishes it easily.

"Right, so, next steps… I need my team to tell us what is happening. We don't even have the full picture yet." She almost whined in frustration.

"I can't do this on my own. I'm not advanced enough with this code. My team will be much more able to handle the investigation," she nervously continued, giving him more information than he needed, "The data breach protocol demands that I notify upper management before engaging anyone else to assist. I tried telling Mr. Jones, my boss, and Mr. Crinchfield, via text, less than hour ago. Mr. Jones texted me back and told me to wait until their board meeting breakout session was over," she unknowingly repeated.

Christoph's face hardened, and she could tell he was upset. He particularly didn't like managers who blew off such a critical notification, even if it was on a development server, but right now he couldn't focus on their ineptitude. The breach needed to be addressed quickly. These systems were connected to the Argon private systems, and he needed answers, fast.

He pulls out his phone again and sends a text message to his Argon security team to perform an instant lockdown on all Argon systems, while he says to Susan, "Fine, no problem. Consider upper management notified. I'll handle that. I need you to notify your team now. I'll have my secretary put together the NDAs – the non-disclosure agreements, and let's get them started."

"Okay, sure," Susan says, only just a little startled by his quick movements and sudden commands. She immediately uses her cell phone to send an email to her team. Before finishing, she asks, "Where should we tell them to meet? All the meeting rooms have been taken over for the board meetings and breakout sessions."

"Tell them to go to the main executive conference room. I'll have it cleared out by the time they get there," Christoph responds, as he begins typing yet another text to make sure the room is cleared. He calls a halt to the remaining board meetings and initiates the data breach protocol of locking down all GTS systems. Christoph then calls his Vice President of Operations to give him the verbal explanation of the security breach. "Lock down all departments and cancel the remaining board meetings. Speed is paramount, given the type of data breach. And get Mr. Jones and Mr. Crinchfield in my office immediately," he said, before hanging up.

Christoph needs to talk to the Argon board as well. It is imperative that he gets them working on securing the facilities against any further breach attempts while they are vulnerable. He quickly composes and sends a text to his head of security to forward a corresponding notification to the Argon board, as he is locking down the Argon system. He then sends an email to his private secretary with instructions for the non-disclosure agreements.

Christoph looks at Susan, who is finishing up her email to her team. "Do you think you're okay to go back to the office? I think you should go home and get some rest," he prompts.

"No, I'm fine. I need to work. I would go crazy if I was at home not knowing what was going on," she explained.

At that moment the door opens and a tall, burly, bald man in a black suit walks into the room. He looks to be about six foot five and is so thick, she can't imagine anyone being able to knock him down. "Sir, I'll be escorting Ms. Caldwell today until we can arrange to have others flown in," he explains.

Christoph nods in agreement and turns to Susan, "Susan Caldwell, this is George Simpson. He'll be your escort today. He's the head of my private security team, and he is the best there is." Christoph pauses, not knowing what else to say to alleviate the fear he can clearly see in her face. "You can feel safe with him," he tries to reassure her.

"Hello George," Susan says as her professional instinct takes over, and she puts out her hand to shake his extremely large one.

As his hand engulfs hers, he firmly but easily shakes her hand, without crushing it, saying, "It's a pleasure, ma'am."

"George, I think that Susan might be in a little bit of shock. She was with me in the deli when it was attacked. She wants to continue to work today. She's going to be assembling her team in the main executive boardroom to continue to identify the root cause of the breach, and the damage that has been done. Actually, she and one of her team members are the ones who found the code breach. Please escort her anywhere she would like to go," Christoph requests of his most trusted security team member.

"You can count on me, sir," George replies. "I'll be waiting just outside this door over here, when you're ready, ma'am," he says as he exits a different door than the one Christoph brought her in through.

Susan just stares at George's back as he retreats from the room. She is in shock and doesn't know what to say or what to do. Her mind is a jumble of thoughts, yet blank at the same time. She feels like crying, but she also feels like yelling and screaming.

Christoph watches her and sees the confusion, pain and fear in her incredible green eyes. She's simply the most beautiful woman he's ever seen. He feels compelled to look after her and protect her, so he asks, "What would you like for lunch? I'll have somebody run out and get you something. I'll have it delivered to you in the conference room."

She looks at him with a sincere thankfulness in her eyes. She says, "I'm not sure I'm very hungry anymore, but I know that I should eat."

"Yes, that would be best, especially after taking the pill for the shock. Are you sure you wouldn't rather go home and lie down for a while?" he asks. His voice is laced with concern, and he touches her on her arm when he asks.

There was no actual shock from his touch this time, but she still feels the almost electric energy flowing between them. It's unlike anything she's ever experienced before. He's so warm. She wishes she could fall into his arms and have him hold her for a little while. She's still so afraid.

She was almost killed at that deli. She's still not sure what to think. She replies, "No, I couldn't be at home; I'd never sleep. I would be too worried. I need to keep busy, at least for now, if that's okay."

"Of course that's fine, but let me get you something to eat. What would you like?" he requests.

"All right, how about a bowl of chicken noodle soup and a roast beef sandwich. Lettuce, tomato, cheese, mayonnaise, mustard, oil and vinegar, please." she replies. It's the easiest thing to think of since that's what she was going to order at the deli anyway.

"Okay, that sounds easy enough. I'll have it sent up to you. Are you sure you wouldn't like to lie down for a few minutes here? There's a massage room, just off in the back corner. You could lie down for a while. I could even arrange for you to have a massage if you like," he offers.

'Where is this man's generosity coming from?' she wonders. He's being much too kind to a stranger. Why would he even want to help her? He must be this nice to all his employees. But no, she can't accept, she needs to brief her team. They're probably all in the conference room by now. "No, thank you. I really need to get up to the conference room to brief my team. I'm sure they're anxiously waiting and wondering what is going on." She pauses for a moment before she asks, "What do I do about my bosses, Mr. Jones and Mr. Crutchfield? Do I keep them briefed? I'm not sure how to handle this."

"Leave them to me. Do not talk to anyone else in management. Only provide your status to me and me only," he stays sternly. "Do you understand?"

His tone made her look twice at him. He was so forceful, as if she would face dire consequences if she disobeyed. Of course she had no problem agreeing. "Yes, of course, I can do that. But how will I reach you? Email? Phone?"

"Here, hand me your phone and I'll program my personal phone numbers and email," he says, as he holds out his hand for her phone.

She readily gives it to him and he programs his personal cell, his desk phone, and his personal email into her phone. He didn't want her messages to go to any business line, but directly to him. She was too important. Plus, he wanted to keep his interest in her secret, at least for a short time. He wanted to get to know her better, now that he was certain she was human. How could she not be human with those amazing green eyes?

He hands the phone back to her. "There is all my information. Call my cell first before any other number, and use the email for any documents or links that you want to send to me. I'll personally be handling this breach protocol, and all communications regarding it. Do not tell Mr. Jones anything about it. He'll be waiting in my office by now. I'll let him know to leave you and your team alone. Don't worry, he won't be bothering you. If he does, tell me immediately. Understand?"

"Yes, I'll keep to the conference room. Thank you for all your help and support," she says with a genuine look of warmth in her eyes. She gets up and starts for the door, leaving him staring at her and the door long after she's gone, only seeing those mesmerizing green eyes in his mind's eye.

He is frantically trying to finish copying the original scripts back. The mind control is weakening; he isn't able to remember all the commands. He is flipping through his notes in a frenzy, trying to find out exactly what he is supposed to do next. There is a burning, intuitive urgency inside him that is driving him to search for the commands. His life depends on it; he knows for certain. He doesn't know how he knows his life is in danger, but he doesn't question it.

His monitor beeps at him. He looks up to see words on the screen showing the status that the UNIX file replication, finally, has successfully aborted it. Relief floods his mind. But he isn't finished; he has to get all of the scripts replaced before he is booted off the system with the lockout.

His desk phone rings. From the caller ID, he sees it has to be an interoffice call. Absentmindedly, he picks up the phone to answer while still searching through his folders for the paper with the commands written on it. He punches the speakerphone button. "Yes," he abruptly barks into the phone.

"This is Mr. Baldric's personal secretary. He would like to see you in his office immediately," the voice projects from the phone base. Silence waited for his response.

"Yes, okay," he says back.

"Thank you," the female voice says before hanging up.

Shit! He doesn't have time now to find the commands and replace the scripts. He must leave to go to the CEO's office. Thank goodness he was able to stop the replication.

Chapter 4

Christoph watches Susan depart. Once the door closes and locks behind her, he makes his way toward the swimming pool. On the other side of the pool, he walks through the facade that looks like a mirrored wall. It is simply an optical illusion. On the other side is the entrance to the Argon underground command center.

Christoph strides to the moving sidewalk and begins walking on it at a brisk pace, nodding to others he passes along the way. After several minutes, he exits the sidewalk and walks through a door he accesses with hand and retina recognition.

The door locks behind him. He approaches a pedestal and types in several sequences of numbers. One section of the wall lights up in a bright blue hue and a door slides open, exposing a small pod. The control panel in the center of the pod is accessible from either of the two seats. A dim blue light brightens the interior. As Christoph sits down, the seat belts automatically secure him in place. He touches a control to activate the pod, and the doors slide shut.

The computer voice states, "Hello, Commander. Preparing for liftoff in ten, nine, eight, seven...." When the computer reached one, the pod seemed to lift off and rise into the sky in a shaft of blue light, so fast that the naked human eye would be unable to see it.

Christoph laid his head back and closed his eyes. He had just a five-minute journey from Earth to Spirit's Destiny, the Argon colony ship, which was cloaked in invisibility, and orbiting the Earth just outside of any human satellite range.

The pod navigated by a type of tracking beam straight to the colony ship. Once the pod docked, the lights brightened, the seat belts retracted and the door slid open. The computer said, "You have arrived at your destination. You may exit."

Christoph left the pod station and headed toward the only door in the room. It opened into a corridor, much like those in the command center on Earth, except that on one of the corridor's sides there were window panels looking into Space. He could see the Earth's moon, which was close, but he could also see Earth in the distance.

He stepped on the moving sidewalk and briskly walked for a few minutes before stepping off and turning toward a door, which automatically opened as he approached. On the colony ship, there was no need for security scans. All Argons carried special recognition chips that provided them automatic access to all areas where they had personal permission to enter.

Christoph entered into a large boardroom, in which at least fifty people were milling about, drinking and socializing. The emergency Argon colony board meeting was set to start as soon as he arrived.

"Good afternoon, Commander," a uniformed attendant greeted him as he entered the room. "Would you like something to drink?" she inquired.

"Hello, Janeen. No thank you," he said, before making his way to his normal seat on the side of the long table as he nodded greetings to the others in the room.

The others saw him enter the room, and everyone moved immediately to take their seats. An eerie silence overcame the entire room as the others quickly broke off their conversations to take their seats. Everyone was anxious to hear what had happened on Earth to warrant an emergency meeting of the Argon board.

The man sitting at the head of the long conference table cleared his voice. He looked like an older version of Christoph, with gray hair. "Thank you, everyone, for gathering here so quickly. Christoph has called together this emergency meeting due to recent events on Earth. Please, Christoph, tell us what brings us here."

"Thank you, Your Highness," Christoph responded as he stood from his seat. "There have been Grogan developments on Earth. Today there was an open shooting at a deli in Boston by Grogan attackers." He shifted to show everyone the shoulder of his jacket, where it was clear that a bullet had torn the material. "As you know, on Earth we wear clothes that will repel normal human bullets and protect us from normal violence – however, this attack on the deli was perpetrated by Grogans with *their* bullets, not human ones."

Christoph paused for everyone to digest the information before he continued, "Several human lives were lost. It is unclear whether the target was myself, or a human who works for GTS. The reason it is unclear is because this human's GTS security team discovered a code breach in the development environment. As you know, our code base was developed by our own Argon computer technicians, and breaching it would be far beyond the capabilities of any human; thus I suspect that the Grogans are behind it. In addition, the human who discovered the code breach was murdered this morning by a car bomb."

"While we don't yet have much intelligence on the car bomb, we believe it was an inside job because the security cameras were disabled. Thus we do not believe the Grogans were directly involved in the car bomb, but were instigators behind it. These are looking to be very similar tactics to the ones the Grogans used when they started the gang wars. We need to address this breach – and the pending threat to humanity – immediately."

The female at the other head of the table, an older woman with silver hair, asked, "Christoph, son, what do you plan to do to protect the humans? What do you need from the Board?"

"I've arranged for extra security and monitoring. The team working on the breach is meeting in a central location so they'll be easier to protect. I need permission to activate our Argon computer scientists to examine and work on this issue. We need to activate those already staffed at GTS so they can assist in locating the source of the breach, as well as finding out where the stolen information was being sent. We need them to determine what the data was, and what it is being used for."

The gray-haired man at the head of the table asked, "This is a simple request that could have been handled without an emergency meeting. Why call this Board together?"

"Yes, sir, Father, I understand your concern. It is the sequence of events that have happened so closely together that concerns me, and the fact that Grogans are using their own force and their own bullets in public. There is more to this than a simple code breach. We need to know the current status of all of our efforts around the globe to suppress Grogan control. It's been three weeks since our last meeting, and I believe there may be clues in the latest information. We, as a group, must be on the lookout for their ulterior motive."

"I see. Well, let's start with Jorge: What is the status for locating more weather machines," the gray-haired man asked, "and disseminating the data we gathered from the one we captured last month?"

"Yes, sir, we are still examining the data, but it seems as if the machine was set to heat the Earth, not cool it as we would expect of Grogans. However, the machine does have the capability to cool the Earth to a frozen tundra," Jorge explained.

"How large of an area can the one machine control?" Christoph asked.

Jorge replied, "It looks as if it can impact at least one quarter of the Earth's surface. We have to assume that there are at least three or four other machines like it out there. Also, we've been able to determine this machine was definitively built on Earth with local materials."

"What about the status of our cross-breeding efforts? Are there any clues there?" Christoph asked.

A younger blonde woman several seats down on the opposite side of the table spoke up, "As you know, for some time now, we've confirmed that by using the supplement that is needed to match our blood acidity level to that of humans, all our experiments continue to be 100% successful. The offspring that have been developed continue to be healthy and have the intelligence levels of normal Argons, which is much higher than that of humans. However, they share the Argon intolerance for the same foods, like wheat and dairy, which are normally poisonous to our systems without the supplements.

But, just like full-blooded Argons, when taking the supplement they can eat whatever foods they like."

The Argons found that they were enough like the humans that cross-breeding would actually strengthen their race. They'd been experimenting with it for centuries, and now they could ensure success – without creating genetic blunders or infecting the population with monstrous repercussions.

She continued, "Our most surprising recent find has been in the experiments we've conducted that show an incredible, equal ability in emotional levels in both male and female offspring. Our scientists are amazed at the level of emotion the females are showing. It will totally redefine our current social standards as we more fully integrate with humans."

From the other end of the table, Christoph's mother added, "Yes, it is a great discovery, and it only solidifies our goal for the Milky Way to be our destination for the new Argon. How soon will you be able to publish your findings, Linda?" she asked.

"We will be ready to publish our findings shortly – within about eight weeks – to share with our other colony ships, so that they can begin charting a course for this solar system," Linda concluded.

This was the most crucial information that Christoph wanted to know on a personal basis. After meeting the human siren, Susan, his thoughts had been pulled in the direction of integration more and more. More than that, as Planet Commander in charge of all Argons living on Earth, it was crucial information for his race. With more emotions for females, the impact was going to be phenomenal.

Christoph asked, "What about the conservation efforts? Are they still on track?"

The Argons have been on Earth throughout the last two millennia, thanks to exploratory missions from their home planet, Argon. Although they have kept their presence secret from humans, they've been instrumental in fostering, or planting the seeds of, every major scientific advancement during that time. Their scientists had taken years, painstakingly prodding and pushing the human technology along so that the Argons were able to prevent extinction of all endangered species on Earth. The Argons had found that simply by stopping the hunting of a few key animal species – like whales, dolphins, and elephants – they were able to adjust the entire Earth food chain so that eventually it had positive impacts on panda bears, white lions and other special species.

A short man, sitting a few seats down from Christoph, answered in a small, meek voice, "We continue to prove with every experiment that the life force on Earth is almost identical to that of Argon. The food chain works exactly the same way. Over the last month, we believe that we've finally completed our study of the above-water food chain, as scheduled, with the last of the rainforest insects identified. However, we still have gaps in the plant life in the oceans. As you know, all species identified by the humans have long been organized in the chain. It has been a challenge to ensure there is nothing left unidentified."

The small man paused before continuing, "Our main focus is examining the impacts of those species that have become extinct, and how that will affect the other areas of the chain. We are still unsure of the long-term harm to the health of Earth. In addition, we continue to fight to regrow the rainforests; as well as, re-introduce bees. No one realized the damage that would be done to the planet with the near destruction of rainforests worldwide. If we had not introduced hemp plants when we did, and made sure the humans accepted them, the planet would be on a fast decline that we would not be able to stop."

Christoph replied, "Thank you, Tim, this is good news. Congratulations on completing your research. That's well done. What about environmental impact studies on the effects of the gang wars instigated by the Grogans?"

Tim replied, "That study is still ongoing, but our preliminary findings strongly lean toward showing no impact. Because most of the harm consisted of physical damage to buildings within the cities, the destruction did not hurt the natural environment. If anything, it helped. It reduced emissions in all those major cities. Now, as humans are rebuilding, we continue to be involved to ensure that all is done in an environmentally sound way. You were right when you stated that the Grogans' aim was for the humans to destroy themselves through hand-to-hand combat, starvation, and isolation of communities, not through the environment. But what has me worried is the weather machines being set to heat the planet," Tim said.

"How so?" Christoph asked.

"Well, sir, if the world is heated too much, then certain species will begin to die off. The oceans and lakes will begin to evaporate. Slowly, the environment will be killed, thus resulting in the eventual extinction of the human race. It is my personal, as well as professional belief," Tim stated confidently, "that this is what the Grogans' aims are for heating the Earth with their weather machines."

"Yes, that theory does make sense, Tim. However, assuming this is all tied together, I wonder how the code breach is going to lend itself to the Grogan plan to eliminate humans from the Earth?" Christoph wondered aloud, not expecting an answer. "I need you all to examine your specialty areas for any correlation."

The Argons needed to keep the planet healthy and able to sustain human life – and thus able to sustain Argon life. Since their solar system had been destroyed when their sun blew up and became a black hole, it was critical that they bring all their colony ships to one location. So far, The Spirit's Destiny – the colony ship that came to Earth – had been successful in proving that they'd found a new planet suitable to support Argon life.

Since this Milky Way sun was a dwarf star, it would not explode – but naturally, over time, it would dim into nothingness. The Argon scientists calculated that this would not happen for several million millennia – long enough for their people to gather together and integrate with humans on Earth.

Christoph contemplated the updates and information he'd gained in today's emergency session. "I assume we continue to be on track with rebuilding the cities ravaged by the gang wars?"

The leader, his father, replied, "Yes, those efforts continue as planned. There have been no blocks, have there, Jonathan?"

Jonathan, sitting next to the leader, replied, "No blocks or signs of further Grogan interference on our end, sir. We're advancing technology as subtly as we can, and the cities are improving on pace, just as reported last month. With Christoph's help in Africa, we have a significant jump start on restoring that entire country."

"We need to appoint a task force to examine what the Grogans' motives could be to infiltrate the Earth's monetary systems, other than the obvious," Christoph replied. "As you know, since the Grogans aren't that smart, it could be just the obvious. I'm going to need help, since this breach is at my arm of the firm. I need to be involved on the human level right now. Jon, can you appoint a task force, and let's convene in a week's time?"

Jonathan was Christoph's most trusted counterpart on Spirit's Destiny and was also his cousin, next in line to the throne after Christoph. When Christoph volunteered to command Argons on Earth, it was natural that Jonathan would become second in command, after Christoph's father, on the colony ship. Jonathan and Christoph were great friends and worked well together. If Christoph could count on anyone, it was Jonathan.

"Certainly, my friend," Jonathan replied. "I'll get to work on it and send you the details as they become available."

"Thank you, Jon. I need to get back to Earth now. I have humans waiting for me in my office that I need to interrogate about the code breach. As soon as I have more information, I will notify everyone. Be warned, this is bigger than just a code breach. I can feel it. We need to be on guard," he warned, as he got to his feet, nodded to everyone and left the room.

Chapter 5

As soon as Susan arrived in the executive conference room, she saw that her entire team was assembled with their laptops ready. The lockdown had already taken place. Her team wouldn't be able to log into the system until they'd signed the non-disclosure agreements and their IDs were activated.

The agreements had already been handed out to them, and one of the company's special security support specialists was in the room, ready and on standby, to grant access to those on the NDA list. Susan was more than impressed by how quickly and efficiently the company was acting upon this breach protocol.

After ensuring everyone understood a breach protocol had been implemented, it was quick work to explain the NDA agreement to the team, not needing to stress to them that this was highly secretive work. It was easy for them to understand. They were a security team in a security company; they knew that things like this happened, especially when dealing with money, personal data, and surveillance of the world's most secured locations. Obtaining their agreement was simple – explaining how the breach occurred was another issue altogether.

Susan tried her best to explain what had happened by drawing a diagram on the board. The breach was so convoluted that it was difficult to understand, even with a drawing. Several of her team members got it right away, and they were able to help her explain it to the rest of the team. As a designer and manager, she didn't have to be fluent in the code language – and it was encouraging to her when her senior team members caught on so quickly.

Luis was a very junior programmer who had only been working at GTS for a short time, though it was longer than Susan had. The senior programmers were quick to help their peers to understand the breach. It didn't take long before the entire team was way ahead of her, and they had logged into the systems to investigate.

They worked tirelessly for two days, without stopping, dividing themselves up into shifts, day and night. On the beginning of the third day they found something. They called her over to show her the evidence in the startup scripts for each server. They had found a definite link to the production data files, and it seemed as if the files had been copied and stored in the development databases. But why was someone putting them on Dev servers? Were they planning to copy them?

The team wasn't able to investigate why until they disabled the code responsible for the intruder's access, and also refresh the development databases, to make sure that only mock data would remain. They had found the malicious code in the all the main production server startup scripts. It all had to be disabled and cleaned up before the root cause could be investigated.

For now, they seemed to know how to put out the fire. It included other areas of code that needed to be checked, like the shutdown scripts and the DR (disaster recovery) scripts. It was going to take time for them to review it all and make the adjustments. But the errors they were correcting and finding were extremely advanced.

Susan was impressed with the code breach. Whoever had done this had placed time-specific "crontab" entries on each of the production servers, which did health checks, using deeply hidden scripts, on the integral components required for the code to function. So even if she thought she had cleared the virus, it would be reborn every time the servers rebooted. They were definitely dealing with a determined hacker, someone who really wanted this sequence to work. Susan directed her team to comment out the malicious code in the reboot scripts, just in case this criminal decided to add health-check scripts to watch his health-check scripts. It was going to take time to track and note down all the changes.

Susan knew that Christoph needed to know what they'd found and how much longer it was going to take them to clean this mess up. She decided to text him.

Susan texts Christoph:

:: Discoveries made, path fwd clear/time consuming.
:: Let me know when you want full status rpt.

Susan's phone immediately rang. She picked it up to answer it seeing Christoph identified as the caller. "Hello," she says.

"Hi, tell me the discoveries. How long to fix?" he abruptly spits out.

Susan is used to high-level executives. They don't always pay attention to niceties and general politeness, but it's not personal. She calmly stated, "We've had some developments."

Before she can continue he says, "Ok, that's great, what is it?"

She decided to get to the point, "we found the breach code, but we think it had more malicious intent. We also found a counter in the reboot scripts. The counter is set to activate something; we don't know what yet." She paused.

"Good, that's good. When will the counter on reboots be activated?" Christoph asked.

Susan replied, "After two more automated reboots. It looks like we have about six weeks before the mysterious activation will occur," she explained urgently. She continued, "We need to figure out what is going to be activated and how to stop the counter."

"Can your team do this?" Christoph asked.

"Yes. They think they can handle it, but it is going to take time to investigate. If we can keep the systems locked down, we should be okay," she said.

"Keep them working. I need you to come to my office. I'll see you in five," he said before hanging up.

Susan stared at the phone after he suddenly hung up. 'What a high-handed jerk he is being,' she thought to herself. 'Oh well, it's typical male behavior,' so she really wasn't actually surprised. Maybe she was just hoping for some compassion or personal touch. She shook her head at herself as she made her way to the elevator to go to his upper floor, where the executive offices were located.

It wasn't the top floor, as that was the CEO's penthouse apartment. The executive offices were located directly on the floor below. As the elevator opened on the executive floor, the tall, slender brunette who was standing at the receptionist desk greeted her: "Susan Caldwell?"

"Yes," she responded. Susan had never been to the executive floor before and was glad somebody was there to show her where to go.

"This way, please," she said. "Mr. Baldric is expecting you," as she led the way down the white marble tiled corridor to a door the same color as the dark, slate-gray wall. She immediately opened the door and stood to the side so that Susan could walk through as she announced, "Ms. Caldwell, sir."

As Susan stepped into the office, she was accosted by the brightness of the room, and she suddenly felt dizzy. She put her hand to her head and thought, 'it has to be the fertility medication I'm taking.' She swayed slightly as Christoph approached her.

"Susan, are you okay? Here, come sit down," he said, as he took her arm and directed her to the couch.

She sat down and looked around her in bewilderment, examining the room.

Christoph's corner office had solid glass walls on both sides, with the sun shining, bringing a brightness to the room that was almost blinding – but the windows were tinted in such a way that the light fell just short of that. The floors were of deep-red mahogany, with plush Tibetan handcrafted carpets strategically placed all about.

The desk he'd just vacated was a deep, rich, red mahogany, three times the size of Susan's kitchen table. On the right end facing away from the windows was his computer station, with three monitors and a pullout drawer that held his keyboard at the perfect height, so he wouldn't have to slouch or reach to use it.

On the other end of his desk were various works of what looked to be African art. He must have just unpacked them from his trip. There were too many for them to have a permanent residence on his desk. Besides, they were sitting directly in front of the other chairs, where he would have wanted people to sit at his desk and talk to him.

In the middle of the large room, there was a luscious white sofa, so inviting she wished she could just lie down and sleep on it. She was so glad he suggested she sit here. It was so comfortable.

As soon as she was settled, Christoph asked," Are you okay, can I get you anything?"

"I'm good, but honestly, I'm exhausted, and I've been taking a new medication that puts me off a little bit," she explained, breathlessly.

"Let me get you a drink. What would you like to drink?" he asked, getting up to go to the opposite side of the room from his desk, where the spacious open bar was laid out with assortments of liquor, wine, sodas and juices, all clearly visible in the glass-front refrigerator.

"Sparkling water, please, if you have it," she requested. Getting right to the point, she started, "This has been a tremendous effort by our team to find how this code is connected to the production systems, and what it is doing." Susan stopped and sighed heavily before continuing, "We're still not sure of all the scripts we're looking for." She briefly closed her eyes.

He pours her a sparkling water, giving her time to relax and take in her surroundings. Christoph wonders if she's had enough sleep to deal with the shock she's had. He doubts it. Plus, now he finds out she's taking special medication and his protective instinct rises again. He crosses back over to her and hands her a cold glass of Pellegrino, her favorite. He even puts a wedge of lime in it, also her favorite – which he'd seen on her company profile, thanks to his team's research.

Absentmindedly, she squeezes the lime and takes a grateful sip before saying "Thank you so much." She sits back with another sigh and briefly closes her eyes.

"Have you been getting much sleep?" he suddenly asks.

"No, not really. I try to nap in between shifts, but I'm here for just about all of the shifts now, since my team is working around the clock," she states, matter-of-factly. "I can't justify not being here for them."

Of course, he already knew the ungodly hours she'd been keeping. His personal security team had been reporting back to him on her hours and whereabouts. He could see the dark circles under her eyes, and he was concerned that she seemed to have lost weight in the past few days. He couldn't have her continue to run herself into the ground like this, but he didn't know how to stop her. The news that he had for her wasn't going to be pleasant, either.

"I have some rather bad news," he said solemnly, as he took a seat in the armchair closest to her end of the couch. He watched her face as she opened her eyes and watched him sit.

"Your suspicions have been confirmed by the detectives and forensics: Luis Perez was the one in the car that was blown up three mornings ago," he tried to say gently, as gently as one can impart bad news while confirming such horrible but accurate suspicions. Nobody had heard from or seen Luis in days, but the detectives had told Christoph that they wanted to be sure and check all avenues while they waited for forensics to confirm the bomb victim's DNA. That confirmation took longer, which is why it had taken so long for Christoph to share this with Susan.

Susan was visibly shaken. She stared at him with her green eyes unnaturally wide. She had been valiantly pushing aside her suspicions, ignoring them and the horror they implied. She'd had experience in ignoring tragedy – pushing it off and out of her mind. Stunned, she tried to set her glass down on the coffee table without spilling anything, but her hand was shaking so badly she was lucky she was able to set it down at all. "I see," she finally responded.

Her mind flitted to the youth and eagerness she remembered in Luis. He was just getting started in his career. He was so naive to life, just the way she had been when she first graduated from college.

Susan had graduated from college with a 4.3 GPA, and she had earned her pick of jobs, with any corporation she wanted, to begin her career. She had been ready to spread her wings. She was going to be a professional businessperson, working in a high-rise in downtown Chicago, just as she'd always dreamed. She was ready for it all... single and looking forward to a successful career.

In college, her close, but not numerous, network of friends was constantly inviting her to parties and setting her up on blind dates. They were always throwing men in her direction, but she was too busy with her studies to take much notice. She always thought she'd have enough time. Maybe if she'd had a steady hookup, she would never have gotten into the situation she had. The same goes for Luis, she thought sadly.

Luis had just had a terrible breakup. That's why he'd volunteered for the third shift. Maybe if he hadn't been working the third shift, this wouldn't have happened to him. "I just can't believe this is happening," she said absentmindedly, without realizing she'd spoken out loud.

Christoph couldn't stand seeing the shock in her eyes any longer. He got up from his chair and moved to sit next to her on the couch. 'Screw sexual harassment,' he thought to himself. He put his arm around her, and tried to soothe her by rubbing her back as he said, "Are you going to be okay, Susan?"

"Uhh... yeah," she said, with no emotion. She just sat there and stared into space while he gently rubbed her back. It felt so good. For a moment, Susan just closed her eyes and enjoyed simply being touched. Her mind was in shock. One thing at a time.

He knew that the sleep deprivation and stress were magnifying the shock of the news. Intuitively, everyone knew it had been Luis in the car. Hearing it was sending her over the edge. He knew she needed sleep, and possibly also a massage. How he would love to give her a massage and tuck her into his bed, so that she could finally sleep! But his mind briefly entertained what it would be like to feel his naked body pressed against hers.

"Susan, why don't you get some sleep?" he asked.

"No, I can't, there's too much to do. They're about to have a shift change, and I need to be there," she tried to explain.

"Let them do the shift change on their own. Your team has already found the major problem, at least that we know of for now." He knew there could be other demons in the code that they hadn't found yet. The specialist team from Argon had been closely following the work of Susan's team.

From the looks of what he and his security team had seen so far, he doubted that humans were behind the breach. He couldn't tell her that right now, and there wasn't much more that she, herself, could do. Her coders were doing all they could – while his own security team searched for the culprit. That left her without such an urgency. He could finally send her home for some sleep.

"You are in shock, and you need to get some rest," he was saying, as she turned to look at him.

When she turned to face him to tell him she needed to stay at work, she looked into his eyes and forgot what she was going to say. He was so close to her, and he was still slowly rubbing her back with his hand. It felt so good, she didn't want it to stop. And he was so close. Her heart sped up a bit as she wondered what it would feel like to kiss him. His lips looked so soft and inviting. Her sleep deprivation had lowered her basic defenses.

She was leaning into him – or was he leaning into her? She didn't really care who was doing what when his lips met hers. She was lost in the feel of his kiss – and in the magnetic force that seemed to be fogging her mind and overwhelming Christoph.

Christoph knew he wouldn't be able control himself when she turned to look at him with those pleading, beautiful eyes. During the last few days, he'd thought of kissing her a million times. He didn't even give it much thought – he simply leaned in and kissed her. She felt so incredible to him. Feeling her energy was truly overwhelming to him. He just wanted to pull her up close and feel how their energies combined.

He already knew they were a match by the magnetic force he could feel drawing them together. His race was fine-tuned to those aspects of life. In addition, the males of his species were able to exert control over that magnetic force: it was all part of their fine-tuned mating abilities. But still, he knew it was unfair to use them on Susan when she had no idea he was purposely manipulating their energies to create a more powerful, combined force that only she and he were able to create together.

Still, he couldn't resist her and he couldn't resist just tweaking their energy movements just a little bit. Unlike human men, who did this manipulation unconsciously and based purely on instinct, he was trying to justify a reason to continue. It wasn't hard when her lips felt so good. He easily decided to probe deeper. He opened his mouth slightly, and her lips followed suit. He gently pushed his tongue into her mouth – again, she responded in kind.

When Christoph touched her tongue with his, she thought that her head was going to explode. The chemistry between them was amazing, and she wanted more. She wanted to feel him pressed against her. She unknowingly moved closer so that her body was touching his. At the same time, she encouraged him to pick up the pace of the kiss. He responded, and kissed her back with an urgency that she couldn't help but reciprocate. She was intoxicated by him, and she pushed a little closer as she put her hands on his shoulders.

Christoph slowly pulled back and gently pushed her slightly away from him. He had to collect himself; he'd only known Susan for less than three days. He couldn't just take her to his penthouse and have his way with her. As much as he'd like to take advantage of her lack of sleep and shocked mental state, he couldn't do that to her. Susan was his responsibility, and after that kiss she was his – even though she didn't know it yet.

"Susan, I'm sorry. I didn't mean to offend you like that," he tried to apologize. He wanted to give her a graceful way out.

"Oh, I... I... Uh," she stammered, as she collected herself and pulled herself back. She was completely embarrassed. "Uh, no, please... it's my fault," she began as he face started to turn red. He stopped her from continuing by placing his finger to her lips.

"Shhh, no, it's okay. It was me, I'm sorry. You're in shock. I took advantage," he finished. "Now, you need to get some sleep, no questions." He was adamant that she get some rest. He stood up and walked to his desk to pick up his cell phone, giving her a moment to compose herself. "I'm going to text George and ask him to take you home now, so that you can get some rest," he explained.

"No, that's not necessary, I drove. I have my car. I can drive," she protested.

"Susan," he began sternly as he made his way back to the couch to stand above her. "You are in shock and I'm not going to let you drive, much less be alone right now. I would take you myself, but I have to go to a charity function in less than thirty minutes," he said as the door opened and George walked in.

"Sir?" George questioned, with a nod of his head.

"George, would you please take Susan home so that she can get some sleep? Also, please stay there as an extra precaution, and bring her back here to work when she's ready. I know you have others stationed to watch her house, so let's leave them in place, okay?" he requested. "I'll escort her down now, via my private elevator. Please have the car waiting at the back entrance."

"Yes, sir," George nodded. Looking at Susan, he continued, "Whenever you're ready to leave, ma'am, I'll be waiting at the back entrance," as he left and closed the door.

Christoph turned to Susan. "Here, drink some more," he insisted, as he handed her the glass. She took a few tentative sips, and a few deep breaths. She couldn't believe she'd kissed her CEO. Susan could feel her face heating up and turning red again just remembering it. She felt *so embarrassed*!! Gratefully, she took a few more sips of water and let it help cool her face back to normal.

When her color returned to normal, Christoph bent to pick up her hand and draw her to her feet. "Come, let's get you down to the car. I'll take you down myself," he said, as he put an arm around her to guide her out of the room and down the hall to his private elevator.

The Grogan watchmen didn't see Susan leave the building. She'd been escorted down the elevator via the CEO's private elevator and into a Cadillac Escalade with dark-tinted windows and the watchmen never thought to pay attention to the vehicle coming out of the alley. Those vehicles came and went all the time. The company's limousine garage was located back there, so it wasn't unusual to see the executives going in and out all day. Since Susan Caldwell wasn't an executive, they never imagined she'd be in one of the limos.

The Grogans had been watching the building's comings and goings for weeks now. They thought they knew what to look for. But Grogans weren't always the smartest of beings.

The Grogans are like an advanced human race, except with all the possible negative traits in place and more often than not, not very smart. While their characteristics are based on human ones, they are definitely not human. Their skin is a putrid green color, and they have elephant-like trunks for noses, but the trunks only come down as low as their chins.

While their grotesque looks are totally different to humans, their personalities and characteristics have all of the strong and superficial characteristics of humans, twentyfold. Imagine taking all of the aggressive, destructive and selfish traits of humans, and multiply that by twenty – that is what Grogans are like. If you pleasure them, you will survive.

They survive on brute strength, as they were the strongest beings in their former universe. They craved power and domination. Their leader has waged wars in their old universe, Baldracon, because they wanted to take over the other planets and make all other species their slaves.

The Grogans wanted sex slaves, house slaves, machine slaves… the list was endless. The Grogans' appetites and desires were massive. The beings on their planet were easily manipulated into thinking that if they followed their leaders into battle, they could have whatever they could get their hands on from the alien planets.

Grogan fighters came back with many treasures from alien planets. But they were never able to conquer a single planet and keep the planet whole. Twice during the wars' reign, they had come close to conquering a planet, only to have the planet blow up for some reason or another. The Grogans couldn't figure out that the destruction they'd brought on had actually made the planet self-destruct, due to the instability of life caused by their warring.

As their wars waged across their former universe, they knew their chief nemesis was on the planet Argon. The Argon species was the only one with enough fighting power, intelligence and high-level technology to defend themselves.

The Grogans would not even attempt a full planetary invasion of Argon. They did, however, send out raiding parties, sneaking down every now and again, but it was rare.

During the Grogans' attempts to conquer the universe, they found out from a captured scientist that their sun was about to explode – and that it would suck all the planets in their universe into a black hole, if any of them survived the explosion. With this information, the Grogans began looking to see what the Argons were doing to counteract the sun explosion. All they could find were these huge ships being built. There was a fleet of at least sixteen ships – enough for every being on the planet Argon.

Just after all the ships had been built, the Grogans got lucky and kidnapped the lead Argon scientist and his family. They used him for intelligence, learning that the ships the Argons were building were made to evacuate their planet. The ships were floating colonies to be sent to other universes, with plans to find a suitable planet for their species to relocate. The floating colonies were called Space Domes. The Grogans immediately made the Argon scientist teach them how it all worked, and also oversee their own construction of Space Domes.

The only problem was that the Grogans were too late in getting started on their own Space Domes, and their manufacturing process was too slow. They had only built three when it became evident that the sun was about to explode. When that explosion was imminent, it was all the Grogans could do to get their ammunition and war machines loaded onto the modified space domes. Due to their miscalculations, they were only able to load about a third of the planet's population into the space domes before the sun exploded.

Their space domes didn't have any particular destination, nor any communication plans. They blindly set out to find whatever they could. The ships were able to communicate with each other, but there were no rules, laws or regulations imposed upon them.

When the lead ship intercepted an Argon communication signal, they were unable to decipher it. They decided to follow the initiating end of the communication, and they found themselves upon an Argon space dome in the Milky Way galaxy, in Earth's orbit.

Earth would make the perfect ice planet. Earth was perfectly positioned to its sun, with the right atmospheric conditions for the Grogan weather machines to function optimally. Even though the Grogans sought an ice planet, they needed sections to be free to support the oceanic fish and plants essential to Grogan survival. The other planets were too close to the sun, and the ones that were farther away didn't have the right crust to support the oceanic life that the Grogans needed to survive. But now that the Argonians had led them to this planet, they wanted the planet all to themselves.

The Grogans didn't want to share it with humans, or any of the other life forms. The Grogans needed to freeze the planet – but they were having problems reaching their goals because of the Argons.

Due to Argon interference, the Grogans had changed their tactics. Their first attempt at instigating gang wars so the humans would weaken and eliminate themselves had been a failure, thanks to the Argons' interference via their GTS firm. Now, the Grogans were going to do a switch on the humans and Argonians.

Instead of freezing the planet, they were going to heat the humans off the Earth and into extinction, through drought, disease and famine. Melting the ice caps and flooding the Earth, along with the false storms the Grogans' weather machines could create, would eventually bring forth the end of the human race. The Grogans would then be able to turn their machines back to the cold setting for which they were originally designed, and freeze the Earth to the perfect temperature for their own survival.

But first, before they could accomplish this feat, they would have to overtake the Argons so that the Grogan weather-making machines could do the work they needed. Recently, they'd lost one of their machines to the Argonians.

The Grogans knew they would not be able to defeat the humans and the Argons by sheer numbers and brute force alone, because there were too few of them. For the first time, the Grogans had to fight an intelligent war based on strategy and brains – something they did not collectively excel at. Only their aristocratic leaders could make this happen.

The Grogan colony leaders had been working on implementing their heating strategy for several decades. Every attempt had been met with failure, and counteractions, from the Argons. But this time, they were working on counterintelligence by hacking into the Argon computer systems. They were attempting to infiltrate the Argon databases and weaken them through false information. In addition, they were slowly and methodically working to eradicate the Earth of all Argons, one at a time. But they had to find them first. Access to the GTS system would hopefully help them identify who the Argons are, and where they are hiding on Earth. This added strategy would take time and require the Grogans to use and develop more of their cloaking devices so they can blend in with humans more than ever.

The human cloaking device was the only way Grogans had been able to integrate with humans to carry out their plans. Their captured Argon scientist had developed not only human cloaking devices for Grogans so they could blend in on Earth, but also a human mind-control device. The Grogans were able to take captured humans, and control their minds and actions for twenty-four hours. They had just begun their first serious use of a human operative. It was all part of the strategy to infiltrate the Argon systems for intelligence data.

The first step in the strategy was to select and develop a human operative from the GTS security management team. They needed somebody who could easily get root access to the systems. For several years, the Grogans had suspected that the Argons were behind the eradication of the human gang wars and the shift towards global digital monetization. It matched too closely with the structure used on the planet Argon. The Grogan leaders knew they had to get inside GTS to investigate, and eventually take over the Earth's monetary supplies, in order to cripple the humans. Capturing and developing a human operative with the proper permissions had been vital to their scheme. At first, everything worked smoothly and without a hitch.

Then their operative made a mistake. The mind control was waning, and it was almost time for his to return for reconditioning when he started trying to get logged back into the system and turn off the copies that were running. To complicate the situation, the operative was summoned and questioned by GTS's CEO. He hadn't had enough time to copy back all the original scripts, even though he'd turned off the replication. The humans wouldn't be able to figure out where the replication was going, or even that the data was being replicated in the first place. Those types of traces didn't exist in development environments – at least they didn't exist in human-created development environments. Since this human's mind control was weakening by the minute, he was unable to remember the commands to find and replace the original scripts. He missed many of them, leaving those in place. That meant there was a trail.

The Grogans needed to stop the scripts from being discovered. They thought they'd taken care of the problem when they eliminated the original programmer who had found the breach. Then they found out that his manager also knew about it. They'd already tried to eliminate her once, but it hadn't worked. She was still working on it, and now her entire team was working on it too. There was a company-wide lockdown, and everyone now knew there was a breach. Something had to be done to stop them and keep them from discovering the truth.

Chapter 6

Christoph calls Susan on her cell, "Susan, this is Christoph Baldric. I'm coming to pick you up. Pack a bag and be prepared to be gone for a while. There's been another accident. I have to get you to a safe zone. Don't leave George's protection," he told her urgently. "I'll be there to pick you up in half an hour, and I'll explain everything then," he said, before he hung up. He didn't even give her a chance to reply.

Susan's mind was running a million miles a minute. 'What in the world could this tragedy be that is so great that he would wake her up?' She looked over at her clock, and noticed she'd only been asleep for an hour. It seemed longer, but it still wasn't enough, and she wanted to roll over and go back to sleep. Just then she heard a knock on her bedroom door.

"Ms. Caldwell, this is George. Mr. Baldric called and asked that you pack a bag and be ready to leave in thirty minutes. Is there anything I can help you with?" he asked through the closed bedroom door.

"No, no thank you, I'm getting up. I'll get in the shower and then get packed," she replied. "But wait," she started. "What am I supposed to pack for? It's fall: it can be really cold some places or really hot."

"Pack for hot, plus air conditioning," he replied.

Forty minutes later she opened her bedroom door, rolling her suitcase out behind her. George was there immediately, "I can take that for you, ma'am. Is there anything else?"

"Yes, a small case by the foot of the bed, but I can get it if you take this one," she offered.

"No ma'am, I can get them both. Please go downstairs. Mr. Baldric is waiting outside for you. I'll be right behind you," he said.

"Wait, what about my dog? I can't just leave him here. I haven't even made arrangements to have him looked after," she balked.

"No need to worry, ma'am. We have that all arranged for you. He'll be watched after by Peter, twenty-four/seven. If you have any special instructions, send me a reply email to the one in your Inbox about your dog," he responded, matter-of-factly. "I'll make sure everything is handled."

Susan's head was spinning. It seemed that they'd thought of everything. She had nothing else to worry about: not her job, not her dog, not even her safety – as she had personal security guards around her all the time. She wasn't quite sure she was comfortable with this arrangement. 'What else can I do? I was almost killed in the deli,' she reasoned with herself. And her co-worker *was* killed!

She descended the stairs carefully. Even though she'd taken a shower, she was still dead tired, and she felt a bit disoriented. The medication had really made her dizzy. She needed more sleep – and badly. She made sure to hold onto the railing all the way down.

Another security guard was waiting at the bottom of the stairs by the front entrance, ready to open the door for her when she arrived. Before he let her walk through the door, he checked it out himself to be sure that all was clear before escorting her to the waiting vehicle. Its motor was already running. The guard took her around to the passenger side, and opened the front door for her to climb in.

She looked into the Escalade when the door opened, and saw Christoph in the driver's seat. Susan reached inside for the handle and climbed up into the huge SUV. She didn't like the ominous sensations she was feeling. The security guards had never followed her so closely before. The sun was so bright that she was temporarily blinded when the security guard shut the car door. She vaguely registered another person sitting in the back seat, but it was too dark for her to recognize who it was until her eyes could adjust. She focused on fastening her seatbelt.

The back doors to the Escalade opened, and George stowed her luggage safely. He closed the doors and walked around to the driver's side window, which Christoph rolled down. "Sir, all the luggage is stored." George announced. "Peter will be staying to watch after Ms. Caldwell's dog, and her property, while you're gone. Is there anything else?"

"Yes. I need you to follow us to the airport. Make sure the security team has our ETA and is ready to escort us when we arrive. Double check that the island security team is on standby," Christoph outlined. "As soon as you get the downtown headquarters locked down, I need you to call me so we can review your team's findings on the bombing investigation."

"Yes, sir. I'll be right behind you," George reassured him.

Christoph rolled up his window before backing out of the driveway.

As he started driving them out of her neighborhood, he asked her, "Did you get any sleep?"

"Yes, about an hour. What's going on? I know something happened. Tell me," she insisted urgently.

Christoph was silent as he negotiated the turns needed to enter the expressway. He briefly looked over at her anxious expression before saying, "There's been another bomb."

He looked back over at her and saw that her face was now as white as a sheet. He continued, "It happened at 6:20 p.m., during shift change on the twelfth floor in the executive conference room."

There was no way for him to candy-coat it, he had to tell her flat out what happened. "All the programmers who were in the conference room at the time were killed instantly. It was shift change when it happened. Only one survived, Juan Cortez. He's in the back seat now," he finished, with a nod of his head toward the back seat.

"Juan, are you okay? What happened?" she automatically asked, as she turned to look for him in the back.

"I'm fine. I don't know what happened, ma'am. We played our normal Coke game – the one we play during shift change. I lost this time. Carrie Hamilton-Geiser wanted a Red Mountain Dew, so I had to go down to the fifth-floor break room to get it. You know that's the only floor with a Pepsi machine?" He paused for a moment, and swallowed before continuing. "That's when I heard the boom and felt the entire building shake. I was terrified that it was going to crumble to the ground," he finished frantically, his voice still shaky from the incident.

"Everyone died?" she asked in awe.

Christoph replied, "Yes. So far we've not found any survivors. The bomb was quite powerful. The entire upper levels of the building have been compromised. We've evacuated the building, and we will be repairing it before anyone is allowed inside."

"But everyone?" she asked again. Clearly the shock was setting in.

Christoph continued as if she hadn't spoken, "Juan says they'd already checked in the code. It was locked down and fully backed up, off-site, before they even started shift change, so the systems have been secured."

"Yes, ma'am," Juan confirmed, "we did just like you instructed for every shift change. We already had the code secured before the next shift even showed up. We were just waiting for the clock to chime at 6:30 p.m. so that we could officially leave for the day. You know we always finish the security procedures early; that's why we play the Coke game between shifts."

"Everyone?" her saddened and terrified mind questioned again.

She couldn't comprehend that everyone was gone. Susan knew that her teams were very good at following her security instructions and the procedures she'd set out to maintain the integrity of the code between shifts. She'd even been the one to introduce them to the Coke game. It gave the team a chance to socialize, and talk about any developments they'd found during their shifts. It was a chance for an informal shift change before the official change occurred.

It hit her as slightly ironic that Juan had lost the Coke game, yet that fact had saved his life. If he hadn't lost, he'd never have been down on the fifth floor getting the special soda when the bomb went off.

The thought of another bomb left her numb. Everyone was gone. She was at a loss as to what to think or what to do.

Susan was in such shock that she couldn't think of any more questions. She didn't even ask where they were going, although she knew they were heading toward the airport. She knew it wasn't the main international airport, though, because that was in the other direction.

Her mind was a jumble and a mess. All she could think about were the lives that were lost. All of her innocent team members. She would have been there too if Christoph had not made her leave to get some rest.

Just then, Christoph offered a short explanation: "I'm taking you both to a secure location so that you can continue to search the code. I need to be sure that you'll both be safe, which is why I'm taking you to my private island compound. It'll take us about thirteen or fourteen hours to get there, but it's our safest bet to keep you safe at this time and on such short notice." Of course, there were the secure Argon compounds that he could take them to, right here in the city, but so far no humans had been there.

Now was not the time to expose his race to them and introduce any more shock than they'd already experienced in the last several days. His urge to protect Susan was his number-one concern. He had teams of his alien security experts to handle the code breach.

His Argon security experts were already working on reviewing the surveillance videos to see if they could pinpoint how the bomb was planted. They were also primarily concerned with insuring that the Argon computer systems were secured and safe, before they turned toward the GTS monetary systems and surveillance data.

Christoph was confident all was in motion to protect GTS and Argon systems, but Susan was another matter. A personal matter. Christoph felt it his place to ensure her safety, which meant taking her to a safe location. He pulls the car into an obvious special airport entrance. It is a small, private airport. He pulls right up to the building entrance and stops the vehicle.

Before she can register what is happening, Christoph is opening her door, releasing her seat belt and helping her down, out of the Escalade. She follows him into the building.

"Where's your passport?" he asks her.

She fumbles through her purse, produces the booklet and hands it over to him to show to the security guard. She puts her purse on the security belt and walks through the metal detector. She wonders why this is necessary if they are flying a private plane, but she doesn't even think to question what is happening. She just goes along and does as Christoph instructs.

At this point, she doesn't even really care where she is going or what is happening. All she knows is that she wants and needs to sleep. She is calculating in her mind when he said the bomb went off. She'd barely been home for ten minutes when it had exploded. If she had delayed leaving any later, she might have been in the room.

It could have been her too. Her team. Gone. The shock is setting in and the devastation is beginning to register. Tears start falling unchecked down her cheeks as Christoph leads her down an escalator, and out a door onto the tarmac.

"This way, Susan," Christoph says to her, as he takes her by the arm and guides her to the steps leading up to a private jet. He notices her tears and knows she's in shock. There had been no easy way to tell her what had happened.

She can barely see anything. The tears are silently overflowing, down her face. 'How am I going to manage those steps?' she thinks to herself as she peers up them to the door of the large private plane.

Christoph looks down into her face when she pauses at the steps. She is still in shock, and he realizes there is no way she can see anything through the tears that are falling down her face. Out of a protective instinct, he exchanges his case for Susan. Setting his case on the ground for the security team to grab, he picks her up and takes her up the steps into the jet. He nods to the pilot and flight attendant: "Hello Tom, Hi Valerie. Valerie, can you please bring me two tumblers of bourbon, neat?" he requests, before he walks to the back and sets Susan down on the couch. He hands her a box of tissues so she can wipe her eyes. The tears seem to have stopped for now.

"Is there anything else I can get you?" Valerie asks, as she hands him the tumblers.

"No, thank you, Valerie," he replies. "We're ready to take off when Tom is. The sooner the better." He moves to sit next to Susan and hands her the glass. "Here, drink this," he coaxes. "Drink it all – it will help."

Susan takes the glass and drinks the bourbon down in one gulp. She coughs a little bit, but it is smooth, and she feels the warmth all the way down to her stomach. She automatically hands him the empty glass.

Christoph finishes his bourbon in the same fashion before saying, "Here, let's get your seatbelt fastened." He leans over her and pulls out a buckle, which he attaches to the strap in between them. He tightens it a bit, saying "Just relax, we'll be taking off shortly."

Takeoff was prompt and fast. The jet climbed to a cruising altitude of 35,000 feet within minutes. As soon as it was safe, Christoph was again sitting next to Susan, asking her, "Is there anything I can get you? Are you hungry? Another drink?"

"Is there someplace I can lie down?" she requests. "Someplace quiet." He looks at her and can see that the shock is still on her face, but along with the emptiness in her eyes, he can see the dark circles still there from lack of sleep. He takes her hand, helps her stand up and leads her to the middle section of the plane where there are bunks in the wall with privacy curtains. "Here, take this bunk, Susan. Get in," he says, as he holds back the curtain.

She peeks in, and the bedding area looks positively delightful. There is a duvet and several soft feather pillows. All the linens are 1000 thread count; she can tell by looking at them. Everything is white, and it all looks like a fluffy cloud welcoming her. She slips off her shoes and climbs in without question. She feels wonderful and soft as she nestles under the duvet on one of the most comfortable beds she's ever been in. Before Christoph can stow her shoes and pull the curtain closed, she's fallen sound asleep.

They were flying to Christoph's private island in the Pacific, just beyond the coast of Korea. You could only reach the island via boat or air. It is the most secure location he could think of at this time – at least the most secure place that he could take humans. Up until now, he'd only ever needed to keep Argons safe. This was the first time he was, personally, protecting humans. Without telling them about his alien race, his options were limited.

About forty-five minutes before they are to land, he hears shuffling in the bunk where Susan is sleeping. He goes over to listen, and hears her shifting back and forth and rustling the covers. He hears her barely whimpering, "No, no, no, don't touch me." He throws back the curtains to see her alone. Alone in her nightmare, trying to push at the air and thrashing back and forth.

He sits beside her on the bed and gently touches her shoulder. He whispers her name: "Susan, Susan, wake up. It's okay – wake up," he says, as he gently shakes her shoulder.

Chapter 7

In her dream, she's lying there helpless.

She's trying to move her arms, but they're not moving. She's trying to move her legs, anything on her body, but nothing will move. The loathsome sailor guy is back and he's trying to kiss her. She moves her head to the side, but it doesn't stop him from touching her breasts and removing her bathing suit. She can't stop him. Then she feels another person at her shoulder. 'Please make him stop,' she thinks to herself. She tries to look to see who it is, but when she turns, the ropes of the canopy press harder into her back. "No, stop, please," she pleads, except her mouth isn't working anymore and the words don't come out.

Christoph notices her getting more and more anxious. He literally gets into the bunk with her to reach her other shoulder and pull her into a sitting position, trying to jostle her awake.

She opens her eyes and stares at him with horror in her eyes. She looks terrified, but at the same time, her green eyes are blank as if she's still in the midst of her nightmare. "Susan, wake up. It's me, Christoph. Wake up, you're dreaming."

She wakes up, looking at Christoph. She's sitting up in the airplane bunk. Christoph is on the bunk with her and he looks concerned. "Are you okay? Are you awake now?" he asks.

"Uh," she pauses, and takes in her surroundings again. "Uh, yeah, I think so," she says, as the dream fades into the background. She puts her hands to her face as if to wipe the nightmare from her eyes. It's the same one, over and over again. It leaves her feeling so helpless and ashamed of herself. She doesn't even want Christoph looking at her. She quickly puts her hands over her face to try to block herself from him for a brief moment. She says, "Can I have a few minutes alone?"

"Of course. Are you hungry?" he asks. "We'll be landing in about an hour. You've been asleep for almost thirteen hours. Come, have something to eat before we land. You slept through dinner," he explains, "and I didn't want to wake you."

Before words could answer, her stomach growls. She's never slept that long – ever. She wondered if he put something in her bourbon. But she replayed it, and he couldn't have. She relaxed a little.

She faintly acknowledges him as she says, "Okay, yes, I'm famished." She shuffles around under the covers, embarrassed at hearing her stomach growl again. "Give me a few minutes?" she pleads, mainly with her eyes. He steps back from the bunk and secures the curtain to give her the privacy she needs.

———————————

They land on a tiny airstrip in the middle of the small island. From the air, Susan sees a huge complex on the island's east end.

As she steps to the door of the plane, she is immediately hit with a huge wave of heat and humidity. She can feel her hair already kinking and curling up. 'Wow, it's really *hot,*' she thought. She took off her blazer while she descended the airplane steps. Once they were on the tarmac, guards led them to an open-topped red Jeep.

Christoph tells her, "Go over to the passenger side, Susan. Juan, you can get in on the driver's side, here," he says, as he pulls the driver's seat forward so Juan can get in the back. "Don't worry about your luggage. The crew will get it and bring it with them to the complex," he explains.

Once they are on their way, Susan takes a moment to look around and get her bearings. It's beautiful, just like the pictures in the magazines, except on the ground all she can see is brush and trees. It's like a dense rainforest, and the dirt road is bumpy and rutted from rain. She actually has to hold on to the bars in the Jeep to keep from being thrown out.

In about five minutes, they reach a more level, barely paved road that runs alongside the ocean. As they approach the complex, she is in awe of the beauty around her. There are palm trees and mangroves on the white beaches. The water is crystal clear, and you can see all the way to the bottom of the ocean. It's gorgeous, and everything you can imagine an island should be, including the massive mansion sitting on the top of a cliff.

Christoph reassures them how safe the island is, "We're the only ones here. I have a special security team in place, and nobody else can land on this island by plane or by boat without our knowledge." He explains that they have the access and tools necessary to keep working on the code. "You'll be surprised at how modern we are here on the edge of the Pacific: with satellites and microwave technologies, we've been able to simulate New York City in response times." He paused as he negotiated a particularly sharp set of hairpin turns as they climbed to the top of the hill. "While you both will be working on the code, I'll be focused on my other business and on handling the fallout and media attention that the bombing has caused."

When they arrive, Christoph introduces them to Alan, his housekeeper. "Alan, please take care of Susan and Juan. Give them a tour around the house, the pool, the exercise room, and show them how to get to the beach. We'll be setting up computers and such in the dining room for them to work on. In the meantime," Christoph requested kindly, "please show them where they can sleep."

The housekeeper was a short five foot nine, and he had a jolly look about his face as though he smiled all the time. He had a rotund but solid figure. He worked out, but he liked his beer, too. Alan found it odd that they would be working on computers in the dining room. "Why aren't they using the secured area for all their work?" he wondered.

It wasn't for him to question his Commander. He was here to do whatever is asked and needed. The security team had already told them the Commander was bringing humans to the island. It would be a nice change of pace to be able to socialize with humans – quite different from interacting only with Argons on the ship. Thank goodness Christoph had opted to text him well in advance of their arrival, so he could quickly call in the maid to help ready the two extra guest rooms. In the meantime, he was looking forward to getting to know Juan, who was extremely good looking – and hopefully single.

The next morning, at 6 a.m., Juan can't stand to stay in bed any longer and feels the need to do something. He decides to work on the code fixes.

Juan is about five foot ten, with thick, black, wavy hair and dark, golden-tanned skin. His face has the chiseled, classical features of Renaissance paintings, but his personality is blatantly gay – of which he's not ashamed and which he sometimes flaunts to the discomfort of his fellow colleagues. Many times, Susan had a good laugh about some comment or other that Juan had made about a man. Truly, his acceptance of who he is was very refreshing.

However, Juan is not used to the time change being upside down. He's wide awake at 6 a.m. He feels as though he was forced to sleep through the day – and in reality, he was. His normal time, back home, is 5 p.m. He's anxious to get back to work – and to see the handsome housekeeper.

Luckily for Juan, Alan starts his morning at 5:30 in the morning with a nice pot of coffee, continental breakfast, and the news. When Alan looked up from his reading, he was taken aback by the handsome man coming his way. A moment later, he remembered it was actually his *job* to get to know the coder. 'Oh and what a chore that will be!?! NOT!!' he thought to himself, as he welcomed Juan and offered him a cup of coffee.

By 10 a.m., the entire house is in full movement. Breakfast has been served, Christoph has recently finished his last Western interview on the bombings. Juan and Susan are busy working on finding evidence of who might have infiltrated their system.

At 10:30 a.m., Juan finds code evidence that points toward Susan – and Carrie, the intern – as the culprits. He is showing it to Susan when Christoph comes in. "Did I hear you say you found out who did this?"

Juan stumbles on what to say and stutters, "Uh... well... uh... I found something that seems to point to responsible parties, but... well... uh... I'm not sure." Juan was very shy and a bit overcome when talking to the CEO. Not only because he was the CEO, but he was so handsome. Even though the CEO wasn't gay, Juan was still in awe of him.

"It points to me. The intern and me," Susan blurts out, directly cutting straight to the point. "The entries in the startup scripts implicate us. It doesn't make sense. You have to have root access in order to make those changes, and neither one of us has ever requested root access." She shakes her head and stares at the screen some more. "This should be easy," she states adamantly, "as I know it wasn't either one of us."

Susan insists, "I'm going to get to the bottom of this and prove it isn't either one of us. I just need to get the root access requests."

Suddenly the impact of the tragedy hit Susan. Carrie is dead; she died in the explosion. Carrie, bless her heart, was only an intern and barely knew how to check out a script. Beyond that, Carrie was a seasonal intern, and she was still pretty much on coffee duty. Or rather, she had been.

Susan had to stop a moment to collect herself. It was so sad and wasn't fair at all. Carrie had recently gotten married, and she had a wonderful, three-month-old baby boy. She was so in love with her husband and her child. She had a most unusual life for women these days. Although, her life couldn't have been any more perfect – and then "BOOM," it was all over for her.

Why couldn't it have been herself instead? Susan thought glumly. All she had was a dog, and her sister would have looked after him for her. Soon, she'd have a baby, but she didn't have one now. It's amazing how life can turn on a dime and leave you to wonder what the hell you're even doing here.

Susan usually didn't bother wondering what she was doing because she always had an immediate goal. Graduate from college, get a job, and now have a baby. Simple. Although there'd been some occasions where she wondered about trying for more than a hookup with a guy.

There had been several men she might have liked to continue a relationship with, perhaps even a partnership in raising children. For some reason or another, though, those relationships never worked out. It didn't matter to her; she was ready to have children of her own, and she was excited that soon this would become a reality for her. Like most of her friends, she didn't need a man to have a family. Besides, she didn't like men much anyway and ultimately she didn't trust them.

Since men were mostly hookups, they were just something to satisfy that basic instinct. However, it had been nice to have a steady hookup every once in a while. She figured her regular hookups had eventually realized that any time she had any physical contact with them, she had to be buzzed or drunk. She always left before morning and never let a man spend the night. She kept men at bay as much as possible. If by some chance a man did spend the night, she was always awake before him so that he couldn't touch her. She had no idea that she was acting this way; it was her automatic defensive actions to protect her from getting involved.

She kept men at arm's length, and basically used them just for sex. It was the way of the world anyway, so she wasn't doing anything out of the ordinary. Very few people had long-term relationships or marriages anymore. Carrie was an exception to the norm. But not Susan, she was content to follow the norm of society.

She was determined to have a family on her own, just as many of her friends did. She'd signed up for the best fertility clinic in the country and resigned herself to wait until her number came up. Otherwise, just her dog and her job – that was all she needed. It was the deciding factor in her relocation to Boston, where the clinic is located.

Moving to Boston was no big deal for her. It was an easy decision, plus she'd finally landed the job at GTS Security. She'd interviewed for two months. It had taken her nine months to find a job, and finally she'd found one at GTS. She was looking forward to a fresh start, meeting people, learning the city. Plus, one of her closest friends from college lived nearby in Cambridge with her two little girls.

Thoughts of holidays spent with them made her smile. She always enjoyed her visits, making her look forward to when she could have her own child. The butterflies started in her stomach again as she contemplated how soon she would be able to have her baby. And that reminded her to take her daily medication.

Susan got up from the computer and went to the side table to pour herself a glass of ice water. Taking it back to the table, she sifted through her purse to find her meds, then popped the necessary pills. Satisfied that she was ready to get back to work, she tried to focus on the screen and the problem at hand.

It took her a minute or two of staring at the screen to pull herself together and get on with searching for evidence to vindicate Carrie and herself. It was just a short time later when she found what she needed.

Susan pulled all the root access requests, and verified that neither she nor Carrie had ever requested that level of access. From there, it was clear that the log entries had to have been falsified. It was easy to find the trail of evidence held within the timestamps. First, the month and day were wrong. The system timestamp used the new world standard timestamp, which follows the old European pattern: dd/mm/yy. These timestamps had the day and month switched.

Susan was relieved she'd found it so quickly. The miscreant had re-entered the systems by using a back door, and had set up more scripts to overwrite the log files using her and Carrie's own IDs! Since Carrie had never really logged in before, it had been easy to identify where her ID didn't belong. Unfortunately for Susan, she had to log in frequently to check on her team's activity. It had taken slightly longer, but by pinpointing the root commands, she was able to separate the real records from the fictional data. Thank goodness she had never had root access.

Chapter 8

Finding this evidence definitely eased the tension in the house, and everyone seemed to fall into a groove over the next few days. Juan was seeking out the company of Alan, the housekeeper, as much as he could. It started easily because the dining room has an open doorway to the kitchen, and the housekeeper's office was nestled in the back corner of the kitchen.

One day, after Alan had brought them lunch. As soon as he was out of the room, Juan sighed as he said, "Oh yeah, now *that's* a hot booty."

"JUAN!" Susan exclaimed. "How can you say something like that?" she asks, in feigned disbelief. They both laughed.

"He is something else though," Juan said, as he sighed, staring off in space, absentmindedly toying with his fork.

"Are you hitting that already?" Susan asks in true disbelief.

"No, honey, but I wish I could. That man is so fine, he makes me hard just thinking about touching him," Juan confessed rather crudely. But that was Juan.

Susan shrugged her shoulders, "I'm sure that it's not from a lack of trying, eh?" She loved teasing him about his dating adventures.

"I'm dedicated if nothing else. You'd better believe your sweet little muffin that I've been trying. I kissed him last night," he said, on another deep sigh off into space. He had this silly, goofy grin on his face as he obviously replayed the scene in his mind.

"Well, spill the beans," she prodded. "How did it happen?"

Juan suddenly focuses and leans over to hunch down between their computers as though he's about to tell a secret. "He showed me the hot tub last night, and I convinced him to get into it."

"Hot tub, huh? Are you sure kissing is all that you did?" she guessed. She already knew that every day, Juan would slip into the kitchen to eat an early dinner with Alan. After that, they went out walking or hiking before the sun went down, so she wasn't surprised to hear this from Juan.

But at her question, Juan's face suddenly went completely red. She didn't want to poke at him; he needed to enjoy the moment. It really wasn't any of her business anyway. She needed to ease his mind.

"Never mind, Juan – sorry I asked. That's none of my business." She paused as she saw him visibly relax and smiled in his direction. "Enjoy yourself and be happy," she said encouragingly. "Eat," she said as she took a bite of the delicious chicken vegetable pasta salad that Alan had made for lunch.

For meals the first couple of days, Susan ate whatever Alan brought to them whenever he brought it in. Alan kept a schedule every day and it was normal hours, so she couldn't complain. It was actually lovely not to worry about what to each for lunch or dinner.

In addition to their regular meals, they kept a jug of water, an ice bucket, sodas and glasses on the dining room sideboard, along with some fruits and nuts. Occasionally, Susan would go into the kitchen to fix coffee or tea, sometimes even fruit juice. She only ever saw Alan or Juan in the kitchen area. She didn't know what Christoph did for dinner. She hadn't seen him in the kitchen at all when she was working, but then again, she had kept the door closed to keep out any distractions.

By dinnertime, Susan realized she hadn't seen Christoph around, so she'd email him an update instead. Not really knowing where he was or what he was doing in and around the compound, this would be easier. She really didn't know much about where he could be in the compound. Her slight tour she got from Alan on the way in was very limited and she hadn't had any time to explore since she'd been here.

Would she ever have time to laze at the beach? Shouldn't they be working on this twenty-four/seven? It just didn't seem possible to enjoy her location with so much stress on her to do something she couldn't do. She didn't know the code well enough – only Juan did – but there's no way he could do it all by himself. She needed a new team.

Trying to figure out how to approach Christoph to tell him they needed help was causing her some concern. The thought was making her frown as she selected food from the dishes that Alan had left for dinner. She turned to put the plate in the oven to heat and bumped into Christoph, nearly losing everything in her hands.

Christoph saw Susan turn just in time to steady her and keep her from dropping her plate of food. He smiled into her captivating green eyes. 'I've definitely missed looking into those eyes these last couple of days,' he thought to himself. As he looked closer, he could see flecks of gold highlighting the green. They were amazing – *she* was amazing. He just wanted to pull her close and kiss her again before proceeding to bed her in every way he could think of. She turned him on like he couldn't believe.

Christoph was vulnerable to the humans in general, but Susan caught him on a level no one else ever had. He had a fascination with humans, and he was a major proponent for integrating more quickly with the humans. He could never pinpoint exactly what it was about Susan, but he desired her like no other, and he wanted her to be his mate. He had not had a personal relationship experience with a female who had emotions. The females in his species didn't have them. Susan was a new challenge to him.

Christoph was willing to risk it all to have her and integrate her into Argon society, giving her the special treatments and medications necessary to extend her life to equal that of an Argonian. But until then, he needed to blend in and be like a human male would be.

Since he was so much like a human in the physical sense, it wasn't too difficult. But it was things like human decisions that he tried hard to emulate. It was difficult due the shift in human relationships, with marriage at an all-time low. It had him concerned because his views were not the same as human men. Hookups were *not* okay for him. It didn't work that way on Argon. Marriage was a necessary partnership for raising a family. The humans, though, were taking on a new way of life with their fertility clinics and single parents. Trying to incorporate his actions with that of a human with these views had Christoph at a distinct disadvantage, which is why he needed to get to know Susan, quickly.

Having Susan at the island was his best chance to get close to her. He had his Argonian computer specialists working on the code. He primarily had Susan and Juan here to keep them safe while his specialists figured out who was behind this, and why. He didn't need Susan and Juan to work on the code, he just wanted them to feel useful.

When Juan found the most recent false evidence pointing toward Susan and the intern, Christoph had found out in less than thirty minutes that it was falsified log records, and that the two women had never had root access.

Christoph couldn't tell Susan, or else there'd be too many questions about how he could find out so quickly. Eventually, he would have to tell them he had another team in place. For now, though, he had to find a way to lessen their stress so that they'd take some time off and relax. If they continued at this pace, they would burn out in no time.

His hands were still holding onto Susan to keep her from falling and spilling her dinner. "We have to stop meeting like this," he joked as he removed his hands. At that moment, he made up his mind that he would protect her at any cost. Right now, that meant stepping out of her way and trying to get to know her.

"Excuse me," he said, as he stepped out of her way and reached to open the oven door for her.

"Oh, of course, yes, thank you, oh… sure no problem, you just startled me," she finished breathlessly. She was barely able to slide the plate into the oven without her hand shaking. She couldn't believe she didn't spill everything! Her heart was racing up in her throat. He's here, and he's touching her. He felt so good.

Every time he's near, she becomes jittery, clumsy and overly excited. He wonders if he really does have that effect on her. He would love to be able to make her squirm like that on a regular basis. "Sorry about that, I was just coming to get some food. What's for supper?" he asks, trying to shrug off the incident.

He turned to the counter and surveyed the dishes: ham, green beans, baked asparagus, and carrot hash cakes. It was a typical Argon meal: all natural, no wheat, no dairy, no rice, no corn. It's not that Argonians couldn't eat those foods, but for many it caused upset stomach, diarrhea, and gas. There had been a few deaths for those who were highly allergic, very similar to the humans.

Susan was calming down as she took a deep breath and said, "There's a salad in the refrigerator. I'm going to have some while my food is heating. Do you want me to get you one?" she offered.

"Yes, that will be great. I'll get some wine. What kind would you like?" he asked.

"Red. Do you happen to have a Cabernet Sauvignon? If not, a Merlot will do nicely," she replied.

Christoph retrieved one of his favorites, a Mirror Cabernet Sauvignon, from the wine rack and opened it. He poured her a glass and handed it to her, asking, "Now that you've proven it wasn't you, it seems there's no immediate threat to the computer systems, right?"

"We've fixed the startup scripts so we don't have that deadline. We still don't know who did it or why," she continued. "We also don't know what they were going to do with the data in the development databases."

He thinks for a few moments and compares her comments to what his security team has already briefed him on. She's right, but what she doesn't know is that it's bigger than her human world – and that there's more there than she and Juan can handle.

"At the moment, our company is operating in the emergency lockdown mode. It is only impacting internal operations, but we are still processing funds, collecting data and performing surveillance. Only a select few are allowed on the system at this time, which is how we are controlling it. We cannot afford any downtime," he stated emphatically.

She looked a little shocked at the vehemence in his voice, but she had no idea what was really entailed here. Sure, she was a target, but his Argon computer systems were the bigger target. He couldn't explain that flat out to her. He decided to take the tack that he would put together another team.

"I'm having my senior computer engineer VP put together and head up a special security investigative team to search for the reason why, and to help confirm that there is no other code," he explained.

"What? Why? Does that mean I don't have a job anymore?" she panicked.

"No, no, of course you have a job," he reassured her. "It's just that your entire team is gone; you don't have anyone to manage. We need another team of security specialists. You're in danger, and you don't have access to put together that team, or even to interview people. The VP is going to pull experts from within the company from several different divisions to fill in until your team can be assembled for you," he added.

"But what am I supposed to be *doing*? And what is Juan supposed to do?" she queried him.

"You both will still do what you're doing, but there isn't going to be such urgency. You don't need to work around the clock. Take weekends off. Your safety is in danger, but you can't stop living your life. We don't know how long it will be until we find the culprits and it's safe for your return," he said solemnly. "You will burn yourself out if you continue at this pace. The code is secure for now." He was confident his alien security specialists already had everything under control. His certainty transmitted security to Susan.

The relief Susan felt at his words was immense. She took a sip of the wine and thought about how she didn't have to tell him her weaknesses. He already knew them. It was as though he already knew she was going to ask him for another team. Well, she's the doofus: of course she should expect to get another team. Replace those she lost. It just hadn't occurred to her yet. While it did now, she wasn't ready to deal with it yet. The deaths were too recent. The tragic thoughts of them immediately silenced her and made her mind draw a blank. She stared into space for a moment before the oven buzzer started.

Susan didn't say anything as she stopped the buzzer on the oven and took out her plate. She didn't know how long she was silent. She hadn't even gotten her salad. He'd distracted her with wine and talk of a new team. She wasn't ready to face that yet. She wished she didn't feel responsible, and that she herself had to find the problem. But she knew she couldn't do it. She was wasting her time – it was not her forte. She was a much better manager and designer, as she had an excellent knack for strategic thinking and molding her job to help the big picture. They needed experts – and more than two people. At least she didn't have to do this on her own.

"Are they going to come here to work?" she asked. The relief on her face was clearly evident. It was as though she became ten years younger in a heartbeat.

"Not at this time. We're going to train them and get them set up back in Boston. If something else occurs, we might have to move some of them here," he said. "For now, you need to take tomorrow off. It is Sunday and you shouldn't be working. Sleep late, relax, enjoy the island," he cajoled.

Trying to change the subject to something light, he asked, "Do you like to swim? Snorkel? Scuba dive?" He looked at her with a smile, hoping she'd take the hint to change the subject.

Susan didn't need a hint to change the subject. She gladly grasped his concept with gratitude, answering, "yes, I like all those things. I think I like snorkeling the best since the water is so clear. Scuba diving always gives me a bloody nose, or messes up my ears for a few days. Plus, you have all the hassle with the equipment and the tanks." Finally, she can think of something fun. She looks up from pushing her food around on her plate and grins at him, "Snorkeling is so much more freeing. Just you, your swimsuit, a mask and snorkel, no fins required. You can go whenever you want, from any point on the island," she said with a wistful look in her eyes. She was lost in memories of times at her friends' house in the Caribbean. She'd spent so many springs there. The carefree ease of going swimming whenever you wanted, not dependent upon a boat or any scheduled activity. She and her friends just loved the freedom of it.

"You're talking about something you know well. When and where did you snorkel in the past?" he asked. He was admiring how beautiful she looked when she was speaking of her memories. But he was taken aback when a frightened look changed her face completely.

Suddenly the memory of the tragedy that happened to her there flitted through her mind – and she started to frown before answering, the mood completely gone, "Oh, just in the Caribbean, some friends have a house, they invited me every year in college. So, what is the snorkeling like here?" she asks brightly, trying to change the subject back to swimming here on the island and not the other islands. She didn't want to think about the Caribbean.

"The snorkeling is great. Just out there, down at the lagoon Alan showed you on the first day, is the best place to snorkel. There are masks, fins, and snorkels in that shed you saw just off the path as you reach the lagoon," he explained.

"Mmmm… okay, I'll think about it," she says with a smile. "So, are you going to be taking tomorrow off too, maybe sleeping in?" She could just imagine the bliss of being able to sleep in with him.

"I never sleep late, but I do have some international conference calls at 3 a.m. and 5 a.m. After that I have some issues to deal with here, but I'll be around." he said. *Yes, around, watching out for you.*

Susan finished her dinner before he did. She got up to rinse her plate in the sink and load it into the dishwasher.

As she was opening the dishwasher, he said, "No, don't do that. Alan will get that. He's very particular about how things are placed in the dishwasher. Please just leave everything in the sink." he offered.

"Okay, no problem," she said, as she turned off the water and gently placed the plate and silverware into the sink. "Uh, well, it was nice chatting with you, but I'm going to head to my room. I'll see you tomorrow, maybe," she said hesitantly.

He was instantly disappointed she was leaving him and going to her room. He wanted her company. He wanted to look at her while they talked and drank wine. He wanted to make her smile. But he also knew she was tired and she needed rest. His desires were going to have to wait until another time. He wanted to be sure he had her full attention.

"Okay, enjoy your late morning and day off," he said, with a brief nod of his head, as he forked another bite of his dinner into his mouth, signaling that conversation is over. Reluctantly he watched her as she left.

Susan smiled gratefully, nodded her head and didn't say another word before she turned and left the room at a faster-than-normal pace.

She needed to get away from him. Her heart was racing; she didn't even know how she'd eaten her dinner. His presence was so intoxicating to her. She wanted to reach out and touch him, not only with her hands but with her body. She had this urge to press herself against him and kiss him the way they'd kissed in his office.

She had to control herself. For now, escape was the easier route for her to take. She was exhausted, and she didn't have the best control over her senses and reactions. She needed to sleep and to be clear headed. She was looking forward to sleeping late the next morning.

She was so relieved that the urgency was over. He was getting her a new team. He didn't expect her to fix everything. Now she could relax.

Chapter 9

When Christoph attempted to meet up with Susan in the kitchen Sunday night, he found her with Juan and Alan drinking wine and laughing around the table. He'd missed dinner, as they all had clearly finished eating, even dessert.

Feeling loose and enjoying the easy company of Juan and Alan, Susan said, "Let's play a card game." Christoph overheard the suggestion as he was filling up his plate with the leftovers.

"Yes! Let's play Yukor," Juan requested. "Do you know how to play, Susan?"

"Yes, I've played before. Some friends in college taught me how to play," she said. She remembered the late nights at the villa playing Yukor and drinking endless rum drinks until 2 or 3 a.m. Of course it was all interspersed with dancing and quick dips in the pool to cool off between hands. They'd had such a great time. The stereo system at the villa was incredible, and the music always encouraged dancing. She couldn't imagine Christoph being that spontaneous or even that drunk to just get up and dance.

Christoph came to sit at the table with his food, just when Juan said, "Yeah, but we really should have four players. Hey, Mr. Baldric, you wanna be the fourth person?" The alcohol had given Juan the courage to just blurt it out as if he'd known Christoph for years, making Christoph smile.

'Ah, humans when they're drunk,' he snickered to himself. With all outward calm and reassurance, he replied, "Sure, I'll play." He was up for an excuse to spend some more time with Susan. At least this way, he'd be able to get to know her in a more informal setting instead of always talking about work.

"I'll go find some cards, I think I might have brought some. Be right back," Susan offered as she quickly got up from the table.

Christoph watched her walk out of the room as he kept eating his dinner. He was breaking his rule about trying to get involved with her, but he couldn't resist. He had a rule not to 'dip his pen in company ink.' The last time he got involved with somebody remotely associated with work, it turned out to be a colossal failure – mainly because the woman he thought was human turned out to be a Grogan.

It had been a while, but he knew the Grogan temper and their vain attempts to act normal, so he should have known she wasn't human. The CEO of Pegasus Technology, Eva Sinclair, came on strong toward Christoph, but she had seemingly uncontrollable mood swings. He'd been investigating her firm specializing in supply-chain software because they were using a suspiciously advanced technology. He and his team, under the guise of a buying expedition, went in to see what they could find out. He hadn't seen personalities like it since he'd last interacted with the Grogans. It was eerily similar. Thankfully, he was able to confirm his suspicions when George stumbled upon the evidence they needed.

George was waiting for Christoph outside Eva's office one day; sitting on a bench across from the elevators. The doors opened and three men walked out. The older, gray-haired man in the middle looked right at George and literally pleaded for help with his eyes. George recognized the man as the senior Argon scientist and computer engineer who had been kidnapped by the Grogans before their sun blew up.

Seeing the captured scientist verified the technology of Pegasus Tech was definitely not of the humans' making. It was also clear indication that this technology company was run by Grogans, thus confirming their suspicions. It turned out that the entire supply-chain technology company was a front for them to build their weather machines. Christoph had barely made it out of the sales discussions without her knowing he was Argonian.

Some few months later, Eva did find out Christoph was from Argon, but he still isn't sure how. But once she had that information, it is clear that she guessed that GTS is linked to the Argon computer systems. Christoph is certain she is behind the intrusion.

The recent attacks were definitely Grogan tactics. He was surer with each passing minute that Eva was behind the infiltration. Every time he went over the events in his mind, he could see the Grogan patterns and decision making, down to using real Grogan bullets at the deli that day. The thought of the event made Christoph frown.

Absentmindedly, he finished the last of his food with a frown on his face. He wasn't paying attention to the dialogue around the table, but Susan hadn't been there and had just sat back down with the cards.

What a refreshing sight she was. Susan had gorgeous curves, and Christoph just wanted to run his hands all over her. Of course, he was always lost in her green eyes with flecks of gold. Now that she was back, he was intent on turning his attention toward her and giving her a chance to open up to him. For now, he knew he needed to pay attention to her and figure out this game.

Susan selected all the face cards and aces they'd need for the game. Juan had retrieved the six and four cards for scoring, passing one of each to Alan. They were divided up as partners by who was sitting across from the other. She was partnered with Juan, and Alan and Christoph were a team. The rules were explained and they began to play in earnest.

Twice, she and Juan took every single trick, receiving a "No fair" from Alan. The wine was flowing and there was laughter to be had by all. But then, on the next hand, Christoph surprised them all by bidding for and taking every single trick in the game himself. The back and forth was amazing.

When the fun game was over, Susan and Juan had won by a mere two points, which in Yukor is a very close game. Susan felt so good and was so thankful for all the laughter tonight. She'd needed the relief from all the stress and danger. Tonight, she'd had a little more than her normal quota of wine and decided to call it a night. "This was really a lot of fun! Thank you so much guys, but I need to call it a night," she said, as she stood up.

"I'm heading that way; I'll walk with you," Christoph said, as he too got up from the table.

"Good night," she called back to Juan and Alan, who were still sitting at the table with glasses of wine. Susan waited for

Christoph. She didn't want to be rude, they were walking in the same direction.

It wasn't an unusual request for him; his quarters were just past hers and they both had to go outside to get to their part of the villa. Juan's rooms, on the other hand, were down a different corridor, inside the main building with the kitchen. Susan didn't give it a second thought as she nodded her head in acquiescence when he met her at the doorway and held the door for her to go out. However, her heart was racing; he had been playing havoc on her senses all night long. It was only a short walk, she could do it.

When he came up to walk next to her, she instinctively wanted to lean into him. She fantasized that he would put his arm around her and they would walk down the path together. She shook her head at the crazy thought, knowing it was the wine, so instead asked, "Did you have a good time playing that game?"

"Yes, it was quite fun, but I still cannot believe that you beat us," he exclaimed.

"It certainly didn't take either of you long to catch on. Otherwise, you would have beaten *us*," she declared.

"It was fun," he said with a smile. He looked down at her face and paused before asking, "Did you swim or snorkel today like I suggested?"

"No, I slept late and didn't feel too much like swimming. I sat in the shade at the pool, read a book and napped. I really felt like I just needed to sleep," she said.

He figured as much. He'd asked Alan to put some of the special Argon emotional relaxation compound in her and Juan's breakfast food so that they could sleep and let their systems deal with the recent trauma. It was harmless to humans if taken in the right doses. It helped both humans and Argonians process emotional stress more easily and quickly. For the next twenty-four hours they would be recovering without knowing it, and tonight they would both sleep very soundly.

Susan felt great after such a relaxing day. It was clearly evident on her face, as the dark circles under her eyes were gone. Her complexion was much more peachy, thanks to the island sun. She was simply beautiful and glowing. Smiling, she looked up at Christoph, "Tomorrow is Labor Day in the U.S., and we're supposed to be closed. Since you said to keep normal hours, I thought it would be a perfect day to spend at the lagoon on the beach," she finished.

The thought of her in a bikini that he could easily take off, sent shivers through his body. "Yes, of course. Definitely, you should take tomorrow off. Maybe I'll even join you at the beach," he said.

They approached her rooms. As she turned down the path to her door she said, "Sure, that'd be great. Have a good night." Then she was gone, into her rooms.

He stood there on the path for a moment in disappointment – but from what, he wasn't sure.

———————

The next morning, the only reason Susan woke up was because the sun had shifted into her eyes. She gasped when she looked at the clock: it was almost 11:00 a.m.! She'd slept more than twelve hours. She couldn't believe it. She hadn't even dreamed, she thought with relief. She was amazed, as she usually doesn't sleep that long, ever.

She slowly got out of bed and went to her sitting room to start to brew up a cup of tea. She decided to grab one of the blueberry muffins that Alan baked fresh each day. This one was from yesterday but it was still delicious, and she was ravenous. She couldn't even wait for her tea before polishing off the whole muffin. Once her tea was ready, it was divine as she sat looking out her window.

It was such a beautiful day, not a cloud in the sky, so after her tea, she decided she definitely wanted to spend the afternoon on the beach with her book. Once the decision was made, she quickly changed into her swimsuit, gathered her beach gear (hat, sunscreen, towel, book, blanket) and headed to the kitchen to gather some food for lunch...

In thirty minutes, Susan was relaxing on a chair in the shade, reading her book and sipping on a frosty rum drink. It was the perfect day. Not too hot, yet with a slight breeze to keep her cool. After she finished her drink she fell asleep again. She woke up and looked at her phone for the time. She'd only been out here for less than forty-five minutes. She couldn't have slept long. She lay back, still a bit sleepy. A swim would be nice, and would wake her up. After she had a good workout swimming in the lagoon, she could eat and have another drink.

She went to the small beach shack and rummaged through the masks in the bin. There was a huge fridge in the corner with bottled water, juices, and frozen "just add rum" drink pre-mix. When she couldn't find a mask she liked, she reached in the fridge and grabbed some water. She immediately open it and chugged half of the sixteen-ounce bottle while she looked around for another mask that would work and anything else she might want.

Tucked neatly into cubbyholes along the front wall, beneath the opened window, were other swim masks, smaller ones, and what looked to be swim shirts. "Yes, perfect," she thought, She loved swimshirts because then she wouldn't have to worry about not being able to reach her back with sunscreen. She always snorkeled with a swim shirt, but she hadn't brought one with her. She picked what looked to be a man's medium, and slid it over her head. It was definitely body-slimming and tight, but it was supposed to be. She just shrugged it off as normal.

Susan had no idea how sexy she looked as she left the beach shack. The white Body Glove swim shirt hugged her figure everywhere. It barely looked like her chest had a chance to breathe. Casually strung over one arm, she carried a small swim mask for eyes only and a snorkel. She had her half-finished water in the other hand. She finished off the water on her way to the shore and tossed the bottle back into the shack... and yes, "Two POINTS!" the bottle made it through the window. Well, it was a rather large window that pretty much took up half the side of the shack, but still, she wasn't a basketball player and that was a good shot. She laughed at herself and patted herself on the back.

As Susan waded into the water, its perfect temperature welcomed her. It was cool enough to be refreshing but warm enough to not chill you. She couldn't wait to start swimming. She quickly fixed the mask, wet it and put it in place. Then she wet the snorkel and knelt on the sand as she put the snorkel in her mouth and lay face down in the water. She used her hands to walk herself out to the deeper areas of the lagoon.

She loved being suspended in the water and watching all the sea life beneath and all around her. She surveyed the area, and when it was deep enough to swim, she swam to the furthest corner of the lagoon. Her aim was to the swim the circumference of the lagoon, and then maybe a few laps back and forth. This was heaven to her. Finally – peace and quiet.

After an hour of much needed quiet time, Susan emerged from the water, a short distance further down from the shack. She had definitely had a good workout, but she was more tired than she'd anticipated. Normally, she wouldn't suddenly feel so incredibly tired, she thought. She felt as if she'd struggled to pull herself slowly but steadily out of the water.

As she made it up the beach, Christoph appeared in front of her. He was furious: she could tell by how his hands were clenched at this sides, his tense body, and the expression of fury and fear in his eyes. She took a step back – it sort of scared her.

"Oh, Christoph! Geez, you scared me," she tried to apologize, as she backed up another step. She stopped when she saw some sort of relief in his expression, but not in his voice.

"What. The. Hell. Do. You. Think. You. Were. Doing?!" he spat out at her.

Susan gasped, but saw again that his tension seemed to be easing. Maybe he didn't know where she was. She'd made that mistake once before. Her friend had gotten so mad at her because she'd gone snorkeling for an hour while he was drinking and entertaining his friends at a beach bar. He had no idea she was going to be gone so long. He didn't talk to her for the rest of the day after he chewed her out like a child. She didn't want to be chewed out like a child this time. "Yes, I was swimming," she said defiantly.

"You know that it is not safe alone," he barked at her as he got closer to her.

For a moment she thought he was going to grab her arms and start shaking her like a rag doll. She stood her ground and even stood a bit taller and said, "I know that, but after the close calls I've had lately, I figured it was worth the chance." Sticking her nose a little higher in the air as she started past him, she said, "When it's my time to go, it's my time to go." She turned around to stalk off.

He grabbed her right arm and whirled her around to face him as he caught her other arm in his other hand, holding her in front of him as he growled, almost fiercely, "No!" Her face immediately went pale and she looked like a frightened rabbit. He realized his anger and how he was holding her.

He loosened his grip but did not let her go, as he tried to say gently and below his breath, "I cannot lose you now." Louder and more calmly, he said, "We've done so much to protect you, I wouldn't want to lose you to a shark or a curious barracuda." He smiled at her, and now that she was closer, he could feel her heat and increased breathing. He'd scared her. Good. She'd scared the life out of him when he couldn't find her.

Susan's pulse was racing. He was so close to her. He'd scared the living daylights out of her, he was so angry with her for swimming alone. But weren't there security guards stationed all over, everywhere? Surely they knew where she was, and what she was doing. Christoph was still extremely irritated with her. She drifted a little closer to his body and looked up at him with her sweetest Southern smile and purred, "I'm sorry."

She couldn't think of anything else to say. She was so elated that he cared. He was mad because he cared, and she just wanted to kiss him.

Susan leaned in and reached up to put her lips on his. She pulled his head closer to her and he shuddered with goose bumps. Oh God, she felt so good. He immediately put his hands around her waist and pulled her to him so her body would be flush to his and he could feel her complete body heat. He kissed her back, he met her tongue with his, and he plunged and tasted and teased.

Back and forth they caressed and tasted with their tongues. They couldn't get enough of kissing each other, and it was starting to affect her in other places. She caught herself about to push her chest further against his and grind her hips right into him. It startled her, and she stopped abruptly.

He was shocked when she pulled back, and he didn't understand. "Are you okay?"

She wiped her mouth with her arm and said, "Uh, yeah, I'm sorry. I won't go swimming alone again." She turned and picked up her snorkel and mask and made for the beach shack, leaving him standing alone on the beach, puzzled.

Christoph stood there wondering what the hell she was doing to him. She was driving him crazy, that's for sure. There wasn't anything else to say to her. He voiced his grief; she apologized, acknowledged it and promised not to do it again. But why did he feel so uneasy about it all? Why did he feel like she was hiding something?

'That arrogant oaf!' Susan thought. She slung the mask and snorkel into the basket and went back to her chair to gather up her things. She was stomping up the path back to her room when he returned to the shack. How dare he dictate to her? He didn't have any hold on her. If she wanted to drown because she went swimming alone, then so be it. She seriously doubted that she was ever alone on this island anyway, especially in his compound. So, how dare he?! She was irate.

Susan didn't want to go back to her room just yet, so she swung around and headed to the pool. She could take a seat in the back corner to have her lunch and read her book. The shade was perfect there, and it would be obvious that she didn't want to be disturbed.

She settled down and actually had a nice lunch. Alan came out and brought her a fresh rum drink and an ice water. Relaxed and finally at ease, after she ate, she just wanted to lie there and think about kissing him again. There was so much passion when they kissed. How could she let herself be so weak to his charms? But *she* was the one who'd kissed *him!!!* She was starting to feel truly mortified, the more she thought about it, the more she had to drink.

If she had the chance to do it all again, she wouldn't care how high-handed he was. She would simply take the opportunity and kiss him again. It was so delicious, and his body was so hard and muscular, she just wanted to touch him all over.

Susan was starting to get really hot and bothered with her thoughts of touching him and pressing herself against him. She needed a dip in the pool to cool her off. Surely Christoph wouldn't get all bent out of shape if she got wet in the pool. She just sighed as she entered, it was so refreshing. She was also sighing because she was imagining what it would be like to touch more of him...

Chapter 10

Christoph saw her get up from her chair and enter the water. He didn't mind her swimming in the pool. He was able to watch her from his office desk. He knew her every move. She had no idea that the place she'd picked to relax and read was in a perfect line of sight from his desk chair. He preferred having her in his sight whenever possible.

His obsession with her seemed to explode with that kiss on the beach. He knew he needed to do something to repair any damage he might have caused. He called down to the kitchen from his desk phone, "Alan, hi, it's Christoph."

"Yes sir, what can I do for you?" Alan responded, willing to please.

"Would you fix beef stroganoff and baked garlic asparagus for dinner, with a tomato and avocado salad to start? I'll be dining, privately, with Ms. Caldwell tonight in the formal dining room," he finished.

"Yes sir, certainly. What time do you want to have it ready?" he asked.

"What time does Ms. Caldwell normally eat dinner?" Christoph shot back.

"She normally eats about 6:45, almost 7:00, sir."

"Okay then, dinner at 7:00. We can start with salad if she's early."

Susan had taken another nap after showering from her long day at the pool. She couldn't believe how much she was sleeping, but somehow she needed it. After her nap, she felt so good that she decided to dress up a little. She put on a nice white cotton tank dress, very short, but she layered a see-through, floor-length white t-shirt over it. It was simple t-shirt material, but it looked very island dressy. She styled her hair in an easy ponytail since it was so hot, and put on a touch of mascara and lip gloss. Perfect island makeup: very little to none at all. It made her feel even better to take just this small effort. She doubted she'd see anyone anyway. Alan and Juan always ate so early, and she'd only seen Christoph in the kitchen a couple of times.

Shortly before 7 p.m., Christoph saw her walking toward the kitchen/bar area, and she looked like a dream. The wind was blowing slightly, and it ruffled her long, see-through cotton dress against her legs so that the long slash up to her mid-thigh gave him a peek at her muscular and shapely leg. She took his breath away. Her hair was on top of her head in a simple ponytail, with strands flowing down and around her neck. It made him want to kiss her neck and touch her shoulders. He even noticed a touch of makeup and lip gloss. She was gorgeous. There was no way he was going to make it through the evening without putting his hands on her, he thought as he watched her approach.

She puzzled at what was going on as she walked into the bar area just off the kitchen to get a glass of wine. She had noticed as she walked down the open breezeway toward the kitchen that the dining room was set with lighted candelabras all around. Two places were set at the table. When she got to the wine bar she noticed Christoph already sitting there.

"Good evening." Christoph greeted her with a sensual smile as she approached the bar. He was sitting on the other side of the bar with a glass of red wine, and looked to have been reading something on his tablet.

"Hi," she said shyly. She was still mad at him, but she was more embarrassed by the way she had blatantly kissed him. She thought it best if she said as little as possible.

"Are you hungry?" he asked. "Would you like a glass of wine?" he probed.

"Yes, please, I'd love a glass. And yes, I'm starving. I am just going to fix a plate as soon as I get a glass of wine," she explained.

"Here," he said as he handed her a full glass, "bring your wine, we're going to eat in the dining room tonight," he said, as he directed her with his hand outstretched towards the dining room. "After you," he said gallantly.

Susan was surprised but followed along. Still not wanting to say much after initiating that kiss, she didn't know what to expect. He was still being a bit high-handed, but this was more gentlemanly than his attitude from earlier today. She figured he'd still be mad at her for swimming alone. He'd never said anything about the pool. His change puzzled her, and she was at a loss as she approached the dining room.

It was a lovely island dining room, done in muted peach tones, with heavy, thick, dark-red mahogany furniture. Christoph held out a chair for her and motioned for her to sit down.

After she was seated, he seated himself and began serving them dinner. "I hope you will like dinner tonight," he said, knowing that just about every item was her favorite. He'd found out from the research he'd asked his team to do on her. It was in one of the "company outing" files, when her team had been playing one of those "get to know you" games. Little did she know that they kept all that information filed away on each employee. It is what determined what he ordered for dinner.

Christoph held a large serving bowl for her. Susan peered over into the dish and said, "Beef stroganoff. My favorite," she said, as she served herself a sizable portion.

He presented her with the next dish and removed the lid. "Oh, baked asparagus... ohhh, that's my favorite, too!" Then she stopped, while serving herself a portion of the vegetable, and looked at him.

"Did you do this?" she asked pointedly.

Feigning innocence he said, "No, I don't cook, Alan cooked all of this."

"Yeah, but you told him what my favorites were, didn't you? How did you know? Better yet, how much *don't* you know about me?" she asked, in pissed-off awe of him.

Trying to calm her down, he said, "Easy, it's part of your employee record. Anyone could look it up; it's on your personal wiki page. Every employee has one. We use information from the company outings and the surveys you fill out. Relax. Please enjoy the food," he pleaded.

She considered his response and back at her plate, and the aroma was too intoxicating, much like his kisses. For now, she didn't care how or why her favorite food was here – she was going to eat it and enjoy it. Finishing off her second glass of wine after devouring her food on her plate, she sat back and sighed. "That was incredible. I will have to thank Alan profusely for such wonderful culinary skills."

Christoph knew she was goading him, by mentioning that she'd thank Alan and not himself – for it was he who had thought of it. Either way, the outcome was the same: she was comfortably sated, and perhaps in a forgiving mood. Time for him to try to get closer.

"It's still early, how about some cards?" he asks.

Susan considers his request. She didn't like spending all day alone and she wasn't tired at all, not after all the naps she'd taken today. He was trying to be nice. Besides, she needed some human interaction and company.

"Sure, I'm game if you are?" she bantered back at him with a smirk.

Christoph grabs a deck of cards and another bottle of wine before returning. He dealt the cards and continued to reach for ways to get her to open up so he could get to know her better. They made small talk about this and that: family, high school, college, past loves. He tried to pick normal human topics while they played "Rummy."

Since Christoph picked the first game, it was her turn to choose, and she picked one she hadn't played since she was a little girl, "Spit," which led to "War" and other childhood games. She was enjoying herself and teaching Christoph her childhood games.

Next thing you know, they're finishing the second bottle of wine, and she's laughing at him because she's beat him again. But it was late and she was more than buzzed, so she tells him,

"It's late, I'm ready to get some sleep. Thanks for a fun night and a great dinner, I really appreciate the diversion."

Knowing she figured out that in his process of getting to know her, he was also diverting her thoughts from work and her recent tragedies. He sighed before saying, "Of course, it's my pleasure."

Before he could say more, she quickly said as she got up, "You don't need to walk me to my room. Take your time with your wine, I'll see you in the morning." She skirted out of the room without giving him a chance to say more than a cordial, "Goodnight."

The next day after lunch, back at work, a call came through on the main line they used for GTS business. Susan answered, "Hello, Susan Caldwell."

"Hi, Susan, this is Mark Parsons, I've been recently assigned as your Tech/Dev team lead. I wanted to call and introduce myself," he said,

"Hello Mark, it's nice to meet you. How have you been doing wading through the files I emailed you?" she asks.

"Yes, the team and I have already gone through all those files, so I think we're up to speed on where you found the code breach and the actions that were taken to comment out the code. But does anyone know what was happening to the data once it was brought over to that development server database?"

"No, and I'm pleasantly surprised at how quickly you've come up to speed. It's good, because I want you to add this to your priority list. Right now we have two main priorities. #1: What was happening to the data after it was copied, and #2: Who did this?"

"Okay, yes, I've got it. We will work on that. I understand that Juan is there with you," Mark requested more than stated.

"Yes, he is, but he is going to be reporting to you directly. Circumstances, as I'm sure you're aware, led to his being here with me." She paused briefly and took a deep breath as she realized what had transpired in just a few short days. "Would you please schedule a meeting with him tomorrow so that he can get direction from you on what he needs to do?"

"Certainly, I will do that, and I will also consider the time difference. Do you work normal business hours in your time zone," he asked, "or do you keep to Eastern Time zone?"

"We're on regular business hours for this time zone. I believe it is Korean time zone, so whatever it is in Boston, add an hour and change it either to a.m. or p.m. At least that's the trick I use to keep it straight," she explained.

"Okay, great, I will get on that. I wanted to let you know that I've also contacted the network team and asked them to provide us with the tracer logs so that we can cross-reference our log entries to IP addresses and locations. It is going to take considerable time and some of my team will need to come up to speed, but we are hoping to figure this out by the end of the week," he finished confidently.

"That sounds promising, but I won't hold my breath. This is as sophisticated as it comes. All of my team was surprised at how complex the links were between servers. Please provide me with a status update each day via email," she requested in her most professional manner.

"Yes, of course. Thank you for taking the time to review our priorities with me. I'll be in touch," he added, before saying his farewells.

Susan couldn't believe how quickly things were falling into place. She hoped that her new team found the breach soon, and who was responsible. Now that she wasn't as stressed about having to do all this work with just her and Juan, she could relax. And when she was relaxed, and felt safe, she didn't have the nightmare.

The night after the kiss on the beach was the second night she didn't have the nightmare – only the second peaceful night's sleep she'd had since she drove to work and found that Luis had been killed. The other peaceful night had been the night before. She felt as if maybe she'd been drugged, but how could that be? She'd never heard of a drug that gave you peace. Well, there were illegal drugs that made you love everyone, and there were some mood-altering drugs like anti-depressants, but they usually took a week or two to begin working. Maybe it was the fact that there wasn't an immediate threat looming any longer. Plus, she was safe on the island and seemed to frequently be in the presence of Christoph.

Over the next few days, when she was working, Christoph started coming into the room and would sit to do some of his own work. He would interrupt them for lunch, and make them take breaks. It seemed as if he might have an ulterior motive, but Susan wasn't clear what was happening with Christoph.

While Susan noticed she was spending more time with Christoph, sharing dinner and playing cards afterwards, she was determined not to get romantically involved with him. She continued holding him off. Although, Christoph was wearing on her. When she was not working, she was never alone unless she was in her own rooms.

Christoph was always around. It's not that she minded, but he was slowly becoming like her best friend. She was spending so much time with him, and it was hard to keep holding him off. She wasn't interested in any man right now, although she would entertain a hookup with Christoph. But that might be too complicated and she still had trust issues.

She didn't trust men to keep her heart safe, or to even really want to be with her longer than it took to get their rocks off a few times. But that is the norm these days. She certainly did not expect anything more. She'd learned over the years to be comfortable alone, as did all of her girlfriends.

She knew she didn't *need* a man to have love in her life. She had her dog, her friends, her family and her ability to give it back, which she used graciously. Occasionally, her subconscious berated her for her mistakes in life and it was difficult to stay positive amid all the tragedy recently.

Susan knew she had to ignore the tragedy as best she could. There wasn't time to grieve. She was in danger, and she had a job to do. Plus, being forced to be in Christoph's presence, it was imperative that she present a positive front. She acted as much as she could.

She found that by just pretending to relax and pretending to have a good time, that she actually *was* relaxing and having a good time. Gradually, she wasn't thinking of ways to avoid him. She started looking forward to seeing Christoph, and making the most of their time together.

They talked and joked about everything. It felt good to have somebody to lighten the load, when most of the time all she could think about were the colleagues she had lost in the bombings, or else worrying about her ineptness at this code base.

Three nights after their intimate dinner, Susan was beating Christoph, mercilessly, in the card game "Spite and Malice." She was teasing him as she got up to get a snack and a glass of water: "I can't *believe* you played that ace knowing I had a two on my play deck." She could feel the wine still going straight to her head. She was feeling great.

He followed her across the room for a snack of his own, saying, "Well, maybe I was being nice."

"Huh? Yeah right?! As if!! I don't believe that for a minute. It's down to the wire, I only have a few cards left and your deck is practically full," she parried.

She accidentally bumps into him as she turns around to go to the refrigerator.

He almost knocks her down. Reacting by pure instinct, he catches her. Suddenly, he is holding her in his arms. Christoph had been wanting to touch her since she kissed him on the beach.

She is stunned, and stares back up at him while he holds her. She doesn't know what to say except, "Uh...sorry."

Split-second decision made, he moves in to steal a kiss. It is gentle and sweet, unlike the one on the beach. He'd been mad as hell then, and if he was honest with himself, scared shitless when he'd seen she was swimming alone. He reacted on instinct then, as he is doing now. He's been waiting for days for the right moment to make his move. Holding her head tenderly, he keeps his arm around her waist as he slowly coaxes her to open her lips.

He felt so good against her; she couldn't help but comply. Their tongues met and it was as if they'd known each other forever. She unknowingly became a willing participant, kissing him back with all the desire she had been feeling for him. She started to melt into him, molding her body against his. When she realized what was happening, her mind screamed at her 'NO!'...she started to panic, pushing away from him abruptly. "Please, no," she said breathlessly. As she caught her breath, she said, "I can't do this with you." She turns to pick up her glass of water and says, "It's late, I'm tired, I'm going to go to bed. Good night."

Christoph watched as she escaped to the safety of her room, leaving their card game unfinished on the table.

———————

The next day Susan was planning to spend more time working, but unfortunately, Juan and she were at a standstill. They were having to wait for a backup, which would take eighteen hours or more before they could continue again. Basically, work was over for the day. She didn't know what to do with herself. All she knew was that she wanted to avoid Christoph.

After the kiss last night, she felt she needed to put some distance between Christoph and herself. If he kept kissing her like that, she was going to give in to the idea of a hookup. The safety of her room offered the most privacy, given their confinement to an island. Instead of staying in the common areas, she went to her room and spent the afternoon napping and reading a book. She'd had plenty of time to think, and to go over how she'd even gotten into this position in the first place.

She got up to get into the shower, as she thought about how it had started with her job. She thought, 'Everything was looking up when I got this job after being accepted on the Boston Fertility Clinic wait list.'

She had been so excited over the acceptance, then the job just started falling into place. Susan wasn't afraid of risks or new adventures. Perfect example: moving to Boston to be close to the fertility clinic and landing this job. Now, though, after the tragedies, she'd had enough adventure to last a lifetime. Her job and life was not turning out to be the nice, controlled, sensible existence she expected.

A low-key life and raising a child was the perfect life for her, but almost being killed twice and wanting to sleep with her CEO is *not* low-key! She had to stay within the confines of what she could control. Moving to Boston allowed her more control by being close to the clinic. Raising a child on her own would allow her more control. For now, she controlled the fact that she didn't have a man in her life.

Her problem was that right now, she didn't have any control over the current situation – and she needed *this* man, Christoph. She needed him to keep her alive. Hell, she couldn't even get home without his assistance. She wasn't exactly "free" to leave. Susan pushed aside those fears. She was grateful for his help. If he hadn't stepped in, she'd be dead and nothing would matter.

But here she was, alive, playing nightly card games with this man who's become her best friend over the last week. She hadn't let herself get close to anyone, almost ever. She was definitely treading in uncharted waters here. The indecision made her uneasy.

She finished up her shower, contemplating her options and reviewing again the sequence of events that had brought her here. She really did have Christoph to thank for saving her she thought as she dried her hair and dressed to go over to the kitchen for some dinner. She needed to eat and her hunger was escalating her anxiety.

When Susan arrived in the kitchen, the object of her avoidance was there, pulling lids off the dishes on the counter. There was no excuse she could think of on the fly to stay away from him; she'd really been counting on the work excuse. 'Shit, shit, shit, double shit,' she thought to herself.

She tried to think of another reason to stay away. She thought maybe she could claim to be sick, maybe cramps or something. But Susan knew he'd knock on her bedroom door and make sure she had any over-the-counter drugs she might need. Having him show up at her door was too dangerous, so she decided to go ahead into the kitchen. Plus, she was starving and needed to eat. Maybe she could pretend he hadn't kissed her last night, and ignore the fact that she'd kissed him back.

Christoph says, "Good evening. Hungry?" He is hoping she will open up to him on her own. He noticed that she'd avoided him today. He also knew she'd spent the entire day in her rooms. He didn't want to push her, so he was letting her have her space, today.

Smiling sheepishly at him she answers, "Yes, I'm starving actually." She leans over the counter next to him to examine the dishes of food. "Mmmm," she murmured as she looked over the food: cole slaw, BBQ ribs, carrot and squash casserole, and green beans.

"It looks like a good combination for tonight," he said.

"Yes," she said, her mouthwatering when she saw the bacon and fat chunks in the green beans. 'Real Southern-style green beans! YUM!' she thought. She couldn't wait.

He hands her a plate and says, "It's all still warm, so we really don't have to heat up anything tonight."

Susan made her plate and went to sit down with the glass of wine he'd poured for her. She immediately tasted the green beans and they were delicious, just like their maid, Belle, had always made when she was little.

Christoph didn't engage her in any more conversation, and they ate in comfortable silence. He poured her another glass of wine, knowing that soon, she'd be able to open up. Wine always did that for her.

Susan was enjoying the dinner and wine. She was mostly nervous, more than anything else, because of the kiss they'd shared last night, but she was beginning to loosen up a bit. She drank her second glass of wine down much faster than the first, and she still had some dinner left on her plate. Not knowing what to say to him, she didn't say anything. She was scared, but she didn't know from what. She wanted him so badly, she didn't know what words to even use. She'd never experienced this before and she had no clue what to do.

Noticing her indecision, finally, his patience gave out. He broached the subject, asking her, "Why are you trying so hard to resist me?"

Feeling definitely fueled up on liquid courage, Susan wondered to herself, 'Why *am* I? Why *am* I scared?' She contemplated a few seconds longer as she finished chewing her food. 'What does it matter if I answer him?' she wondered.

She'd been treating him as a friend, and if he was going to *be* a friend, shouldn't she try to open up? 'Ha!' She's never had a serious conversation about her personal feelings with a man. Who was she kidding?

The hookups she'd dallied with never really cared enough to ask. She'd never let them get past being a hookup to even ask. It was part of her control. Christoph was the first one to ever ask her difficult questions like this. And they weren't even difficult, just simple questions about her feelings.

Hell, when she was having trouble in college, even the psychiatrist her parents hired didn't ask her any questions about her feelings. All he wanted to do was hypnotize her and let her figure out what she needed to do on her own. It was the norm in this day and age, because people had become so self-sufficient and independent.

'Damn, is it always this difficult?' It is no damn wonder people say relationships are hard, and stay away from them.

She decided to step out of her comfort zone and open up to Christoph. "I don't think it's a good idea for me to become physically involved with you?" Immediately she berated herself. 'Shit. That's the worst, lame-ass answer I could have given,' she thought to herself. 'Seriously? Is that how to open up? You idiot!' her self-conscious continued its assault. She could have kicked herself.

"Why?" he asked. Of course he asked. She deserved his obvious question.

'Damn!' she thought. 'What the fuck do I say?' She paused a few moments and took another sip of her wine before venturing, "First off, you're my boss, the CEO of the entire company. I don't think it would be a good idea. I might find myself without a job."

She stopped and took a sip of her wine. When he only stared at her, she added, "And I'm not interested in "friends with benefits" or a "hookup." I don't have time for it and it's too complicated for me."

"Who said anything about *'friends with benefits'?*" He was beginning to get irritated.

He hated the term, and the concept. These humans and their "hookups" and "friends with benefits." They'd lost all identity with love, compassion, and relationships. Not that Argonians were much better, because their females had little to no emotion.

But the relationships the men developed were deep and caring. Some men preferred only male partners and some men preferred female partners and had the urge to procreate. It was about forty percent to sixty percent, relatively speaking. Christoph had the DNA and urge for procreating, and he loved the female body.

When Christoph decided to take a woman to his bed, he wanted only her. Right now, he wanted Susan in his bed, and in his bed only. He knew he was very possessive – and he wanted more than friendship with Susan. He made the decision when he was pulling her through the alley after the deli shooting. He wanted *her and only her*, always. It was an intuition common to Argonians along with their propensity for possessiveness. He knew Susan was the perfect mate for him.

"I'm not interested in a simple hookup Susan," he said as he leaned closer to her and put a hand on her cheek. She automatically curled her face into his hand. He looked into her vivid, gold-flecked green eyes.

She didn't speak, all she could do was return his stare.

He didn't elaborate on his comment. He slowly leaned in and gently kissed her, while cradling her head in his hand.

Susan was stunned by the gentleness of his kiss. She was feeling so vulnerable, yet so safe next to him. His warmth and his touch were intoxicating to her senses. She wanted to be held, and she wanted to be gently caressed. Slowly, his arms were wrapping around her. She unconsciously followed her instinct to press her body against his and be as close to him as possible....

She wants him to touch her. She wants to touch him, to feel his naked skin pressed to her own naked body. Head to head, chest to chest, toe to toe.

The pleasure she would feel when he slowly slips inside her... 'Oh God, could I *be* more horny!' she thinks to herself.

'Even if all he wants is a hookup, I'm in,' her subconscious affirms for her. She can't allow her doubts or second thoughts about whether he wants more to stop her. Even though he said he didn't want a hookup, that's the normal mind-game men play. Men said fanciful things and made empty promises, it was a game of pretend when with a hookup, everyone understood that.

It's been a long time since her last hookup. She was extremely horny since it'd been a while. Besides, she almost died twice in the last month, so she needs to enjoy this opportunity while she can and take advantage of the benefits this situation has to offer.

She lets him kiss her. She can't believe how good it feels to kiss him again. It's as if they were made for each other. As he's caressing her back, she subtly rubs her body against him. He replies with a moan of his own, and he tightens his arms around her.

The passion intensifies between them as they eagerly devour each other's mouths. Their tongues dance, then he is sucking on her tongue and vice versa. Every time she feels the need to be deep in his mouth, it happens, and he was there, deep in hers.

Kissing like this was so erotic to her. She loved being held in his arms. Because he was returning her kisses so passionately, she wasn't sure if she could stand any more. She just wanted to melt right then and there. Anything he wanted was his.

He began to kiss her neck and began to unbutton the buttons of her shirt when she half-heartedly protested once more, "No, we shouldn't be doing this." Then he started kissing her again, and she didn't push him away.

"I want to make love to you," he whispered to her. In his mind he was saying, 'and I want to brand you and make you mine.' Of course, he was thinking of the Argon customs.

In Argon society, men branded the women they wanted by getting them pregnant. The humans' maturity level as a species hadn't yet reached the point where their sexuality had increased to Argon levels, but in another few hundred years, they'd be there. For right now, Christoph had been put off too long by Susan and he was more than ready.

Christoph could feel that Susan was the right one for him. He'd never imagined that a human would give him this calling, but it was physically possible. He just didn't know if she could survive his strong sexual appetite. Regardless, he was going to brand her. He could smell her ovulation. This was the perfect time. "You're mine," he said, into her mouth.

"But, wait, wait, Christoph please!" she begged.

He stopped long enough to take her hand and pull her in the direction of their rooms. She stumbled along behind him, still wanting to be in his arms.

"Come with me, be with me, never leave me," he said, as he pulled her through the door to his suite of rooms.

"Stop, for goodness sakes, Christoph! You can't be serious?" she said in bewilderment as she stepped away from him and, unknowingly, closer to the bed. She'd had three glasses of wine and was really feeling horny. If she were honest, she would want to forget about tomorrow and just touch him. She can handle another hookup, no problem, but he was pushing this playacting a little too far. The intensity and things he was saying weren't normal for a mere hookup.

She backed into the bed and sat down. She was so confused. She knew what she was supposed to do – which was run out the door and lock herself in her bedroom – but that's not what she wanted to do. She definitely wanted him.

Christoph just looked at her with desire in his eyes so strong, she could swear it was emanating from him in a purple light. She just wrote it off to it being dusk, with no lights on in his rooms. He pulled his shirt out of his pants and began unbuttoning it to take it off.

She gasped when he took off his shirt. He was the most magnificently sexy man she'd ever had the pleasure to see in the flesh. And he was hers for the taking. He was walking toward her as he removed his belt and unbuttoned his pants. As he got close, she put up her hand as if to tell him to stop, but he took the opportunity to walk into her hand so that she was touching his muscled abdomen.

"I know we shouldn't," she mumbled as she looked up at him. "But, I just don't want to say 'No'." She paused for a moment as his pants dropped to the floor.

"Susan, darling, be mine," he said, as his right hand caressed her cheek while his left hand guided her hand up and across his chest. He leaned over her and pushed her back onto the bed. He kissed her neck and up to her mouth, where he kissed her with a slow, loving tenderness, unlike any kiss she'd ever had.

Her melting was complete. The wine had gone to her head and made the decision so much easier for her. She acquiesced, wrapping her arms around his shoulders and pulling his body down on hers and holding his head in that tender kiss. Before she knew it she started kissing him back, and their passion escalated once again.

He made quick work of removing her clothes and his boxers. He slowly and gently caressed his way from her ankles up to her shoulders with his mouth and hands. Then he started back down again, stopping at her nipples until he made her come. She was panting, and overwhelmed at his ability to find her most sensitive places and gauge her reactions.

He began kissing her neck and captured her ear in his mouth, and so overwhelmed her senses that she started coming again as soon as his hand touched her.

She couldn't believe how adept he was at coaxing that reaction from her. She didn't care – she wanted more. She touched his arms, his back, and she ran her hands up and down his sides, feeling his entire backside.

He spreads her thighs with his knees and easily maneuvers until he smoothly enters her in one single stroke. She is so wet and slick, he knows and feels he made the right decision. She is his, and he is going to make sure she stays that way.

He thrusts in and out only a few times before Susan is coming again. It has been so long for her that it just floods throughout her body, and she can't hold it back. Her muscles clench him so hard that they push him out when he pulls back.

She is so tight when he thrusts back in that he knows it won't take him long. He takes a few more strokes, helping her ride through her orgasm. Just as her muscles are beginning to relax, he pounds into her one, two, three times and comes with a force that is dizzying for him. Christoph has never released his reproductive sperm before. It was more than what he had heard. He was completely amazed, and it depleted him as nothing ever had – while at the same time, the release impacted his soul. He could feel it.

Argonian men were able to control the release of their reproductive sperm, and had been able to for several millennia. It was well documented in the history of his people that through controlling their own bodies' energy they could control certain outcomes. But they had to merge with another's energy and Christoph had experienced blockages because of Susan's trust issues.

In Christoph's case, he could feel Susan's distrust for men. He knew she didn't think he wanted more from her than one night. With his attempt to overcome her thoughts, he wanted to be sure that she never spent a night away from him again. After this night, she was his. He knew humans didn't do it that way, but he was determined to convince her otherwise. As far as getting her pregnant, she didn't have to know right away that he had done that on purpose.

He was only following the unspoken human rule of consensual sex when it came to pregnancy. They hadn't talked about prevention beforehand, so he knew pregnancy was on the table for her and that she was willing to take the chance that it would happen. It made it easier for him to rationalize the unfair advantage he had, because he could smell her ovulation. Now, it was done and they were both comfortably sated for the moment, until his desire overtook them again.

As Christoph lay next to Susan, he curled her up beside him. He held her as he drew the sheet up over them. She slept, and he contemplated what life would be like with her and the children they would have. A female with emotions would be a new challenge for him.

Chapter 11

Susan wakes up the next morning in his bed. All the French doors are open, and the breeze off the ocean is blowing the curtains. She doesn't recognize where she is at first, but then she remembers. He had been kind, gentle, and very passionate. He'd made her come so many times, it's a wonder they got any sleep. She knows they both fell asleep in wet spots.

Susan giggles to herself and stretches out. She feels so wonderful and so sexy waking up completely naked. She never sleeps naked when she's by herself. Remembering how wonderful and sweet he'd been, she felt blissful just thinking about it. For now, she just wanted to relish in the aftermath, and think of how good it was. As far as hookups go, this was one of her best ever, even if his playacting was a little over the top.

She looked over at the clock; it was almost 9:30. Ooops, she slept a little later than usual! They must be wondering what was wrong with her, but then she recalled it was Sunday. Nobody would expect her until around noon, as Susan usually spent Sunday mornings reading in her room. She decided to stay in his comfy bed and enjoy the moment a little longer, remembering precisely how it had felt to touch him and be touched by him last night. Then she realized that she hadn't had the nightmare last night. But then, how could she? She didn't exactly sleep very much, more like short naps before he'd coax her awake and start all over again. 'It was marvelous,' she thought with a sly and very satisfied Cheshire cat grin.

At about noon, wearing her swimsuit and cover-up, she makes her way to the kitchen for coffee and a muffin. She's decided that when she sees him she's not going to pretend that nothing happened last night. She wants him again and again, and for as long as they can make a hookup arrangement work. Why not? It's worth a shot.

Though she's given up on men, she knows an opportunity like this doesn't come along every day and she needs to make the most of it. As she makes her way down the hallway, she tries to remember if he had shared anything with her about his past relationships. She walks into the dining room, and finds both Christoph and Juan hunched over one of the monitors. They both look up when she enters.

"What's going on?" she asks. "It's Sunday. Why are you guys in here working? What happened?" She starts to panic when she reads the concern on their faces.

"What did you find?" she asks. Momentarily she is distracted when Christoph looks up at her and meets her eyes with an intense stare of his own. She still feels a little awkward, since this is the first time she's seeing him after spending the night together.

'Damn, what a workout!' she involuntarily thinks to herself. Her legs were definitely feeling it this morning. Again, the memory brings a bright smile to her face as she looks at them for an answer.

"It looks as though there's been yet another breach," Juan says gravely. "Again, it looks as if you and the intern are responsible. But I don't see how either one of you would have known how to do this. It was more likely that your IDs were the easiest to manufacture, since neither of you were ever regularly in the system," Juan explained.

Susan imagines, although they don't, that both Christoph and Juan view her with suspicion. Her back stiffens and she becomes extremely defensive. She is fearful her relationship with both men is on the line, as well as her reputation. As before, she is determined to find out what happened. "I'm going to get started then. Show me what you found," she demands.

It takes her thirty hours, with no sleep, until she finds it. She is excited and jumps up to do a happy dance. This is the clearest evidence she has ever found that points to more counterfeit evidence in the log files. Not only does Susan find where it alleges she'd inserted code two months before she even worked there, but also where the intern had made changes the day her son was born. It was now very clear, and more than demonstrable, that this was a setup. But by whom?

Juan walks in as she's doing her happy dance and asks, "What? What did you find?"

"Oh, Juan, you're not going to believe this. Look at this..." she says, as she swivels the monitor in his direction. "Look at these dates when this was inserted. Neither I nor our intern were here on those days. It's clear that somebody is going back and changing evidence by altering the logs. The worst part is that whoever did this is still in the system – and is going in behind us and putting the malicious code back. We've been chasing our tail!"

Just then a voice comes over the speaker phone, "Hello, Susan, this is Mark. I'm back. What did you say about chasing tails?"

"Mark, thank goodness you're back. You're not going to believe what I found in the log files," she excitedly informs him through the speaker phone. They were obviously having a working session. "I've highlighted the entries, encrypted the files and emailed them to you. I need the team to take those entries and crosscheck them with the network traces you've been gathering. I think that we're going to be closer to finding the culprit."

"I'm looking at the first file now," he replies. "Yes, I see your highlights, but what is wrong with them again?"

"Look at the dates. The dates don't match. All of the entries that are attributed to my ID happened before I even worked here. The other two entries are under our intern's ID, and they both occurred on the day she had her son. Besides, again, neither one of us applied for, nor were ever granted the root access permissions that are necessary to make these changes."

"Okay. Yes, ma'am, I understand. I will get the team on this right away. Since its morning here, we'll have all day to work through this, and we'll let you know by your morning tomorrow," Mark confirmed for her.

Relieved, she said, "Thank you, Mark. I'll call you."

"Goodbye, ma'am," he said, before hanging up.

It was dusk when she walked into Christoph's office to give him the news. Mark and Juan had confirmed it for her only moments ago, so she was confident. She needed to show Christoph.

As she walked into his office, it was barely growing dark outside, just past dinner, but Christoph sat there eating from a plastic microwave plate at his desk while he read something on his computer screen. She hadn't done much better, eating a cold sandwich Alan had brought to her in the dining room. He'd told her she should get some sleep.

She looked like death warmed over. Her hair was greasy and pulled back in a ponytail. The dark circles had returned under her eyes, and she was pale. She was exhausted. The high of finding the falsifications in the log files was waning quickly. After she told Christoph the good news, she would be heading to bed. She could see the concern in his eyes when he looked up at her as she approached his desk.

She wondered if she looked that bad. Automatically, she reached her hand up to make sure her ponytail was smooth, and that she didn't have freaky hair or anything like that. She said, "Hi."

"Hi. How are you? Have you eaten?" he asked her. His protective instinct was kicking into overdrive. He was concerned for her welfare, and he knew she especially needed to keep up her own health for a healthy baby. She could already have conceived. As she sat down in front of his desk, he could still smell her unique scent. It drew him upright in his chair, and it made him hard just thinking about touching her and tasting her again.

"Oh yes, a few hours ago," she answered. "Alan made me a delicious roast beef sub sandwich and some sweet-potato chips.

It was delicious." She was just staring at him – he was so handsome, and all she wanted to do was kiss him. 'Get your damn act together, you nitwit!' her subconscious yelled at her. 'You need to tell him what you found.'

"Is everything okay?" he asked her, as he got up from the desk and came around to stand next to her chair, offering his hand to help her up. He led her to the sofa and motioned for her to sit, then proceeded to sit next to her.

"Yes, yes – I came to tell you that I found that the log files had been falsified again. The entries were bogus. I have the new team investigating and crosschecking with the network traces to try to identify at least what terminal the changes were made from. If we're lucky, we can then correlate it to the security camera footage," she explained. He didn't seem to be listening to her.

He heard her words, but all he could think about as he watched her green eyes was kissing her again. His head of security had already called him with her findings about five minutes before she walked into his office. All the details of the cross-references they were going to perform had already been explained to him. "Do you realize how beautiful you are?" he said to her, without realizing he'd said it aloud.

"What?" she said. Susan was taken off guard by his comment, which had nothing to do with what she had just told him. His hand was now caressing her face, and her cheek rested in his palm. It was difficult for her not to lean into his hand for more of his soft touch. She couldn't even remember what she was talking about.

He leaned in as if to kiss her, but stopped short, saying, "I've been miserable while you've been working." He waited to see the look of puzzlement in her expression, so he continued, "I'm not used to spending a lot of time with another person, and this was a rude awakening to how much time we actually have been spending together. I definitely felt you were missing. I missed your company. I missed your laugh." He was trying to explain how much he had come to depend upon her company, but he felt he was doing a poor job of it.

Susan couldn't think of a response to his declaration. He was taking the role playing a little too far. He almost sounded serious. What the hell was she supposed to say to him in response? Her feelings were new to her where he was concerned. But she was willing to take a risk. She was always willing to take a risk, but she wasn't sure what to say.

Luckily, she didn't have a chance to respond because he leaned in and started kissing her. He had his arm around her and pulling her body closer to his.

He was like a magnet to her. Once he'd started kissing her, she was lost. She easily fell back into the pattern with him as his kisses were so mesmerizing.

She liked being rendered speechless and didn't want to resist his pull. He continued kissing her and touching her in the most intimate of caresses. All she could think was 'Don't stop!'

Susan is melting against him; she is ready to agree to anything he suggests. It is a risk, and she has already decided to accept. She will never know if she doesn't at least try.

As she is coming to this conclusion, she puts her hands on his shoulders to pull him closer – when she hears a buzz. 'Is that because I put my hands on his shoulders?' she wonders, until she realizes that she's hearing motors. She wonders what in the world they are.

Then she hears the first machine gun shots. They both turn to look out the window at the same time, and in the increasing darkness, they can barely make out helicopters coming at them.

There were men with machine guns, hanging out of the open doorways and firing. Christoph acted quickly, grabbing her hand and literally scooping her up and carrying her behind his desk, then pressing a button so fast that she hardly had time to register where they were before they stepped into a small opening in the bookcase.

As the door was closing, they saw and heard the machine gun fire tearing up the couch they'd been sitting on, with pieces of the cushioning flying up into the air. Glass from the windows spewed across the room, and the blue-lighted bullets flew around, pegging books and shelves, throwing bits of pages and wood everywhere.

Susan was stunned as she watched the door slide shut. Her arms were around his neck because he was still holding her. They could still hear the helicopters and machine guns tearing up the villa. She was terrified.

It had happened to her again – she was almost killed. Again, he had saved her. Her heart was racing, so she closed her eyes and laid her head on his shoulder. She'd never been so glad she wasn't standing on her own two feet. A moment later her body just went limp when she fainted.

Chapter 12

Christoph felt her go her limp as he looked down at her and saw her eyes flutter shut. She'd fainted. Thank goodness he'd picked her up from the couch when he did. He had the ability to move slightly faster than humans. It wasn't too significant, but it was enough that any Argonian could outrace any human at any time. He smirked as he recalled all the Olympics when they'd done just that. It was a fun pastime for his people, these Olympic Games. It was why they had introduced them to the humans through the Greeks.

The Argonians had had a good, long relationship with the now-ancient Greeks. Many of the Greeks' advancements and ideas had come from the many Argonians who had been given a chance to test whether the human race was ready for integration with the Argon society.

But alas, their attempt proved futile, and the Argon coalition withdrew their forces and tempered their attempts when they realized that the Earth's human race was just not mature enough. The Argonians kept the planet under surveillance, and on its list of potential evacuation planets. With the humans, it was going to take time to get them where they needed to be for full acceptance.

Full acceptance – that's what Christoph wanted from Susan. He was already committed to her, and for him, there was no going back. For centuries, the Argonians had had to live on Earth in secret, and he didn't want to keep this from Susan. He wanted her to know who he is, and he wanted her to be aware of her danger. He couldn't insure her safety if she didn't know the danger she was in from the Grogans. His number one personal priority was keeping her safe, which meant getting to the main control room, quickly.

As Christoph hurried down the concrete, reinforced hallway to an elevator, cradling Susan in his arms, he felt certain that the Grogans were behind these attacks. After seeing the laser bullets they were firing from the helicopters, he knew it couldn't be anyone else. He just hoped that Susan hadn't noticed the blue laser bullets.

Given the bullets have confirmed that it's the Grogans again, Christoph can't help but wonder how they found this island. There had to have been a leak in Boston. Christoph's certainty that the Grogans were responsible changed everything. If the Grogans continued this aggressive front, then there was no longer plenty of time. The Argonians might have to reveal themselves to the humans sooner than planned, in order to protect them.

Christoph's thoughts continued to trouble him when he stopped at an elevator. He quickly did his retina scan, but now he needed her to do the retina scan too, so he had to try to wake her. "Susan, wake up, are you there?" he said, as he gently jostled her in his arms. She stirred, but not enough to be truly coherent, yet still he tried. "Susan, here, turn your head." He leaned her over so gravity would help. Now with her head turned, he coaxed, "Open your eyes, Susan, just for a moment. Come on, sweetheart, just one second." She opened and blinked her eyes a few times, but she still was limp in his arms. Luckily the system was able to pick up all three blinks, and put together an image they could process. The word "Processing" was up for a while longer than normal, making him edgy.

His relief was palpable when the green light flashed the word "CLEAR." For a moment he was worried she was an alien. How laughable, he thought. *He* was the alien, hoping that *she* passed the retina scan, verifying she was human or from Argon. He knew Susan wasn't from Argon, but the thought of her being a Grogan in a human cloaking suit did make him shudder as he carried her into the elevator.

The elevator took them down a few levels. When the doors opened, he stepped into a short corridor with a fully functional-looking war room to the right and a moderate living room/kitchen area to the left, complete with an underground wall waterfall in the middle that separated the rooms. It was all very sophisticated, and extremely modern looking.

Christoph moved to his left, toward the couch in the break area. Gently, he laid Susan down on the couch, adjusted the pillows behind her head and extended her legs. He noticed a throw draped across the back of the couch, which he absentmindedly picked up to cover her. It was only about fifty-five or sixty degrees down here because of the sophisticated Argon computer systems, and she was dressed for island temperatures in a halter top, short shorts and flip-flops.

He went over to the kitchen area to find a towel to moisten, and a glass of water. When he returned to sit on the coffee table, he looked at her, seeing her eyes fully open and a frightened look on her face. His protective instinct took over, but he was careful not to reveal much, "Are you okay? Would you like a drink of water?"

Christoph put the damp towel across her forehead, knowing that the cooling effect would help her focus. He said, "We'll be safe here until help arrives, and we have secure communications. The lines down here are satellite, and they're separate from the lines upstairs."

"What are we supposed to do?" she asked.

Before he could answer, his phone vibrates and beeps that he's receiving a text. He takes out his phone and looks at it.

Security team:

:: Helicopters gone.
:: Are you ok? Underground?

Christoph texts back:

:: Yes. With Susan, in command center.

Security team:

:: Alan and one other badly wounded.
:: Transporting to mainland.
:: Compound secure for now. End.

Christoph:
:: Good. Request more patrols to be sent, and add radar surveillance. End.

Susan looks about her in amazement. This is the type of area you see in those movies when they have to take the POTUS to a secure location. It was really unbelievable.

Christoph says, "I have to turn on some equipment and get some communications started. I need to send a text to increase our security lockdown." He bends over and kisses her forehead, and asks, "Will you be okay right here? I'll be over in the other room."

"Yes, I'll be fine," she says slowly.

"Try to relax," Christoph says. "There's everything you could possible need or want over in the kitchen area. There's a TV, magazines, and here's an iPad. Help yourself," he says, as he stands and waves his arm about. "I'll be down those steps and in the main room if you need me."

Susan nods her head at Christoph as he walks out of the ultra-modern break room, which looks more like a luxurious living room. She sits up and looks back at the kitchen area, surprised at how nice it is – with white tile backsplash, latest appliances and marble counter tops, even a marble-topped island.

She turns back around and lays her head back on the couch. She stares into the blank TV and thinks, 'Relax he says! Oh, my fucking God, seriously?!!' She had almost been shot to death, on a remote island, somewhere close to Korea.

How in the hell was she supposed to fucking relax? Shit, she needed a drink – and a strong one, at that! She looked around the lounge area where she was sitting and spotted a cabinet with bottles of brown and clear liquid. BINGO! She'd hit the jackpot.

She made her way over to sniff the various liquors. Deciding upon a foul-smelling bourbon, Susan poured herself a glass, neat. If it was a good bourbon, it would be smooth, and taste nothing like it smelled. The power of the punch would be just what she needed. It's not every day that you're almost shot to pieces. But hell, for her it was happening way too often. She shuddered when she thought of her odds – and they weren't very good.

She lifted the glass and tentatively tasted it. Gag! Oh shit, it was awful... it tasted like Jack Daniel's. 'Yuck! No, thank you,' she thought, as she found another light golden liquid that might be Scotch. She got a fresh glass and poured some from the new bottle. This time, her eyes rolled heavenward in thanks as she took yet another sip. It was divine Scotch. It had a buttery, smooth taste to it, so she didn't even bother with adding any ice. She drained it, then refilled her glass to halfway, dropped a few ice cubes in and went back to the couch.

Susan contemplated her life as she sipped her Scotch, wishing the alcohol would go to her head faster. She thought of those bullets. The devastation was incredible. It was as if there were blue lights being shot at them. It was strange. She'd only ever seen guns shooting in movies. Did they make blue streaks? This was the third time in less than a month that she'd almost been killed. But when she was at the deli she didn't see anything, because Christoph had tackled her to the ground. She wondered for a few more moments about it, when she realized she was having a hard time catching her breath. She had to stop thinking about it and just breathe.

She was having trouble clearing her mind, so she started trying to think of things, small things to be thankful for, besides the one large one... her life! 'Jesus Christ, I can't believe this is happening to me,' she thought, as she finished that drink and got up to make herself another.

Susan took a long draw from her freshly refilled glass. 'Damn, this is so good,' she reveled, as she sat back down on the comfortable couch. She was definitely feeling much looser and relaxed. It was easy to think of the nice things she had to be thankful for now. The alcohol was going to her head, quickly and effectively. She started to feel both sleepy and cold.

She pulled the small blanket over her, and reached in her shorts for her phone to see what time it was. Though it wasn't too late, Susan figured it wasn't surprising that she would be tired. She'd been up for a day and a half, working to prove her innocence. It was no wonder she was tired. The adrenaline of finding the evidence she needed – and then almost being killed – had left her, and she felt drained. She knew the alcohol was helping her exhaustion along. It was exactly what she wanted. She just wants to forget for a while and lie down on the couch for a few minutes and close her eyes...

———

At midnight, Christoph could not do any more than he'd already set in motion. He had to wait for the others to arrive, and for his island security team to be reinforced. He walked into the lounge area and saw Susan passed out on the couch, with an empty drink tumbler on the floor. He looked around and saw she'd found the liquor cabinet.

She looked peaceful. He hated to wake her, but he couldn't let her sleep here all night. It was cold, and she looked like she was shivering. Plus, he knew she hadn't had any sleep in a few days, and she would likely need uninterrupted sleep for quite a while.

Christoph gently woke her to tell her she should go to bed and get some sleep. "Come with me," he'd said.

It was all that Susan could do to acknowledge him. She without question followed his lead and let him help her off the couch. Barely coherent and a little more than buzzed, definitely teetering on the line of buzzed and drunk, she blindly followed him down another hallway and through another set of doors. She let him lead her by the hand, stumbling after him in her drunken state.

Christoph finally noticed her stumbling and realized she might have had more to drink that he suspected. He slowed down and took her past the elevator down a hall to another doorway on the left, which again opened by a retina scan.

After scanning her eye, the door opened and Susan found herself ushered into the most luxurious and soft-feeling room, with a huge king-sized bed. The right-hand section of the room where the bed stood, decorated in shades of blue, was clearly for sleeping; while the opposite end, with the living area, was all in white. White couch, white carpet, white coffee table, white lampshade, white recliner; it matched the break room she'd just come from. The TV and bookshelves were white too. It did a lot to open up the room and give it a more spacious feeling. At the back of the room, in off-white and soft yellow, was the combined kitchen, laundry and eating area. But what really drew her was off the right side of the room, where the plush, dark-blue carpet started.

The bed was a huge, king-sized, deep red mahogany four-poster canopy bed. The duvet cover was a solid royal blue, a few shades lighter than the carpet. The sheets and pillow cases were a soft light blue, but all the tones blended well together. There was dark blue velvet fabric, which looked to be tied back, covering the posts of the bed.

She watched as Christoph went around the bed untying the velvet curtains, then slid them around to completely enclose the bed in darkness.

He stood by the closest side of the bed to her, leaving the curtain opened slightly, and said, "Come," as he reached out his hand. She was so sleepy she didn't even think of disobeying. It simply looked so luxurious and inviting that she couldn't wait to get in and fall asleep. Christoph slowly undressed her and lifted her into the soft bed. He undressed and followed, then he pulled her to him and spooned her until they both fell asleep.

She woke up thinking that she and Juan were almost finished with the code changes and testing. Whoever put the false code there definitely knows by now that they aren't getting video feeds. Neither can they pull data. But she can't think now. Not while Christoph is touching her like this. She forgets about code, and wants to feel Christoph touching her again. She closes her eyes and sighs because she doesn't want it to stop. Was she dreaming? She wondered.

It was indeed a dream – at least she thinks so for a moment. Then she realizes she is waking up. Before she has time to register the dream state versus reality, and her position in bed with Christoph, she feels him pull her close and whisper, "Good morning, sweetheart" in her ear. The fact that he adds "sweetheart" when he says it makes her heart jump. It's odd how a small term of endearment goes such a long way.

She was feeling more vulnerable than she ever had. Holy shit, she was naked! And he was naked behind her. 'Oh shit, oh shit, oh shit' she thought. The last and first time they'd been together, she'd had a few drinks. He wasn't there when she woke up the next morning.

But last night was different. They didn't even have sex. She was drunk, and who wouldn't be after almost being killed – again!? But now, she was completely sober, but so overly tired she could barely think. She didn't even recall how she got here.

She remembered him undressing her. He was very caring in a non-sexual way. He was innocently efficient, as if he was putting a child to bed – except, of course, when he got into bed with her. She was so exhausted that she was asleep almost before he'd set her down in the bed. When he cuddled up behind her, it felt like a dream to her. But now, here he was – and she could feel evidence of how excited he was to be next to her.

Her mind was slowly waking up. And he felt so damn good. He was warm and hard behind her. His caresses were slow and erotic, yet he wasn't pressuring her. It was very relaxing as he stroked her curves and soft skin. It felt so good to have him touching her. And it would feel so nice to touch him.

She lifted her hand to put it on his hip and thigh behind her.... He felt so good. It was so soothing, what he was doing. She relaxed.

Christoph didn't do more than caress her. He avoided all her trigger points. He wanted to do more to her. He wanted to bury himself so deep inside her that she screamed in the inevitable orgasm. He'd heard that human females did that because of the emotion they tied to it. He knew firsthand that Susan was very vocal. He was enjoying having a human female, because she definitely experienced pleasure more fully than an Argonian female.

He loved giving Susan pleasure – but not that kind, not right now. She wasn't ready to be awake yet. He had already calculated it, and she'd still only had less than six hours of sleep. She needed much more than that before he was going to take her again. He gradually stopped, and made sure her breathing was even again, letting her sleep.

Susan slept peacefully until it happened again. The dream was so real.

She could feel the ropes pressing into her back. It hurt so badly. Where was her swimsuit? Why wouldn't he leave her alone? She tried to fight him off, but she couldn't make him stop. "No, no, no, please stop!" she said as she shook her head from side to side to get him to stop trying to kiss her. Oh God, he was so awful, she didn't want him to touch her. She couldn't understand why she couldn't stop him.

Christoph was in the kitchen when he heard her yelling, "No, no, no, please stop!" He quickly went to the bed and threw back the curtains. "Susan, wake up sweetheart," he said as he pulled her into his arms and put her head on his shoulder. She didn't resist him, and soon she seemed to be sleeping peacefully again. But he felt he had to wake her to make sure she was okay. "Susan, wake up. Wake up," he said.

She suddenly felt an unfamiliar softness and comfort, and heard her name being called. She opened her eyes sleepily and looked, baffled, at Christoph. He was holding her, cradling her against his chest. She felt safe.

"Hi you. Are you okay? It was a bad dream," Christoph said, and he brought her back to his body and held her, kissing her forehead.

She pulled back and looked at him with bewildered eyes. "Yeah, I'm fine now. Thanks." She numbly let him hold her. 'Oh God, it feels so good to have him holding me,' she thought. But other urgent matters arose, prompting her, "Uh... umm... I need to go to the restroom."

Immediately he lets her go, as he reaches down to the foot of the bed and hands her a big, lush, white robe. Smiling, he says, "It's on the other side of the bed, through the door. Take your time, I'm making breakfast. It should be ready in about twenty minutes." He kisses her forehead again before he gets up to leave, and gives her privacy behind the curtain.

She smiles back at him and hugs the robe to her chest as she watches him leave. Shaking the dream from her mind this time was easier, and it faded quickly. She knew it was because she felt safe with him and was beginning to trust him. She slips on the robe, climbs out of the bed on the other side and silently makes her way to the bathroom.

Now that he knew she was okay, he was back at work in the kitchen. Christoph was making breakfast, but at the same time he was also on his computer emailing, and had just finished a video chat. He had his cell phone out for urgent phone calls and texts. It was important that he get this breach sorted out, especially now that they had confirmation that the Grogans were behind the attack yesterday. He knew they were behind the deli attack as well, and they were more than likely behind the bombings too. It was clear they were responsible for the data breach, but his Argon security team had yet to find the evidence he needed.

Christoph had been in communications, and on meetings and calls, for the last four hours. He'd had to meet with the Argon council on the colony ship to explain as well. It had been one eventful morning for him. Perhaps Susan had picked up on his stress.

He was worried about this dream she had been having. This was the second time he had woken her from it. What could it be about? He was hesitant to ask her. He was no psychologist or psychiatrist, so he wouldn't have any idea what to make of whatever kind of dream she was having. Given the close calls with her life recently, he couldn't blame her for having bad dreams – after all, she had almost been killed three times since he met her. These near-death misses were enough to give anyone nightmares.

His computer beeped that his next conference call was starting. Luckily, on this call, he just had to listen, so he could mute his end of the line. He plugged in his wireless earphones so only he could hear the discussion about Argon defensive tactics being implemented around the globe.

While he was listening, he continued with making breakfast, putting biscuits on a baking sheet and sliding them in the oven. His mind was consumed by the conversation and planning tactics they were discussing. His team was good at working together and collaborating on ideas to construct a comprehensive plan. He looked up and saw Susan coming toward him, wrapped up in her white robe. Her hair was wet; she must've taken a shower.

"Orange juice?" he asked, as he put a medium-sized glass of OJ in front of her.

"Yes, thank you. What are you making?" she asked. It looked like a disaster in the kitchen. There was flour all over the counter, and a bowl, plus what looked like a biscuit cutter. "Did you make biscuits from scratch?" she asked, incredulously.

"Yes. I also fried up some bacon a while ago. Want some?" he asked, as he put a huge plate of bacon in front of her. Just then her stomach audibly growled, and he laughed, "Well, I guess so… eat up!"

Christoph set the timer for the biscuits before asking her, "How many eggs would you like? Scrambled, fried, omelet?"

"Three, scrambled please," she replied with wonder in her voice. She couldn't believe her CEO was making her breakfast. But then again, she's also slept with her CEO twice, not mention she's actually had sex with him. So, yeah, it's okay that he's making her breakfast. But still, her life has been moving so quickly in the last week, she almost couldn't believe that she was sitting there, watching this happening.

He deftly whipped up about seven eggs and poured it into a waiting, oiled-up pan. He'd learned how to cook as one of his efforts to fit in with humans and he found he enjoyed it. While the eggs were cooking, he recalled the fun he'd had with his cousin taking the classes on Earth, disguised as humans. His mind went back to his current efforts and he made quick work of the messy counter and slid the bowl, spoon, and biscuit cutter into the dishwasher. He retrieved two plates from the cabinet and set them next to where the eggs were cooking. Christoph flipped and moved the eggs around for about a minute before the buzzer on the oven went off. He took the biscuits out of the oven, and turned off the eggs, all in quick, neat order.

But what was strange to her was that it was as if he wasn't even here. His mind was occupied with something else. Then she noticed the ear buds in his ears. He must be listening to something. Then she noticed his laptop behind him on the kitchen island. It all clicked – he was on a conference call.

His mind still on the call, he silently served up eggs, put two biscuits on her plate and handed it to her. The butter was already sitting next to the bacon, so she was all set. She dug her fork into the eggs and rolled her eyes in appreciation, they tasted so good.

She was so hungry anything would have tasted divine. Why was she so hungry? She usually wasn't this hungry when she woke up, but then again, she wasn't usually the target of machine guns. At least she was hoping it wasn't going to be a usual thing.

Christoph walked over to his laptop, punched in a few keys; then he removed his ear buds from his ears and laid them next to the laptop. "Sorry, I had to listen in on that conference call. We're working out the next plans," he said glumly. It worried him that she was involved. He didn't know how to tell her he was an alien, or that aliens even existed. For now, everyone agreed it was best to keep her in the dark.

"That's okay, I understand. I figured you were on a call," she said, as she took her first bite of biscuit. "Mmmmmm," was all she could say. The biscuits were delicious, and they were clearly buttermilk biscuits. A man after her Southern heart, for sure.

"How do you like it?" Christoph asked her and she took another bite of biscuit.

She smiled, her mouth clearly full, chewing biscuit. "Mmmmm ... mmmmm" she mumbled as she nodded her head.

"Yeah, I see, sorry, didn't mean to catch you with your mouth full," he conceded. He wasn't thinking clearly. He was on a mission and had things to do. He didn't have time for niceties, but he needed to be gentle with Susan. He imagined her emotions are fragile after all the attempts on her life.

To ease her mind he shared, "The reinforcements will be here in a few hours. We're still safe here," he confessed to her. "I'll send some medics down today to check you out and make sure that everything is ok, just in case," he said. "You'll need to talk with your team. Let me know if they've found anything. I'll send your laptop down to you. I'll make sure it is already be connected to the wireless receiver down here."

He looked at her with some concern on his face. She was still eating and she was just nodding her acquiescence to him as he was talking and mumbling, "Uh uh" and "Ok" through her food.

"Will you be okay down here today Susan?" he asked. Concerned because she hadn't said much.

Taking a sip of juice to rinse down her food, she said easily, "Yes, I think I'll be fine. But actually, I think I'm a little tired again. Would it be okay to just take a nap?" She looked at him and was suddenly feeling really sleepy again. It must be the full stomach. She'd eaten everything on her plate.

"Yes, of course, please take your time, sleep if you feel the need. There's no urgency. All the systems stateside were locked down and there's been no intrusion. You're safe down here," he implored. Secretly he was glad she was getting sleepy. He'd put a tablet in her juice and she'd almost drained the entire glass. If the pill was working this quickly it just meant that she needed it more. Some of his people who only needed a bit, would not even get sleepy, just pensive for a few minutes and then they'd be cleared up. It'll take Susan some time to get to that level without knowing her physical capabilities.

Christoph got up from the stool next to Susan and held his hand out to Susan, "Come, I'll tuck you in before I go."

Susan could not resist and put her hand in his. He was promising that she could sleep, which is exactly what she wanted to do beyond anything else. She let him lead her the short distance to the still rumbled, but divinely soft looking bed. Christoph bent and pulled the duvet back in one swoop.

He pulled her hand around and maneuvered her into the bed. He flipped the duvet back over her and the bed was neat again. He bent over to kiss her forehead, "Goodnight darling" she thought she heard him say, but she wasn't sure. She was already drifting off to sleep.

That afternoon, Mark Parsons, her team leader, called her through the video line on her laptop. She was sitting at the bar in the kitchen, except that she'd exchanged her breakfast plate for her laptop. She was so grateful when Christoph had her computer delivered to the room when the medics came to draw blood and check on her after she finished her two hour nap.

It was wonderful to sleep until she woke up, refreshed and ready to work. She had not been up more than 10 minutes before the medics showed up. But she'd texted Christoph when she woke up, so he probably alerted them. Either way, she was glad he was so considerate and understanding, not to mention efficient in getting her what she needed to work.

Now, her team was just starting their status call and she was able to join. Mark started, after everyone's hellos were made, "Ma'am, we've fixed all the startup and shutdown scripts. We found that the problem code was in all the primary production server scripts – literally, in every key server that we have. The breach had definitely been initiated on the Apache development server, just like was originally thought."

"So Luis was right," she replied, more as a mumble to herself than to Mark on the other end of the phone.

Mark gave her an update on what the new team had been working on, "And the new security developers we hired fixed all the code. Now that we've figured out all the intricacies of where the breach was occurring, we thought it was safe to fix them." They'd had to call in network security consultants so they could ensure that any firewall or networking holes were closed, and that the intranet within the wall of the company was well sealed and safe from more intrusions.

"Did you save the hacked files in a secure location so we can use them as evidence?" she asked him. Without giving him a chance to reply, she also asked, "And have you had a chance to work the network consultants to cross-reference access points with IP addresses and terminals?"

Mark continued, "We were able to verify that access was initially gained via one of the development servers, which didn't have all the same secure protocols in place that Production had. But we haven't been able to pinpoint much else yet. As soon as the villain was able to access the network, he was able to move around from server to server, hacking any and all standard security measures."

"I see, so it is difficult to track. But is it impossible to track, Mark? What do you and the network consultants think?" she asked quickly.

"It is definitely possible, ma'am. The lead network consultant and his team said it's just going to take longer to untangle, but they are confident that it's only a matter of time before they can identify a workstation," he explained.

"Okay, good. Please call the main security team, and have them ready a team on standby to assist with video evidence when you identify the workstation. I'll email the contact name you'll need to coordinate with," she instructed him.

"Yes, ma'am, will do. Is there anything else?" Mark asked.

"Not now. Please keep me informed on a daily basis. Thank you all for your hard work, and for working so much overtime to complete the fixes," she earnestly concluded before they said their goodbyes and ended their video session.

Susan typed keys to end the session. She flipped screens on her laptop to her email. The last email from Christoph had the security manager's name on it. She quickly found the name and emailed it to Mark. In less than five minutes he replied with the name of the security team leader, and confirmed that they would be waiting.

There wasn't anything left for her to do. The main data breach had been handled. She didn't even have to stress over finding a new team; that had happened practically overnight. She was simply amazed at how quickly GTS HR was able to organize it, despite the sudden tragedy of the accident. It was still difficult for her to wrap her head around finding that many experts in this specific code base in only days. But now, she had a team that she'd only ever seen on video.

There were just several suspicious pieces about how quickly her new team came into being that made her think Christoph was holding back on her and not telling her everything. She wasn't sure she even wanted to know, either. It seemed as if the more she knew, the more vulnerable she was. She guessed she was probably still in danger now, because they hadn't figured out who was behind the attacks and the data breach. At least that's what *she* thought.

Christoph walked into the room he had shared last night with Susan. She was still sitting at the counter with her laptop, but her mind didn't seem to be engaged with the unit. She was staring into space, as if something else was bothering her, and he made a little noise to catch her attention. She turned and presented him with a smile so bright, he swore that the energy radiating from her had blinded him for a moment.

'Oh this is good, *really* good,' he told himself. If his presence could make her glow like that, he was sure he had her. He just needed to be careful. "Good afternoon, how are you?" he asked her, as he approached her on the stool.

Susan smelled so good when he got closer to her that he couldn't resist getting even closer. She was wearing his t-shirt and his sweatpants. Her hair was in a ponytail, so he would have easy access to her neck.

He bent over and kissed her lightly on the neck first, then the lips. He couldn't help himself. His security team had given him a tour of the compound, and he knew she wouldn't have had much of a chance to survive if she hadn't been with him. The thought was sobering.

Susan smiled up at him, "I'm good, but a little hungry I think, Chef Baldric," she teased.

"Ah, so I'm cooking dinner, eh?" he asked her goodheartedly, as he put his arms around her and pulled her closer. He looked down into her face and started to say something, but changed his mind and just kissed her again.

This time, he took his time, exploring every facet of her tongue and mouth, licking her lips, before tasting her again. She tasted so incredible, like the sweetest peach, ripe from the tree. Just then he heard her stomach growl. She should have eaten before now; it was well over four hours since lunch. He groaned as he pulled his mouth from hers. "Okay, I hear the call. What would you like to eat?" he asked her.

Feeling decadent, since she was alive after dodging several attempts on her life – not to mention the news from her team – she felt like celebrating, so she said, "My favorite comfort food: spaghetti and meat sauce with garlic bread."

"Is that your favorite? What's the special occasion?" he asked, teasingly, as he started pulling out pots and pans.

"First, I'm alive. Second, my team fixed all the bugs and completed their trace of the data breach. Third, it goes great with red wine!" she cajoled.

He knew all about the data breach. Of course his team had already notified him. He knew this morning before he left. Susan's new team was part of his special Argon security forces. They were specially trained for this type of work. It's why it had been so easy to get the team together. Travel time from different parts of the world was the only delay. But Susan didn't need to know all that. The most important thing for him is that she feel useful, and not stressed. "Ah, wine it is milady," he teased in a fake accent before he made his way to the substantial wine fridge in the kitchen/dining area.

He grabbed a bottle of his best Cabernet Sauvignon, a 2009 Doubleback vintage, over 165 years old. One thing that the humans on Earth did well was wine. That was one advancement that the Argonians had had no problem teaching them, and speeding along, even while the human race was still relatively primitive. As soon as Christoph removed the cork, he could smell that it was going to be delicious. After pouring two glasses to let the wine breathe, he reached for a younger Doubleback and opened that as well. It sounded as if Susan wanted to celebrate, and he was glad. It meant that she was stronger than he thought and the medicine worked to relieve her.

"Okay, the wine will be ready in about forty-five minutes, just when our meal will be finished cooking. So, tell me what your team found while I get everything else going," he asked.

Susan logged off her computer and closed the lid while she started filling him on what Mark had told her. She was so excited to share this information with Christoph. He could see the excitement in her eyes, and her eagerness to find the infiltrator. But then a frown creased her brown and concern clouded her eyes.

Her brow furrowed further, and she confessed, "I'm so excited the team is doing great, but... well..... It's only... well... I don't feel useful to my team, being away from them. I don't feel that there's much for me to do except take their status."

He secretly commiserated with her, but that was the nature of being a manager and an executive. You took people's status and you made decisions based upon those statuses. If things were going well, you didn't have any decisions to make; you dealt with issues as they arose; you just listened to how well everyone was doing and focused on strategic planning for the future. Of course, this is a big generalization, but she was beginning to feel what it was like.

"Yes, you are correctly explaining the majority of an executive's job. You'll also be responsible for analyzing metrics, and detailing out how your team will help the company meet our strategic goals. Don't worry, there's more to come," he reassured her.

"Yes, but all those types of tasks were done by Mr. Jones. Mark is doing *my* job, and I feel lost." She decided to confide in him. "I can't believe I told you that. Oh my God, please ignore that I said that. I shouldn't have mentioned it to you, I'm so sorry." For God's sake, he's the CEO. She can't say things like that to him!

"Susan, relax, please stop, it's okay," he tried to reassure her once again. "Really, yes, it's exactly how I wanted this to work out," he said. He paused as he scooped up the cooked hamburger meat to drain the grease out of it.

"You did?" she asked, clearly puzzled. "I don't understand."

When he turned back to the stove and added the meat back to the pan, he looked up at her and said, "I knew I was going to fire Mr. Jones the moment you told me that he made you wait to implement data breach protocol procedures."

She watched him as he put all the other ingredients in to make the sauce. It looked so good: fresh garlic, onions, mushrooms, tomatoes, tomato sauce, tomato paste. She wasn't even sure what fresh herbs he was cutting up to put in there, but it all looked and smelled delicious. She watched him, but didn't comment. She didn't know what to say to him. Did this mean he is promoting her? She didn't want to ask. She remained silent, hoping he'd elaborate.

After putting the bread in the oven, he had a few minutes until the pasta was done. He said, "I want you to take over Mr. Jones's job. I'm hoping that you will accept the promotion. I was going to wait until we were back at headquarters, but I'm asking you now," he explained.

"Oh," she said. She sat there for a moment, then started frowning. "Is this because I had sex with you?" Of course, she immediately felt that she'd "slept her way to a promotion." She seriously thought those tactics were a myth of her great-great-grandparents' days, but nonetheless, she couldn't help but feel that way.

Christoph had a feeling she was going to ask that. The glow that she'd had since he walked in the room immediately dimmed when that thought came across her mind. He couldn't let her think that. He knew how weak human men were about standing up for their feelings.

He moved around to her side of the bar and took her hands. "No, absolutely not. My feelings for you have nothing to do with the promotion. I decided all of this back in Boston, before the second bomb went off."

"Your feelings for me? What feelings?" she asked boldly, completely changing the subject. He wasn't supposed to have feelings for her. This was just a repetitive hookup, nothing more.

He bent over and kissed her briefly on the mouth before stepping quickly around the other side of the counter, just as the buzzer for the spaghetti went off. His uncanny ability to time things in the kitchen did not go unnoticed. Once again, it looked as if he was going to have everything ready at the same time.

In a more matter-of-fact tone, Christoph continued, "Of course I have feelings for you, Susan. Don't be obtuse – we're not twentysomething and playing the field anymore," he said, hoping to sound like a human. 'Isn't that something a human man would say, at least an honest one?' he thought to himself. He decided to just go for it.

He handed her a glass of wine. She might need a drink after he told her this. "Look, Susan, I've been looking for somebody like you for a long time." She didn't need to know how long it had been. "I didn't make love to you on the fly; it was very premeditated. And if I have my way, it'll happen again and again and again," he said, adamantly.

She took a gulp of her wine at his emphatic statement, catching her off guard. "I see," she said. Then she took another sip. Wow, that wine tasted amazing. She savored it, and tried to sort out what she thought she had just heard from Christoph. Seriously, was he still trying to role-play for the hookup game? No man had ever been that forthright with her – just out and out telling her what he wanted. Not since that crazy geek in sixth grade wrote her those gross letters. She took another sip of wine and watched him, wearily.

He kept himself busy putting the final items of their meal together. 'Why isn't she saying anything?' he wondered. He looked up at her, and she was taking another sip of her wine. Her glass was almost empty. He grabbed the bottle and poured her another full glass. "Don't you want the same thing? What do you want Susan?"

She looked like a deer caught in the headlights. "Uh, well… umm… I… it just hasn't crossed my mind," she lied easily. She quickly took another sip of wine. "You know it's just not the way things are done anymore." Finally she was starting to feel the courage from the alcohol, but it wasn't enough just yet. What the hell else should she say? She's never been in this situation before, and she has no idea what to do.

"Okay, fair enough," he said. "Come, let's eat," he added, rescuing her from having to reply. He served their meal at the small dining table. The food was so good that she didn't even think of talking. She was ravenous, and they ate in companionable silence.

When she finished, she said, "That was absolutely delicious. Thank you so very much." She beamed at him and raised her glass to toast his. "To the best spaghetti ever," she said.

She had devoured every bit and used the toasty garlic bread to clean up any remaining sauce. He was proud, but he also suspected why she was so hungry. He'd served her enough to feed two people. While he didn't know much about human pregnancies, he knew that directly after an Argon woman's egg is fertilized, her body goes into overdrive and requires larger quantities of food. Wine had proven harmless to Argon fetuses' eons ago, so he didn't even give that a second thought.

The Argon sperm and fetus were very strong. It's as if the embryo starts growing and using energy immediately. He smiled to himself even more. She was his. He just needed to figure out how and when to tell her, he thought as he got up to clear the table.

He took her plate and refilled her glass again. They were already into the second bottle of wine. As predicted, the first one was consumed with ultimate bliss; the taste was divine and smooth as silk. She picked up her third full glass before startling him with the question, "So, how long do we have to be down here?"

Susan got up to wander back to her usual spot behind the bar to talk to him while he cleaned up the kitchen. She didn't feel the need to ask to help, he was just putting everything in the dishwasher. She expanded on her question, "Not that it's not lovely down here, but I was starting to get a little claustrophobic down here this afternoon."

His security team and the Argon cleanup team from the colony ship needed to clean up the compound, and all evidence that the attack had been launched by Grogans with laser bullets, before he could let her back above ground. Christoph knew it was safe for them to return to the surface because the Argon space colony ship had secured the airspace within thirty minutes of the attack, but he couldn't tell her that. He couldn't let her see the actual destruction the laser bullets had done to the compound.

Christoph had to bend the truth for her. "It still isn't safe for us above ground. We're hoping to have everything cleaned up, and the airspace secured, by tomorrow evening," he said, which wasn't a complete lie.

"Get everything cleaned up? By tomorrow?" she asked incredulously. "Was there not that much damage then?" she prodded.

"Yes, I have several resources that arrived this morning to take care of it. Don't worry, it's all under control," he tried to tell her, avoiding giving a direct answer. But he wondered how much she would press him to know. How much would he have to tell her right now to appease her? He should try to change the subject.

"We can leave the island once we know who is responsible for the data breach. You should be safe when we have him or her in custody," he explained.

She thought to herself, and then said out loud, "Yes, I talked to Mark and my team about that today. They're working with the network consultants. They're confident they'll figure it out very soon," she added.

He finished loading their dishes into the dishwasher, and joined her once again on the other side of the counter. He stepped close to her, into her personal space, and asked her, "Are you going to be okay?"

"I don't know. You puzzle me. You don't say normal things. Do you really want to be with me? I thought we were just hooking up, the way people normally do." she countered.

He was surprised at where this was coming from, all of a sudden. But they did dance around the topic earlier in the evening. He factored in the wine and the direction of their conversation, back to where she was waiting and didn't feel useful in her job. Predictable human thought patterns. She'd have to learn that she's useful in her job, but as an executive. But for now, he wanted her to get used to being with him – because what she didn't realize was that she belonged to him now, and he wasn't going to let her go.

"Yes, Susan, you are mine," he confessed before kissing her. Again, he really didn't directly address her question. He just made an emphatic and possessive statement.

With her mind occupied with the sensations of kissing him, she absentmindedly puts her wine on the counter and then wraps her arms around him. 'If only that were true, if only he really felt that way' she thought. To finally have a man who actually wants her, and wants her to be his and only his was mind blowing to her. It is literally fairytale material, and folklore from the past. But this kiss, this kiss was real. Real sensations. She didn't have time for fairytales.

She had learned long before she entered college to not believe in fairytales. She was comfortable living by herself. Soon, she was going to be having a baby through the fertility clinic. She was doing great, but having him kiss her, and sleeping with him, was so wonderful and different. Touching him and being touched by him was heaven in and of itself, at least for now. She decided she would let whatever was going to happen, happen.

She needed to ride with this and see how long his desire for her would last. She deserved a little enjoyment in life, so she might as well take it while it's being offered. She didn't have to say anything back; she didn't need to confess her dreams. Instead she would show him how great he makes her feel by kissing him back with fervor.

He was already hard just being near her, but her enthusiasm was overwhelming him. He was so sensitive to her light, her frequency and her mood changes. It was going to take some getting used to, until he could show her the power she exerted when she changed frequencies. His passion was directly fueled by her efforts. He didn't even give it a thought when he picked her up and carried her to the bed without once breaking the sensuous kiss.

After he laid her down on the bed, he slowly peeled off her t-shirt and sweatpants, kissing her skin here and there along the way. He kissed her stomach as his hands started easing her panties down and off her legs. He kissed down her right leg to her knee, then over to her left knee and back up again.

She squirmed underneath him. She wanted to kiss him again and she wanted to touch him. He was tickling her, kissing her inner thighs. Alas, he was still just teasing her, as he kissed his way back to her bra.

He reached under her, then deftly unhooked and removed it, before giving all his attention to her nipples. He moved back and forth between sucking on one and fondling the other. He knew the constant stimulation was working her up, because her hips had started moving and circling. She was a delight underneath him. But he wanted more now and he needed to get out of his clothes.

Christoph stepped back from the bed to stand and take off all his clothes. He approached her and touched their bodies together, as he started kissing her again. Her legs automatically moved to accommodate him. He slipped inside her easily, because she was so incredibly wet.

He moved slowly at first. He kept kissing her, and exploring her mouth, as he began to bury himself in her. His pace was slow, sensual, and steady, but with each thrust, he seemed to go deeper and deeper.

Susan was beginning to lose her mind. His slow and firm strokes were working her up, and she couldn't stand the slow pace anymore. She grabbed his shoulders and said, "Faster, faster," as she locked her ankles around his hips and buttocks.

He moved faster and gave her what she wanted. He could feel her grip on his shoulders grow stronger with the same intensity as her grip on his penis. He knew she was close when she begged, breathlessly, "Faster! Deeper! Don't stop – please!"

It was all the encouragement he needed, and he released more of the control he had been keeping on his Argon abilities. She started moaning really loud, and she screamed his name when he felt the sudden wetness implode inside her. He immediately slowed his pace to a more human rhythm and depth. Back and forth, he slowed down more, as her hands fell from his shoulders and her ankles relaxed around his back. He could feel her wetness increasing. She was shaking and pulsing with aftershocks.

He bent over and kissed her cheeks, her forehead, and then kissed her mouth again. Christoph kept the pace slow and steady while she recovered. But he wanted more and he wanted to make her come like that again.

Christoph pulled out and helped her flip over on her stomach, pulling her up to rest on her hands and knees. He positioned himself at her entrance, grabbed her hips in both hands so that in one swift movement, he was buried deep inside her. Then, he began the slow motion, back and forth, once again.

He leaned over her, putting his hand between her legs to rub her clitoris while he was slowly moving in and out. She started to pant and moan as he stroked her there. He could feel her muscles start to clench. She was getting close again. He wanted to make her come one more time before he released himself. She grunted at his last push inside her – it was deep, and it set her off coming all over again. This time her muscles actually pushed him out when he got too close to the edge. It was all the sweeter when he pushed back into her hard, causing her to moan again.

She was so wet. He grabbed her hips, and pounded in and out of her at a furious pace for only about fifteen seconds before he felt his own orgasm begin to grab him. She squeezed him at the same time, and came again – as he exploded inside her.

Chapter 13

Pinpointing the malicious mind behind this attack was essential to insure that Christoph could keep Susan safe in the immediate future. Between the trail of evidence in the code maps, the falsified logins and log records that they had uncovered, the video surveillance cameras and all the efforts of the network consultants, Christoph was sure that it was only a matter of hours before they would identify the infiltrator.

At 3:00 a.m., Christoph's phone vibrated. He was very much attuned to everything around him during a crisis. He shifted slowly so as not to waken Susan. He reached over and grabbed his phone, reading the text as soon as he could get past his security screen.

Security team:

> :: We have identified the intruder.
> :: Call crisis bridge ASAP.

Christoph's heart started racing and his adrenaline spiked. He looked over at Susan sleeping peacefully. Of course he had hoped to find the perpetrator, but he was enjoying the time spent alone with Susan. He needed to get to the war room and see what was happening in Boston.

Carefully, he slid his arm from underneath Susan and slipped out of bed. He leaned over her and pulled the comforter around her. He didn't want her to lose any warmth, now that he wasn't lying next to her. She was sleeping peacefully – at least for now.

He threw on his sweats before walking to the counter to write a note to Susan. At least she was going to be under his protection from now on. His only problem was figuring out how to tell her. But first, he needed to focus on prosecuting the perpetrator. When he finished penning his note, he silently left the room while Susan slept, undisturbed.

Christoph made it to the war room in less than one minute. It was now only a total of six minutes since he'd started reading the text in bed next to Susan. That wasn't a place he would willingly leave, but duty calls.

The crisis video and conference bridge was being broadcast on the main center monitor. Other monitors had various security views in and around the island, including underwater checks and views. Smaller screens were stacked to the right of the main screen. Several smaller screens showed people in them, obviously the other participants on the call.

"Sir," one of the team members in the room addressed Christoph. "The head of security in Boston is ready on the main bridge," he explained, as he stepped back and moved to his desk. He was one of the newly arrived technical experts in charge of all the video and phone conferences that Christoph had been involved in for the last day and a half.

Christoph moved to the top center desk in the command room, his desk, and sat down. He looked into the main screen and said, "Hello, what's the news?" Looking down, he opened a panel on his desk and raised a touchscreen control panel for the conference call. He could pick any screen and drag it to the center when that person was talking. He used it often to control meetings. People who attended his meetings knew to talk only when recognized. They could instant message a comment or ask a question, but they never interrupted the Commander when he was facilitating a call. They'd all been around him a long time, and they knew he'd get to each and every one of them in due time. Christoph was very considerate of everyone's opinion and input. That's how he wanted to treat Susan as well.

Christoph didn't like keeping the truth from Susan, but he didn't know how she'd handle it either. He only knew of a few experiences his uncle had had. His uncle previously had been in this same position as Commander of all Argonians on Earth. He too had chosen a human, but that had been well over a century ago. There had been no other humans involved then, and theirs had been the first occurrence of integration. Christoph again considered the pros and cons of telling Susan the truth. He heard somebody clearing their throat.

Christoph realized that nobody was talking, and that he wasn't even looking at the camera. 'What?! What is this woman doing to me?' he thought. "Sorry folks, I just woke up. I'd use the phrase "We're all human," but we know that would be a lie," he joked. Everyone laughed, and the ice was broken for what would become a three-and-a-half-hour call, during which his fellow Argonians would explain to him what had happened and update him on the pending interrogation.

George was in the main security room and spoke up: "Sir, I have an overall update I can give you; then there are others on the bridge who can answer any specific questions that you may have."

"Thank you, George. Yes, then please get started," Christoph said, as he looked down at his tablet control to drag George's picture to the main screen.

"The culprit has been verified to be Mr. Clancy Jones, the Director of the Apache Security team." George paused briefly, giving Christoph a moment to digest that it was Susan's boss who was responsible.

"Before you go further, George, has anyone thought to figure out how Mr. Jones was able to do this? He obviously passed our human assessment tests to get hired, and he passed the continued training sessions. How could something like this happen?" Christoph asked in amazement.

"Yes, sir, we are in the process of apprehending Mr. Jones, and we will be interrogating him. We have already verified that he's human, as every retina scan he's been through has shown him to be," George explained. With Christoph, George knew to get to the point quickly, or it would just frustrate the Commander.

"We are also verifying the recent training sessions and test results. But sir, there's one thing we have found so far. Based upon Mr. Jones's background and training, he didn't have the knowledge to make these code changes. We found video evidence of him making the changes that correspond and crosscheck with the network access traffic. We are positive it was him, but we don't know how he could do it." George had pretty much finished his summary.

Christoph had some specific questions for the network consultants. Moving the one he recognized to the main screen, he asked, "What is your confidence percentage that you have network evidence for Mr. Jones's terminal?"

The woman answered succinctly, "I am 100% positive, because I have evidence not only from that terminal, but from other of his team members' terminals as well. It was how he was able to obtain and use their IDs." She purposefully kept it high level. No need to go into further details because her team was sure, just as they were sure the data from the Apache development database server was being sent outside the company. But to where, they hadn't figured out yet. She didn't want to offer up that information without having the Commander ask about it first.

Christoph took a moment to process her information. They knew it was Mr. Jones from different terminals, but they didn't know how. More importantly, Christoph wondered to himself, why? He asked the network consultant again, "Did you find out if there was any network activity on that development server after the data had been copied over?"

The network consultant frowned, knowing he wouldn't like the answer. "Sir, we did verify that large amounts of data were flowing from the development db server, but we've been unable to determine where it was going. The connection has been severed, probably in an attempt for them to mask their trail. It's going to take longer to determine. We have to use the hidden Argon network tracer files that we have on the network. I have people working on it. It should be a few more hours, sir."

Christoph nodded. That was perfectly acceptable. They'd accomplished so much so quickly already, and he was quite proud of his team. "Yes, of course, thank you Mary," he said, calling her by name before he switched back to George. "What's the timeline to interrogation, George?" Christoph asked.

George went on to describe their efforts to locate Mr. Jones and have him apprehended, providing Christoph with more information than was needed. It gave Christoph time to think. So, the nincompoop tendencies everyone had observed in Mr. Jones were likely all an act.

"…It seems to be that we should have him processed and ready to be interrogated in about 3 hours sir," George finished, just as Christoph tuned back in.

"All right, George, thank you." Christoph paused, calculating how much longer he should let Susan sleep, and how much longer it would be before they could interrogate Mr. Jones. He had plenty of time, so he was going to review the network data with the network consultants. They needed to find out where that data was going – although everyone was already pretty sure it was going to a Grogan computer system.

Christoph knew that the Grogans had to be behind this. He suspected they were using the mind-control laser they'd built, but he and his team wouldn't know until they interviewed Mr. Jones. If he didn't remember certain things, and had entire days missing from his memory, they could be sure it was the laser. "Damn," Christoph swore under his breath. They'd only seen the mind-control laser a few times, but the Grogans were using it more and more to capture humans and take them to their space colony to study them. Sometimes they returned them, and sometimes they didn't. Obviously, their experiments sometimes failed.

Christoph and his team had been battling to keep the humans safe from these Grogan interferences for the last century. After they'd realized that a Grogan space colony had found them, they'd been protecting the humans as best they could. But the Grogans were very good manipulators and puppeteers.

It was because of Grogan influence that the world had been taken over by gang wars. Each city had been on its own. Governments were spread out too thin to have any sort of control. Only in the smallest countries were governments successful in controlling the violence and the senseless destruction of their cities.

Martial law in those small countries was the only solution. At the beginning that worked, until the region would be fought over by gangs larger than its armed forces. In every single case, the countries had lost.

It had taken Christoph two years to convince a global coalition to let his company take back control of the cities for the governments. Christoph had watched the downfall of Earth's global society and the emergence of gangs around the world. The gangs destroyed the inner cities and had begun ravaging the suburbs. It had come to a point where there wasn't anywhere on Earth that was safe. The human governments hadn't been able to enforce law and order. Christoph knew his Argonian warriors would be able to restore order through sheer force and high tech technical strategy.

Christoph was finally able to position the Argonians to step in and eradicate the gangs, city by city, using private alien forces and secret alien technology and methods. It was the most unorthodox use of methods that had ever been used on planet Earth – but it was because they were alien techniques from Argon. They used a combination of political strategies and military strength to digitize money worldwide and apprehend the gang members themselves. It was through GTS that the Argonians secretly worked to use their complex surveillance devices to insure that they apprehended the gang villains – and eliminated them.

The Argonians dealt with the gang members harshly, but the good people of the world were tired of fighting and welcomed the harsh methods. They had lost their sense of fairness and equality throughout the decades of gang wars. They were ready for any kind of relief to stop the violence. The general public cheered the GTS teams, and were careful to separate themselves from the gangs. Anyone associated with gangs was being picked up. By doing this, the Argonians were able to thwart the Grogans' attempts to carry out their self-extinction plot for the human race.

The Grogans weren't idle for long, apparently implementing some new scheme that involved GTS. Now, his number one priority was seeing his company through this crisis.

Christoph pulled Mary back to the main screen. "While we wait for the interrogation, let's see what your team is finding in real-time Mary," Christoph requested. "I'll be right back. I'm going to give you control, and a few minutes to gather them online."

"Yes, of course, sir," Mary replied, as she muted herself to begin gathering her team for an online working session.

Christoph went to the kitchen and started some water boiling to make coffee. He grabbed a muffin, yogurt and a banana to take back to his desk. While he was steeping his French-press coffee, he decided to go back to his room to check on Susan.

He opened the door silently and softly padded over to the bed. Barely opening the curtain an inch, he saw Susan sleeping peacefully, exactly as he'd left her. He was relieved. He had been worried she'd have another one of those nightmares.

He grabbed his watch and his laptop, and went back out and down the hall to the war room to wait for Mr. Jones's interrogation, and to watch the network team as they were figuring out where the communications were going.

It was verified. Mr. Jones had blocks of memory loss. The telling factor was when he lost days. He didn't even know about the bombings and the other attacks.

"I remember waking up the other day to a call from Mr. Crinchfield. He told me not to come in to work." Mr. Jones supplied his last memory of work interaction with his boss. "I don't recall much about specifics. I just know we recently got a new development manager. There had been nothing unusual," he confirmed.

Mr. Jones could give them nothing. He was innocent. He was quickly and easily exonerated by the sophisticated Argon screenings and exams. The Argonians were trying to protect the humans – not punish them for being manipulated by the Grogans. Humans are helpless against the Grogans.

The Grogans had caught Mr. Jones and used mind-control to manipulate him. All the tests had not only proven his humanity, but they had shown the same energy indent on his frequency that the mind-control laser made. There were other pretests the Argonians had done after receiving him in custody, before the verbal questions ever began, but they also indicated a mind control device. The Argon physicians had seen it often enough and knew they needed to send Mr. Jones through corrective therapy, in hopes that he would not suffer ill effects from the laser.

Christoph gave directions for Mr. Jones's therapy. "George, can you please see that Mr. Jones is securely escorted to the mind-cleaning facility?" He paused to remember the network issue as he continued, "So that brings me to Mary... Mary, please ping me when you figure out where the data was going." He waited for a moment to make sure neither George nor Mary had any questions. "Okay, folks, I'm going to call it a day," he concluded. "I'm going to sign off, but of course, as always, the bridge will remain open and be attended at all times. Thank you everyone," he said, before disconnecting his desk video feed.

Confirming Mr. Jones's involvement explained much about the code breach and how it was possible, which did much to ease Christoph's mind. At least they'd confirmed it was Grogan involvement. His technical experts had advised that only Argon computer scientists knew of this code construction they'd built for GTS; it's too advanced for humans to figure out. Yet, it wasn't too advanced for Grogans and especially those with one kidnapped Argon scientist. All the Argon scientists were well versed in the concave code construct equations. It definitely made sense, and brought an urgent light to the problem of finding out where the data was going and what data had been copied. Christoph was eager to get to it, but first thing first and that's to let his network team work. There wasn't anything more he could do for them at this moment.

Christoph needed to relax and try to get some sleep while he gave his network consultant team time to gather and crosscheck their data. Yes, relax. That's what he'd like to do with Susan.

He decides that he's going to go back to his room and see if Susan is awake. He get's up and takes his empty coffee cup, banana peel and empty yogurt container to the kitchen. Loading the cup in the dishwasher, he began to focus again on the fact that there was no immediate danger – at least not outside the normal, everyday dangers he faced being the CEO of the world's bank. All his company did was monitor and house the computer system that facilitated and monitored the data. He didn't have control over the supplies; his company just kept it secure. Ultimately, it was the most important job of all – like the human folklore notion of "having the key to Fort Knox."

GTS was able to provide that security that was essential to a properly run digitized monetary system through their special Alien code. It was secure and under tighter surveillance controls; in addition, it was under strict, Argon-only control for the next few months. He wasn't finished with the breach investigation, nor the aftershocks, but all those would take time. His strategies weren't completely vetted yet. He needed this investigation to finish before he and the Argonian board could discuss their options. In the meantime, he was free to focus on Susan.

He didn't have to keep Susan locked up underground any longer. It was time to wake her up. With a smile he thought about what he'd like to do to her when he found her still in bed. After all it was only about 11 a.m.

Chapter 14

Susan read the note from Christoph when she went looking for something to eat in the kitchen. It was already 10 a.m., and she was famished.

Susan, I had to go to the war room for a new development. Sleep as long as you like, and make yourself at home. Kitchen is fully stocked. Will be back soon. Ping me if you need me. ~Your C~

She opened the refrigerator to see what was in there. She was starving, but she didn't really want to cook. She pulled out a Greek yogurt, grabbed a little tub of blueberries and sat down at the breakfast table to eat. She wondered how long it would take for them to check all the footage and figure out who had done this to their code. It's the fact that it was an inside job that frightened her.

There are plenty of people who want to infiltrate the security company that manages the world's monetary supply.

That's normal. What was not normal was that it actually happened. Little did she know that the Argon-built systems had hidden back doors and monitoring systems that allowed the Argons to pretty much make the security foolproof to any humans.

While Susan wasn't aware of these details, she still knew it was the most sophisticated system in the world. GTS had a reputation in the industry. She didn't have to know all about the Argon involvement to know how well respected and basically foolproof the systems were.

Experience from her own interviews and background check made her suspicious that it really was an inside job. It had taken her over four months to get through the actual hiring process. Once through, it had taken her a full two weeks to get all her accounts set up, plus studying and taking all the required internal tests to make sure she knew all the security protocols within the company. There was even a weekly training call – mandatory – and weekly tests. It was the most intense job she'd ever had. But it was an honor to work for them.

For it to be an internal problem was difficult to believe. She could not imagine how in the world any person could get past all the screenings they were constantly put through. She just stared into space, because any ideas of who it could be escaped her.

She finished her yogurt and decided to do a little bit of yoga. It always relaxed her and brought her peace. The stretching was essential for her. She couldn't miss more than a day or two, and yesterday, she'd missed it.

She went to the living room where there was plenty of carpet. Going through her routine by memory and with grace, she was able to clear her mind and just relax into the stretches and poses. It helped her cope with everything that had been going on. Keeping her focus only on her body movements relaxed her mind. At the end, she had time to be thankful for the here and now, and to enjoy the moment of now. She was sitting cross-legged on the floor in her final meditation state, when the door opened and Christoph entered.

She smiled as she turned to see him coming into the living room, "Good morning," she said. She was so grateful he wasn't there when she woke up this morning. Yet again, she'd been saved from having to be intimate with him without having alcohol, her liquid courage. She briefly wondered if she'd ever be able to trust him enough to let him touch her when she was sober. A small frown marred her expression, but she quickly recovered when she was taken by how handsome he was, just standing there.

"How are things working out this morning?" she questioned with a bright smile.

Susan was glowing again, and she took his breath away. Christoph couldn't help but walk into the living room and bend over to kiss her on the lips. The feel of the energy when he lightly kissed her made him feel even better than he already did.

"Ah, you're so lovely," he murmurs to her, before lightly kissing her again, then again on her forehead as he straightens up. "It seems they've found who was responsible for the data breach. How would you like to go swimming in the lagoon or the pool?" he says, quickly changing the topic.

"What? That's great!" she exclaims, as she gets up and sits next to him on the couch. "Tell me, who is it? How did they find it? When did you find out? Why didn't you tell me earlier?" She bombarded him with questions.

He put his hands on her shoulders and brought her to him to interrupt her questions with another kiss. This time it was a more passionate kiss, one that made her forget everything but the man kissing her. The kind of kiss that made everything else except that one moment in time stand still. A kiss that created the right now, the only thing that mattered. Slowly, he brought the kiss to an end when she was calmer.

Christoph whispered quietly to her, "Come, let's put our swimsuits on and go for a swim. The immediate danger is over, and I need to get out from down here. I'll tell you everything on our way up."

Susan's mind was mush and she would readily agree to anything after a kiss like that. 'Who wouldn't?' her self-conscious said to her. She nodded her agreement to follow his lead. She said, "Ok, I'll got put my suit on." She also was dying to get out from below ground and see some sunshine! If he'd found out who the infiltrator is and he wanted to go for a swim, who was she to argue?

If she was honest with herself, she was a little bit afraid to find out who was responsible. This was one of those times in her life when she was grateful there was somebody else worrying, and dealing with the tragedy and drama. Susan was still having a hard time coping on the inside with almost being killed three times.

———————

Christoph contemplated how much to tell her. He didn't want to lie to Susan, but he didn't want to overwhelm her with the truth. He knew he'd alarm her with the entire story. It wouldn't make sense to her unless he exposed himself as an alien.

He didn't want to have to give up any more information than was necessary. But his feelings were already involved here. He was already possessive over Susan and thought she was likely already pregnant, but he couldn't be sure until the result from the blood tests came back. She didn't know it yet, but he was not going to give her up. She was his, and he was going to be sure he kept her. He knew at some point that he was going to have to tell her who he really is, and who he thinks is after him and why. But he needed more time before he confessed all to her. He needed time to process all the questions he still had.

The questions he had yet to answer would likely require more time than he had. If they returned to the States, where would it leave him and Susan? Could he convince her to stay with him at his secured location? He wasn't comfortable she would be safe on her own. He was going to have to take more risks and chances.

Of course, he wanted to stay here and have more time with her without any interference. Eventually, though, they would have to go back.

Christoph met Susan at the door to their rooms in his swim trunks, carrying towels. She had changed into the only suit she'd brought with her, the turquoise bikini. She was also wearing a short, white cover-up with long, wide, flowing sleeves, open in the front. For a few seconds Christoph contemplated removing all of her clothes and taking her, bending over the back of the couch. He slapped his leg, hard, to bring himself back around. He had to get his Argonian urges under control. He could do this.

"Ready," she confirmed, with a cheery smile. She looked younger than she had since he'd met her. She finally looked relaxed. As they made their way down the hallway and into the elevator, she asked him, "Well, aren't you going to tell me what happened, and who it is?"

Of course he relented and told her about Mr. Jones. He relayed to her all the non-Argon facts. He led her down the path to the lagoon as he told her how the network team was still trying to uncover where the data was going. But again, Susan didn't need to know the details about the special Argon network tracers. The less she knew, the better.

"So, do you think that Mr. Jones was under some kind of mind control?" she asked, out of the blue, as they reached the beach. He hadn't precisely said why Mr. Jones couldn't remember. It was the only thing that made sense to her. Even she knew that Mr. Jones didn't know the code well enough to even log into the systems, nor what ID and permission groups to request – not even the names of any permission groups.

"It doesn't make sense. Think about it: he didn't even know how to log on to the machines," she said, "much less anything about doing what was done to our code."

Oh God, she turned him on when she was smart and intuitive. If only she knew how right she was! What in the hell was he supposed to say to that? "You could be on to something. I'm just not sure how they would do it," he lied smoothly. "Come, let's go for a snorkel," he said as he disappeared into the beach shack to pull out some masks and snorkels, trying to distract her from this line of thinking.

Accepting the same mask and snorkel she'd used the other day, she said to him, "Yeah, but there had to have been some way his mind was controlled. Perhaps we could collaborate with that Pegasus Technology company. They have some very cutting-edge devices, and they might at least be familiar with the researchers in the field," she said as she connected and adjusted her mask and snorkel. "I've heard of experiments recently about mind control, but I thought it was very primitive yet," she finished as she approached the water.

Christoph was doing the same, and he was glad he was looking down at his mask when she mentioned Pegasus Tech. Once again, if only she knew how right she was! The Argonians had been fighting with them for decades because they kept trying to introduce new technology too quickly for the humans to fathom.

Christoph put his mask on his head, "We'll definitely have to check it out, but there's nothing we can do right now. Let's enjoy this time we have," he said as he leaned over and kissed her on the mouth. "Come – the water is perfect."

Susan stepped more fully into the lagoon, and he was right – it was delightful. Not too cold and not too warm. The water was warmer here than it was farther out, away from the island. She wouldn't want to swim out that way anyway. She wasn't familiar with any of the ocean streams in the area, and she didn't want to take a chance. The lagoon was just fine with her.

They swam from one side of the lagoon all the way around to the other side. The fish were huge, but that was to be expected with open water all around. She was grateful that there weren't any sharks or barracudas lounging around for the afternoon. It felt good to be out in the sun and getting some exercise. She didn't know if she'd have been able to stay cooped up in that room for another day. Then it occurred to her, she hadn't noticed any damage from the attack on their walk here.

It was very strange, she thought, for it to have been cleaned up so quickly. It must not have been that bad, she reasoned.

Enjoying the swim, she dismissed it, and had to admit that the immediate threat seemed to be over. The code had been fixed. The systems were still being monitored under protocol law for another six months, so there wasn't anything for most of the company to do, herself included. They weren't allowed in the office building and they weren't allowed on the systems, unless, as she had been, they were part of the crisis-management team.

Her team's work on the crisis piece was completed. It was now in network's hands. She took a deep breath through her snorkel and relaxed a little bit more. At least they all got paid during protocol processes. She'd never heard of it happening before, but she had certainly been tested enough on protocols to know.

She had time to relax. She began to wonder if they would leave the island now. Would Christoph still want to be around her and see her? She hoped so, because she was getting hooked on him. But she still didn't trust him.

It was okay if it was just a hookup – that would be the one normal thing in her life right now. In the back of her mind, her inner little girl secretly hoped that this time it would be different, and she wished for that fairytale fantasy. Hell, the rest of her life was far from normal now – why should her sex life be any different?

Chapter 15

Christoph was more than confident that this was the work of the Grogans; he knew they wouldn't make a direct advance again. But only in the most secure Argon compounds would Susan be safe, at least safer than the average human. She was no longer the average human because she was his, and he was surer by the day that she was carrying his child. Her scent hadn't changed from the ovulation scent, so he still had an opportunity, but most importantly he needed to keep her safe...

His only issue was that she is a human, and no humans had ever been in those compounds – which is why the Grogans didn't know about them. Not even his uncle's human female mate had been there. Once she'd been to the colony ship, but never anywhere else.

It was too risky for them to allow humans any knowledge of their secret Argon compounds, not when the Grogans had the mind-control ray. With this ray, the Grogans could take over a human's mind and have him or her under their control. They can program the human, with the ray's effects lasting for almost twenty-four hours. That is plenty of time to make the human act out their commands, then return for another dose of the ray, a debriefing, and the next set of instructions.

Given his situation with Susan, he believed that he didn't have any other choice to keep her safe. Perhaps if he kept twenty-four/seven security at her home and stayed with her each night, that would be enough. It was certainly worth a try, but it was a tricky proposition to figure out how to stay with her each and every night. He knew she believed this was just a normal human hookup.

He decided it would be best for them to return to the States. With more resources available there, it would be easier for him to protect her. And if worse came to worst, he could take Susan to his home, which was a secure compound.

She didn't have to know that the reason for increased security was that he was the Argon commander. Eventually, he knew he was going to have to tell her the truth. According to his recollection from his uncle, this pregnancy would be very difficult on her.

For now, Susan was out of immediate danger, and Christoph didn't see a reason to put off going back to the States. As long as the Grogans were on Earth, she'd never completely be out of danger.

Susan was glad Christoph was finally taking her home. She was getting bored on the island. There wasn't much to do. Yesterday, he'd taken her above ground to go swimming and lounge with a book at the beach. Christoph never left her side. They'd spent a nice, relaxing afternoon. After their swim, they agreed to not talk about work for the rest of the day. There were no immediate worries, so they would enjoy the moment. They'd started out with frozen rum drinks from the beach shack and ended the night with an expensive bottle of divine red wine with a grand dinner of hamburgers and French fries, another of Susan's favorite Saturday night / beach day meals.

When it was time for sleep, Christoph got a text from his security team and he'd had to go back to the war room. "I'm sorry, but I have to go take care of this. Get some sleep, I'll be back soon," he'd said regretfully as he kissed her on the forehead and left the room. He had been looking forward to slowly removing her clothes and making love to her.

When Christoph stepped into the war room, all the video conference screens were occupied. George, his head of security, was on the main center screen. Christoph nodded to everyone in the room as he made his way to his desk and turned on his conference panel and laptop. "Yes, George, what's happening?" he asked abruptly. He was a bit curt, since his cock was still slightly hard from what he'd been about to start in his private quarters.

George, a long-standing colleague and friend of Christoph's, knew right away what he'd interrupted. "Sorry to bother you, sir, but we found where the data was going. I thought you'd like to know, and to be here while we ask further questions of the network team about their findings," he explained.

This was the highest priority for Christoph right now, except for keeping Susan safe, but she was in his quarters, so that part was handled for now. "Yes, tell me. Where was the data going?"

"Sir," George continued, "the network team traced it to another building in downtown Boston. On the outside it looks empty, but the building itself is owned by Pegasus Technology." George paused for a moment. He had to let it sink in that the company that owned the building was also run by the Grogans. Their suspicions had basically been confirmed. The Grogans were behind it all.

Christoph was staring off into space, processing all the facets of what he'd just been told. Absentmindedly, without looking at the screen, he asked, "How confident is the network team that this is where the data was going? Was it going anywhere else as well? And can you trace the outgoing lines from the empty building?"

George was prepared for the questions. They were standard questions that the commander would be expected to ask, and George was completely prepared with all the answers. "Sir, we are 100% confident that our internal trackers have the destinations correct. Mary can tell you about the communications outgoing from the empty building," he said, as he flipped the main screen control from himself to Mary.

"Yes, sir, we only found the one location. We also checked all other outgoing data transmissions from our building, which as you know would include our Argon communications centers, and all were operating as expected; everything verified. The only anomaly was what we found here with the Apache dev server comms." She paused for only a moment, in case he had a question about that answer.

Mary answered the next question: "The network comms outgoing from the empty building were not found. We couldn't find where they were going outside the building on public lines. However, we suspect they were being sent internally to Pegasus offices, as they are all on the same major network switch. Communications between those two buildings are considered internal, and we wouldn't be able to see them unless we installed a tracer on that switch. Since the switch is owned by Pegasus, we can't even get close enough to look at it," she finished.

"Thank you, Mary. I don't have any more questions for you at this time," Christoph said as he switched the screens and went back to George. "George, have you compiled a list of all the data that was copied, the servers that were infiltrated, and the files that were likely compromised?"

"Yes, sir, we have that to review with you. There's a significant amount, and it will take us several hours," George said.

"Yes, let's do it now," Christoph confirmed. "This is the highest priority, because we need to make sure that we take the proper precautions and measures based upon what data was leaked."

Christoph had surmised all of that when George told him they had found where it was going. George really was a valuable part of his Earth command team. He always knew the questions to ask and either had the answers, or was currently probing to find them.

What George didn't say was that their main focus was whether or not any sensitive Argon data or computer systems had been compromised. They'd yet to determine that. But the immediate threat to Earth and its monetary systems was over. Christoph could return back to the States with Susan.

"Yes, George, let's get started. I assume you've already prioritized the categories," Christoph smiled, as he got comfortable in his chair. He wasn't going anywhere for a while now.

Their flight from the island the next day was uneventful but long. Susan was wrung out. Even though she was getting plenty of sleep in the comfy sleeper bunk, it was fitful. She missed sleeping next to Christoph. Susan had spent last night alone, and she kept waking up, noticing he was gone. She kept wondering whether or not he would want to see her once they were back in the States. They hadn't talked about it, and she hadn't asked. She didn't want to come across as needy. She also didn't want to ruin the mood they had going on the island. It was important for her to just think of this as a hookup, one that happens multiple times. She'd let him go his own way when they got back to Boston.

Susan was still too raw from all the attempts on her life. How does a person recover from something like that? It was a lot for her to take in, not to mention starting a sexual relationship with one of the hottest men she'd ever had the pleasure of touching. She rolled her eyes at herself, but it was true. Not only that, but he was a very attentive lover, and always concerned and interested in her, what she was doing, what she thought.

It was nice being in a "no strings," companionable relationship. It wasn't often that Susan could depend upon somebody and he actually came through. In this case, she wanted more from Christoph. She fantasied about the fairytales for a few minutes, and sighed to herself. Fairytales aside, she might at least get one more night with him. She could settle for one more hookup before he disappeared. Maybe he wouldn't disappear and she'd see him every now and again. Sometimes a woman needed to take what she wanted – and she wanted Christoph in her bed.

Upon their arrival at the business metro airport, Christoph helps Susan get in the passenger side of his personal SUV.

Their luggage is loaded in the back by his ground crew and security team. She notices him discussing something with them before coming around to the driver's side to get in.

"How are you? Do you have everything you need? Ready to go home?" he asks with a delightful smile.

Susan whispers, "Yes, thank you." She is overwhelmed with the warmth in his voice and his eyes. She's so tired, she knows she might be a little touchy and over reactive, but she feels so incredibly special when he looks at her like that. She reaches around to grab her seatbelt and lock it in place.

After buckling his own seatbelt, Christoph says, "Okay, let's get rolling then." He knows she is tired and hasn't slept well. She is still stressed about the bombings. He is hesitant to give her any more of the special Argon drug that would help her move through all that emotion at a much faster pace, but it would make her sleep more than normal. This might be the only thing for her, though. He would ask his physician tomorrow.

On the way to her house, Susan was trying to figure out a way to get him to stay. She had already let her guard down with him, when she woke up sober in his bed and he called her "sweetheart." Though it had been a few days since that happened, she was still in awe of it. She couldn't even remember a time over the last many years when she had physically let a man touch her while she was sober.

She'd spent the last several nights in his bed, and every night she'd had wine, or something stronger, before bed. It gave her the courage to trust him. Plus, she didn't have those dreams while he was with her. She wondered if being back at home would start them again.

Christoph was worried that she hadn't said anything since they left the airport, "Are you okay?" he asked her as he pulled into her driveway. All the outside lights were on; clearly his security team knew to expect them.

"Oh, yeah, sure, I'm fine. My brain feels exhausted but I'm not tired. I just feel strange, is all," she replied, as she released her seatbelt and began to exit the vehicle.

Christoph came around the passenger side to help her and to close the door for her. "Don't worry about the luggage, Henry will get it. Let's get inside and have a drink," he suggested. He knew her nerves were wearing on her. She was clearly worried about something, but could he blame her... coming back home. Thank goodness she'd never been threatened here. If he had anything to do with it, she would never be threatened here. He would never leave her alone or unprotected.

Tonight, he was planning to stay. She might not know it yet, but there was no way in hell he was going to leave her on her own, by herself, the first night back after such tragedy. Hell, he hadn't even had his psychiatrists and physicians look at her properly. He'd just whisked her off to the island.

Christoph was reacting on pure instinct. He hoped he'd gotten her pregnant. He wasn't going to let her go. He needed to keep her safe. For now she would be safe. He would be here, protecting her, loving her.

He had already arranged a twenty-four/seven security detail, assigned to this house and to Susan. He wasn't taking any chances. She was his. He had chosen her. While she didn't quite understand yet what was happening, he was sure she would accept. There would be a lot to learn about Argon life and how advanced their species is compared to humans, but once she accepted it, he was sure in time she could develop the same skills. Their children would be magnificent if they looked anything like her or had her tenacity. He was just concerned over how much she would accept of his society.

In Argon society, when a man chooses a partner, if he finds the sex agreeable, he opportunely starts breeding with her. Once she's been bred, they become mates for life. Some Argon couples, like humans, live together for years but never breed. Those Argons are free to find other mates if they choose. The Argon female generally does not have a preference over which male is her mate, given the lack of emotions.

The Argon females didn't have the advanced feelings and emotions that the human Earth women do. Only the Argon men had emotions. It was the men's responsibility to take care of their women. While their women were smart, their lack of desire for a man or a loving relationship enabled their society to easily reach a utopian level. As the Argonians had been learning here on Earth, the human females have more emotions than the males of their species, posing a significant challenge to achieving a utopian society. They had never seen it in an alien species. Of course, they'd never found an alien species that was so closely related to themselves.

Christoph considered all the differences between the Earth humans and the Argonians truly fascinating. He was imagining what it could be like to be with a female who wanted to be with him, who enjoyed being with him, and whom he enjoyed. A real human relationship is what Christoph wanted, ever since he was a young boy and learned that human females had emotions, just as Argonian men did. Now he just had to convince her to admit to them – which is where he was lost.

He knew the alcohol would loosen her up and relax her. It did that with all humans, as well as the Argonians. He suspected she had some other issues to deal with besides the recent tragedies she'd had to endure, and he wanted to bring her along slowly.

They walked into the living room area, where there was a section for beverages in the corner. Susan immediately walked behind the bar and started to make them a drink. She didn't even ask; she just assumed he needed a strong drink as much as she did. A good bourbon would be just right.

Christoph walked across the living room to pick up the drink she'd finished making for him.

"Bourbon on the rocks, right? Wathen's okay?" she asked, as she handed him the drink.

He nodded and took a sip. The bourbon was smooth going down his throat, and it was exactly what he needed.

She picked up one that looked exactly like his.

While Argonians couldn't actually get drunk from alcohol, it did have a calming and soothing effect on their emotions. He needed to be calm and collected right now. Gently sighing, he turned and sat on her couch, motioning her over before taking another sip.

Chapter 16

Susan sat next to Christoph on the couch. He never seemed to get drunk on the wine they would drink while playing cards, but she certainly did a few times. Maybe he'd be different with bourbon. 'What if I got him drunk and he couldn't drive home?' she thought. 'LAME!' Now she was sounding like a desperate high school student. 'Get a grip, Susan!' her subconscious told her. 'Give him a chance to make a move. Why wouldn't he? He hasn't missed a cue yet, has he?' she asked herself.

As she sits down next to him, he puts his free hand on her knee and starts absentmindedly caressing her knee and leg. She decides to try to be honest with herself and with him at the same time. It was now or never for her. If she didn't ask, how would she know? "What's going to happen now that we're back?" she pauses for a slight moment. She quickly continues so he wouldn't think it's personal, "Do I go back to work downtown?" she stammers out quickly. Just deciding to go for it right away and get to the point. No use beating around the bush.

He looks at her for a minute, wondering what to tell her. He wants her to have whatever she wants, but he wants her to have him too. "Would you like to go back to your job downtown?" he parries.

"It's not like I'm independently wealthy. I have to work for a living, and I spent six months trying to find this job. It's been a difficult year... hell, what am I saying? It's been a difficult *month*. I can't believe I've cheated death three times in the last month," she says, more to herself than to him. She silently contemplates the myriad of events that have taken place.

"I think you might need some time to recover from what has happened. You should take some paid leave, maybe a sabbatical," he says, after finishing his drink. "Besides, with the lockdown in place, the protocol dictates that you get paid as long as the systems are locked down. You'll be able to return to work when it's over."

Christoph gets up to make himself another drink. One wasn't enough to relax him. 'Why didn't he just ask her how she feels,' he thought. As he helps himself to a refill, he says, "Your health is the most important thing right now. You need to take care of yourself and not worry about finances. You've been through some major trauma."

She listens to him and watches him as he makes his way back to the couch. His glass has more bourbon than ice this time. She catches herself staring and thinking about how damn handsome he is. Oh God, I could completely eat him alive if it were possible.' She thinks about touching his shoulders and arms while he is raised above her. Feeling his arms; muscles all tense and tight. He is too damn sexy for her to keep her mind on anything else. No, stop thinking about him like that for now – get a grip,' she told herself. She figures she's just tired, and vulnerable to all the basic instincts right now. But still, how does she get him upstairs?

How does she keep him in her bed? She can't get her hopes up, and what she's been hoping for is extremely unusual. The least she could do now is try for one more night.

He sits on the couch and she replies, "I won't argue with you on the trauma, that's for sure." She is at a loss as to what to say, because all she can think about right now is kissing him and feeling his bare skin. On the flight back she didn't eat much, and now the bourbon is making her feel frisky and bold. She leans into him and purrs softly in his ear, "I think you should come upstairs and give me a personal therapy session." Before she pulls away, she nips his earlobe and sucks on it a little, before lightly sticking her tongue in his ear.

He drew a sharp intake of breath when she teased his ear with her tongue. She knew that playing with his ears turned him on, and he was hard in an instant. He set his glass down on the table and leaned back, looking at her, and said playfully, "You think I can help with personal therapy, huh?"

He took her shoulders and moved her so that his mouth easily took hers. He delved in and took her over. He could tell she was turned on by the way she was moving her body. She was so responsive to his touch, and especially to his kisses. He had learned over the past fortnight that kissing her was the key to unlocking her kingdom. Right now, he wanted her kingdom to be in his kingdom – and he wanted to lock her in the tower and throw away the key.

He leaned her back on the couch and deftly unbuttoned her blouse, pushing it to the side and running his hands over her breasts. He lightly tickled her right nipple, causing it to become fully erect.

She moaned into his mouth and wished he would pinch her nipple and give her some release. But he continued to torment her as he moved to her left nipple and did the same thing. She pushed her chest up at him and into his hand. He knew what she wanted, but again he teased her by putting his mouth over her nipple and sucking lightly, with her bra still separating her from pure pleasure. She moaned again, because she wanted more. She wanted to touch him too.

She grabbed his dark-green t-shirt and started pulling it up and over his head. She was in awe again, as she was every time he took off his shirt. 'He is so fucking beautiful, it hurts my eyes,' she thought, as she blissfully raised her hands to touch his shoulders, and feel her way down his arms and back up again. This time her hands journeyed down his chest, and she felt his full and hard pecs before going down to his waist and around to his back. He's hard and solid beneath her hands. She pulled her body up to touch herself to him. "Oh God, if only we were naked," she thought she said to herself, until to her amazement, he answered.

"Well, we can take care of that." He gets up off the couch and grabs her hand to pull her off the couch. He leads her out of the room and up the stairs, before he asks, "Which way?"

She points to the left; there was only one door. He leads her through and over to her queen-size sleigh bed. It is black to match her nightstands and dresser. He stops with her at the foot of her bed, turns to her and kisses her until her knees are weak and she's practically hanging on to him. He takes off her shirt, then her bra, and moves gracefully down to remove her skirt and panties, leaving her completely naked. He turns her and sits her on the end of the sleigh bed before he quickly undresses himself.

The bed is the perfect height for her to sit down on the end. She can't do much else, as she is enthralled watching him take off the rest of his clothes. He is magnificent. His thighs are nothing but solid muscle. He isn't too hairy, but he isn't completely bare either, with just a light smattering of blonde hair across his chest. He is just right. To her, he is the most perfect specimen of man she'd ever had the pleasure to touch.

When he comes towards her, he pushes her back on the bed and follows, kissing her until she feels dizzy. She's been with him many times now and she likes his aggressive side. He's always gentle, but it turns her on when he takes control.

He spreads her legs extra wide, stretching them to the maximum of her yoga flexibility. Kneeling on the floor, he caresses and kisses her legs, inner thighs and finally her most private center.

'His tongue is fucking magic,' she thinks to herself. "Oh God," she says out loud. The feelings were coming over her, and she was starting to tremble. He held her legs wide, barely leaving her any room to squirm. He forces her to endure his kisses and nips. "Oh, I'm coming," she cries.

He'd already felt it building in her; he felt her trembling and convulsing. As soon as she started coming, he switched his tactics and started to suck on her and drink in all her juices.

She tasted more heavenly than anything he'd ever known. He knew the female human anatomy and he knew what was possible, but he'd never experienced it until he'd met Susan and made her come the first time. When he tasted her, he knew it was something he'd never give up.

He stood up and pulled her hips to him. While the bed was the perfect height for her to sit on, it was also the perfect height for him to easily position himself at her apex and shift himself inside her. Over and over again he gave her what she wanted. He held her legs to him and made her lock them around him, while he held her hips steady and kept moving in and out of her.

She came again, this time almost screaming. He could feel the wetness increase around his cock. She became even more lubricated than she already was. It was dripping onto the bed. But she wasn't finished, and he wanted more.

He abruptly pulled out and moved up on the bed, pulling her up to him. It was obvious he wanted her on top.

She took her time teasing him by touching him and kissing his chest, then his legs, and finally she started licking his balls.

"Mmmmmm," he moaned. At that point, she knew she was doing something he enjoyed because he didn't usually moan much.

She slowly made her way up his body, dragging her nipples lightly across him and up to his mouth. He impulsively took one breast in each hand and held each one in turn to his mouth so he could suck on the nipple. He pushed up at her to signal he wanted to be inside. She freely complied by positioning him at her entrance. Gently pulling her breast from his mouth, she rocked back, and took him fully inside her.

"Ohhh," she involuntarily moaned. He always felt so good inside her. All she needed was to move this way, up a little and down and then – "aaaahhhh," she said. It was perfect. Only one or two more times, in this exact way, before she would explode again. Then, when his fingers started tweaking her nipples, she lost it and she came again without any inhibitions.

It was all she could do to move while she was coming, it was so intense. Christoph took over for her, grabbing her hips and pistoning into her until she was completely spent. By then she was so wet, they were making squishing sounds.

She couldn't help but giggle, because it was kind of loud, and so wet, she was sure it was running down his balls and onto the bed. "What?" he said, as if appalled she was giggling.

"I guess that's evidence of how much you turn me on," she purred in his face before kissing him.

Without breaking contact, he lifted her up and whipped her around so that he was on top. He was so strong and quick that he did it without leaving the comfort of being inside her, and without ending the kiss.

He hastily picked up the pace as he raised himself up, then pulled her legs up so that they were resting on his shoulders. Then he bent over and started kissing her as he accelerated his pace. She was in heaven, and it felt so good that she knew it wouldn't be long before he'd have her coming again.

He could feel it building, but he didn't want her to come without him, so he pulled back and slowed down. He sat up and moved her legs behind him and made her lock her ankles around his back again. He licked and pinched her nipples as he slowly went very deep inside her each time. He knew he was making it build in her again.

It felt so good when he pushed it deep inside her. She was in awe at how good sex is with him, every single time they were together – and even more so in the last few days. She'd been extremely horny, and she'd wanted to do it practically all the time. The depth he was able to reach inside her was perfect. It didn't hurt, and it was perfect enough to make her want it over and over again.

She started to press up into him. She coaxed him into increasing his pace. It felt so good, she couldn't get close enough or deep enough. "Please, more, give me more. It feels so good." she pleaded.

He couldn't resist her anymore. He wouldn't. He would never have to resist her again; she was his. He bent over and started kissing her as his hands pushed her legs to tighten up around him. He continued to kiss her as he quickened his pace. His thrusts were deeper too. His cock started swelling. It was quick and deep each time. He was close, so close, as he started pounding hard into her. After only three hard and extremely deep thrusts, he felt her tightening around him. Then the moisture started. One more stroke and he could let himself go. One more thrust and he was gone. He moaned as his body spasmed into her. One, two, three, four times he jerked, and he came uncontrollably inside her.

He gently lowered his sweaty body down to hers. Her hands came up and gently held him. Then she started caressing his back. She caressed him up and down his back, back and forth.

This never had to end for him. He would have this several times a week and more from now on. She was his and he wasn't letting her go. But how to tell her about him? How to tell her she was bound to him forever by Argon law? How to tell her she's pregnant?

Exasperated by his thoughts and feeling that his body weight was likely crushing her, he rolls over to lie next to her. Realizing it is chilly and storming outside, he pulls the covers up over them and pulls her next to him to lay her head on his shoulder. As they fall asleep, he knows he is going to have to find a way to tell her. He must tell her he is an alien, and he needs to tell her he will never let her go.

———————————

Early the next morning, barely after dawn, Christoph hears someone at the gate, just below Susan's window. She is so warm and soft, cuddled up next to him. He hates to leave her, but he slowly extracts himself from her and leaves the bed without her stirring.

He thinks he hears the back door lock open or close. He puts his pants on and grabs the gun he keeps attached to his pants, and straps it around his waist. He tiptoes out of the bedroom.

He holds silent in the guest bedroom doorway where he has a clear view of the stairs. He sees a figure in black, creeping up the stairs. He aims and shoots. The bullet hits the intruder in the shoulder, knocking him backwards and sending him tumbling down the steps, unconscious.

'Is he still alive?' Christoph wonders as he rushes down the steps to investigate.

Susan opens the bedroom door, dressed only in her robe, to see Christoph running down the stairs. She knows she heard a gunshot. Susan leans over the railing cautiously, just in case. All she sees is Christoph bending over the body. She immediately goes down to him. When she arrives on the last step, Christoph removes the man's mask and then looks up at her with shock on his face.

Christoph immediately recognizes who it is. He has seen him at Pegasus Tech's facilities. He is Yamkov, the CEO's personal security guard. It's a good thing he didn't kill him, because they needed him for questioning. However, knowing this man is not a man, but a Grogan, he has to get him secured, and quickly, before he comes around again and the human cloaking wears off.

Christoph pulls his cell out of his pants pocket and punches a few buttons. He puts the phone to his ear, "George, we have an intruder. I've subdued him, but it likely won't last long. He needs to be taken to Facility One and secured. His wound needs to be looked at. It'll need to be high-alert security level. It's a Grogan."

"Yes sir," George said on the other line.

"Who is this man? You know him; who is he?" Susan asks.

Before Christoph can answer, two GTS security specialists open the front door and approach, carrying a stretcher and a medic bag. They roll the intruder onto the stretcher and open the bag to retrieve restraints that they strap on the intruder to keep him attached to the stretcher. They were the strangest restraints Susan had ever seen. They seemed to click into place with lasers. Once they had locked, a dull glow arched across the man's body from one cuff to the next, as though it was creating a barrier. Once the specialists had him secured, George entered and held the door for them to go outside.

Christoph tells George as he approaches, "I shot him in the shoulder, but when he fell down the staircase, it exacerbated the wound. He needs to be looked after once he's secured."

"Sir, how did he get in?" George asked, looking all around.

"He came through the garden gate and in the side door. I heard the gate; that's what alerted me," Christoph said.

"He must have gotten to Mike. I can't get an answer from him, and he was guarding that side of the house. I'm going to check it out. Will you both be okay here?" George asked.

"Yes, we're going to pack and move downtown to the secured facility," Christoph stated.

George looked back at him dumbfounded, but it only lasted for a moment. Humans didn't go to the secured facility downtown; that was for Argonians only. Christoph must have made a decision. "Do you need me to make any arrangements?" George asked.

"No, George, you take care of things here. I'll make calls while Susan is collecting her things," Christoph explained.

"Of course, sir," George said, as he exited through the hallway to the side door.

Christoph didn't want to explain anything to Susan; he just wanted to get her to safety. She was looking at him expectantly, and rubbing her arms. She must be cold down here with her bare feet on the cold tile floor. "Come, let's get you back up to the bedroom." Christoph tried to coax her, putting his arm around her to guide her with him up the stairs.

"You know you have to tell me what is going on, right?" she insisted.

They approached the bedroom door, and Christoph still hadn't said anything. He didn't want to make a big deal, but he knew it would be a major issue if he didn't tell her – or maybe even if he did tell her. Should he only tell her on a need-to-know basis, or more? If so, how much more?

"What was he doing here? Why would he be in my house?" she asked, in a more panicked tone.

He decided on sharing just the bare facts for now, and as she asks questions, he'll try to answer as honestly as possible. From what he knew of her, he was sure she wouldn't freak out, but one never knew, with confident emotional women, how they would react. Some screamed, some cried, some ran. "He is the personal security detail for the CEO of Pegasus Technology Industries."

"What's a Grogan?" she interrupts.

He had to explain this to Susan, and he knew he had not told her nearly enough. She could not understand the danger with the little bit of information he had shared with her. Christoph wasn't sure she could deal with the danger – or even comprehend it.

"The CEO is a Grogan. The Grogans are enemies of the Argonians. They are after me, not you," Christoph begins. He thinks that going straight and to the point is the best. "Come, sit down, let me explain," he says, as he takes her to the love seat in her bedroom and sits them both down. He reaches for her hands.

She lets him hold her hands. She can feel the warmth in her hands. "What's a Grogan and what's an Argonian? What are you talking about?"

"We all originated from the Baldracon Galaxy. The Argonians lived on a planet that is very similar to Earth. The Grogans came from a planet that was our twin planet, but it was further from our sun and mostly ice. Our two races have been enemies for many millennia." He paused to think of what to say next, but also to quickly gauge her reaction. She looked amazed.

He continued, "Our galaxy was fueled by several suns. But the oldest sun finally blew up. When it blew up it created a black hole and destroyed all the planets in our galaxy. We anticipated the event and prepared as best we could. Both races carried out evacuation plans before the black hole could consume the entire galaxy. Our people are scattered around the universes, looking for planets that can sustain our life with a sun that has a long lifespan still ahead of it."

"Argonians have been visiting Earth since your ancient times, when the Greeks named this galaxy Milky Way. We scouted your planet several millennia ago as a possible re-location site for our species when the time came for our sun to explode into a black hole. We've scouted several planets around neighboring galaxies. When our sun finally was at its end, our colony ships were sent out to these planets." He paused to make sure she was listening, which she was, in seeming disbelief. He continued, "My ship, the Spirit's Destiny, has been stationed a short distance outside your range, on the other side of the moon, since the late 1800s. We've been communicating to our sister ships to let them know what we've found. Most of those ships are joining us here in the Milky Way galaxy because their target planets weren't viable or the sun was too old. The only problem is that an enemy of ours from our galaxy, the Grogans, has found us here in Earth's orbit."

Susan was enraptured by his story. There's no way he could be making this up on the fly. It all sounded very plausible, especially given what she's seen so far.

He continued to explain, "A little over a hundred and fifty years ago, the Grogans intercepted one of our encrypted communications. While they couldn't decipher the message, they decided to trace it and locate each end – thus leading to the presence of Grogans on Earth. They want to claim the planet from us and eliminate all current planet life. Then, they plan to remake the planet to mirror their home planet, Grogg."

Though Susan wasn't fully sure she was comprehending this, she was still curious. "You say this as if you own our planet. You don't own us!" She stunned herself with her reaction. She couldn't stop herself. "So what do you Argeminians or whatever you're called think you're going to do with our planet?" She was so defensive suddenly, pacing across the bedroom with her hands on her hips. She turned to him and said, "Well?" It was laced with such sarcasm and venom he wasn't sure what to make of it. He had never seen her this way.

Hell, for Christoph, he's never seen *any* woman this way. Ooh, he'd definitely heard how the Earth's human females react since they have emotions; whereas the Argon women didn't have emotions, only enough to survive, which wasn't much. It made it very easy for the Argon males to operate society. Their females were still integral parts of society as scientists, physicians and such. They were non-demanding mates, good wives and even better mothers. The Argon society and its rules were structured toward protecting their people and providing for future generations.

Along the way, the Argonian men had developed a knack for enjoying the moment due to their increased emotions. It's why Earth females were so refreshing to him and to other Argonian males. Christoph was looking forward to sharing an emotional attachment with a human female.

However, at the moment he was having difficulty. Christoph now found himself defending his people, while trying to explain to a female the danger she is in. "We, the Argonians, are not a threat to humans. We simply want to find a planet where our people can call home. We cannot live on the space colony forever." He stopped to gauge how she was reacting. He'd told her the main thing she was looking for, that she was safe.

Christoph got up from the couch to be close to her when he said, "Look, Susan, you are safe with me. He took her elbow and pulled her gently towards him, so he could nuzzle her neck. "Darling, you should know by now how much you mean to me. I would never let anything happen to you." He lifted his head from her neck, looked her in the eye and said, "We have no desire to eliminate the planetary life forms. Your planet is very similar to our planet, Argon."

Christoph led Susan to the end of the bed to sit down again as he further explained, "Argonians are almost identical to humans, except that our blood is more acidic," he explained.

He would leave out the intricacies of emotions for now and some of the other advanced techniques the Argons used. "Our only aim has been to be very careful in advancing human life, and not overwhelm you with our advanced technology. We want to integrate with humans once the race is mature enough."

"So, are you saying the Argons are protecting humans on Earth?" She shook her head. "This doesn't make sense. And why was this guy after you?"

"Yes, in essence the Argons are protecting humans. We've successfully crossbred with humans now, and we have learned that we can easily coexist. We feel as if we can merge our races and make both of them stronger." While that was the good news, he felt he needed to be completely honest with her.

"What the hell? This is ridiculous! Get out of my house," she screamed defensively. She stood up to look for a weapon or something she could use. "You are crazy, and *this is ridiculous*," she insisted, adamantly and with distinct inflection, pronouncing the words emphatically.

He had to make her understand, but she seemed to still be processing the fact that he was from an alien race. They needed to get out of here, and get out now. He texted his head of security to be sure the intruder was secured at Facility One by now so that he could get Susan and her belongings, and move them out of there as quickly as possible.

"I know you think I'm crazy, but Susan, please listen to me," he pleaded as he stood up and approached her. She backed away as if his touch was harmful. "I'm not going to hurt you. Have I hurt you yet? I would never hurt you. I love you," he professed, as he reached his hand out to her.

Susan stood and gaped at him with her mouth open. 'Holy shit, Mother Mary, what the fuck did he say!!??' she thought to herself. He loves her! 'Oh my God,' she thought. If he had told her his feelings an hour ago, she would have been on cloud nine. It wouldn't have mattered what she did next. Did she feel the same about him? She knew. She knew, she'd gone and fallen in love with him – but that was before she knew he was an alien.

'Holy shit, he's an alien!' she thought, shaking her head. What was she supposed to do now? He's an alien!

"Look, I don't know what to believe and I don't know what to do here, Christoph," Susan said. She was hugging herself and rubbing her arms as though she felt cold. She didn't want to lose him, and all the trust and friendship they'd built. She felt so secure and safe with him. Her dreams weren't horrific anymore either. It was truly the first time she had ever let her guard down with a man. And now he tells her that he's a freakin' alien, and she's in danger. She didn't know what to believe anymore. Should she trust her instinct and her feelings? "I wish my life was normal again before Luis ever called me about the code breach," she finished, as the she put her hands up to cover her face as she shook her head. She was desperately trying to stop the tears.

Christoph immediately went to her and wrapped her in his arms. "Sshhhh, baby, it will be fine," he whispered into her ear. He wondered if this was even the right thing to do. He'd never dealt with a crying female. He'd been observing humans long enough that he was pretty sure this is what she needed. It would be what *he* needed if he'd been in her position. But still, they needed to leave as soon as possible.

"Look, honey," he leaned back and lifted her chin with his fingers. "We need to leave here. It's not safe. I need to make sure that you're going to be okay. I can't protect you very well here, which unfortunately was almost proven this morning." He paused to tell her, "I promise that we can talk about this more when we get to Facility One."

She looked at him, puzzled and asked, "Facility One, isn't that where you took that Gragin thing… or whatever he was called? Are you taking me to lock me up?"

Christoph kissed her forehead, and thought that if it was the only way to keep her safe, that's what he'd do: lock her up. For now he didn't need to keep her against her will. "No, baby, I'm not going to lock you up. Facility One is our primary underground command and living quarters on Earth." He looked her sincerely in the eye and told her, "I want to keep you safe. I can do that if you're willing to go with me. You do not have to go; I am not going to force you." But he shook his head and said, "But if I'm honest with myself, the way I feel about you, if you said no, I would take you there anyway. I couldn't live with myself if something happened to you," he finished.

Susan could only stare at him. At first she was a bit offended by what he said, but at the same time she was charmed that he would do it because he couldn't bear for her to be hurt. But still that's a bit of an arrogant attitude, as if he owned her. She wasn't sure what to do. He certainly didn't act like he owned her at any time. He had kept her safe.

Susan said, "But wait, if that guy was after you, then why am I in danger? The code is fixed and the guy who is responsible is in custody. Why am I still in danger?" She stepped away from him again. She didn't doubt she was in danger as she began to pull her suitcases out and throw things in them. "Tell me, what did I do?"

"Yes, it's me that they want, but they also want revenge against you," he told her. He knew she would have lots of questions, but he had to get her going, so he said, "The Grogans were behind the code breach. Mr. Jones could never have done anything like that alone. He'd never had the training necessary, but he'd been brainwashed, so to speak. The Grogans know you are behind the uncovering of the breach and they want revenge. You are the last one left; they don't know about Juan."

For the umpteenth time, she stood stunned in her bedroom, gaping at him with her mouth open. She couldn't talk and wasn't sure what to say. She became more terrified the more she put it together. The Grogans were behind all the other attacks... she was in danger if they weren't finished with her. "Wait, you said they were after you though. How does that relate to me?"

"Gather up what you need to be gone for a while. Put whatever doesn't fit in your suitcase on the bed, and my men will come get it and bring it to you," he said, as he helped put her suitcases on the bed. Two suitcases were still packed from the month on the island. He began opening them up for her. "Come with me downtown. I'll answer your questions once we get there and I'll show you our secure facility. You can rest. You'll need to process all this information, and it's important that I know you're safe." He stopped talking and looked at her. "Susan, I love you. I promise I will answer all your questions. It's just too complicated and too long to tell you now. Can you wait?"

"You do realize this is a lot of information to take in?" she asked him. Seriously, she had long ago stopped trusting men and what they said. None of them had ever been concerned with her long enough to want to make sure she was safe and cared for. It wasn't the norm in their society, so it was startling now to find it in this man. Christoph was the only man ever who wanted to know her feelings and was concerned about her safety – and not because she was his employee.

After opening the last suitcase, he walked over to her and put his hand on her cheek. "Yes, darling, I know it is a lot for you to take in. I'm very sorry to have to tell you this way, and with this much urgency." He bent over to lightly kiss her lips, "There is one thing you can count on... the truth. The truth is that I love you. You are mine, and I'm going to do everything in my power to keep you safe," he said, before he gently kissed her again.

'Oh God, Oh God, Oh God – he said it again. He loves me!' She didn't think her heart could take this. She's in danger, a target and he loves her. It was too much. Now she knew why people fainted – and she suddenly wanted to lie down. Their time was upside down from the island. Her mind was like mush. Jet lag can really get to a person. She had to think. She had to get a grip on what the fuck was going on. She was so tired.

The first man she's trusted and the first man she's been with without the influence of some substance and he tells her he loves her and he's an alien. 'Son of a bitch!' she thinks to herself. 'But hell, why the fuck not? Right?' She reasons with herself. 'I've always been adventurous. And what do I have to lose, my life?' Seriously, is he going to hold her captive? He's giving her a choice to go with him; he's not making her go. He has the security detail downstairs, so he could easily force her.

Susan realized in that moment that this is one of those times when you have to take a leap of faith. If you want something, you have to take the actions to get it. Keeping her life and having Christoph were the same action right now.

There didn't seem like much to lose. Didn't people say, "Love is a leap of faith"?

It had been so long since she had faith in another person. If she didn't try it now, she might certainly lose him – or even lose her own life. Even if he *is* an alien, she would never have known if he hadn't told her. He was so much like a human in every way.

'Oh My God, I've had his dick in my mouth!' she thought to herself. 'Breathe, breathe.' He sure didn't seem like an alien when she was having sex with him. If anything, he was a superior specimen of manliness, far better than any human she'd ever been with before.

'What the fuck,' she thought. She might as well go with it. Her instincts were screaming at her, 'Yes, yes, yes, yes!' She felt safe with him. She might as well go and see what happens. At minimum, he'll keep her from being killed.

Chapter 17

Christoph brought Susan to the downtown complex where the company offices and his penthouse apartment are located. It was too dangerous to enter the building because they still hadn't finished repairs to the structure after the bomb. All the floors were closed. They were lucky the entire building hadn't collapsed when the bomb went off.

Christoph was taking her to the Facility One complex below ground, the one that no human had ever been to before. It was completely top secret. It was against protocol to take humans into Facility One, but he was the Commander in Chief of all the Argons on Earth, so he could decide when it was necessary to break protocol. He would make whatever explanations were needed to the council. Luckily, his uncle had already paved the way for him with a human mate. He just needed to get the rules adjusted for *his* mate.

Susan was in awe as she and her dog followed him to his personal apartments. She didn't see much of the complex. He took them from the main workout room, straight *through* the glass wall on the other side of the Olympic-sized pool. It was amazing how the wall just dissolved as he took her hand and walked her through it. It was like liquid metal, and it parted as you walked into it, but it went right back to its shape as you passed thought it. Susan just stared, and rushed to keep up with him. The windows along the hallways were amazing, too. They looked like windows, and when you looked through them they seemed like windows, but they weren't. Christoph started to explain it to her as he caught her stopping yet again at another breathtaking view.

"We call these "picture windows." They are developed to make you feel as if you are actually in that location, including the temperature, the air quality, the smells, sounds, and light intensity." He pulled her across the hall to a tropical beach view and said, "For example, if you stand in front of this window, you can feel the heat and humidity of an island beach. You can feel the slight warm breeze coming at you. You can hear the waves and the various tropical bugs, birds, and animals making noises."

Susan stood there for a moment and became lost in memories. Memories of a time and place she didn't always like to remember. She enjoyed those afternoons with her friends spent on a beach just like this one, after a long snorkel swim in water just as clear. It made her yearn to go again. It's much better to swim with a mask and snorkel, so you could watch underwater as you swim your distance. It's why she liked the lagoon on the island so well. She felt a light tug on her arm, bringing her back to reality. "Oh, yes, I see," she said.

"Come along, let's get to my apartment so that you can get some sleep," Christoph urged her. He knew she didn't have much time left before she would collapse in exhaustion.

Lack of sleep, shock of another attack… an attack *in her home* hit her as Christoph spoke. She was suddenly scared, and extremely glad that Christoph was there with her. He was taking her through what seemed like endless tunnels, with people passing back and forth on conveyors or people movers. Everyone looked human. Some of them, though, seemed to be wearing shoes that propelled them without their actually walking. She was so tired that she wasn't sure what she was seeing, so she didn't even question Christoph.

Finally, they arrived at his apartment. The room was massive, with a very similar layout to the one in the island underground complex. It was all one open room with one corner serving as the kitchen/laundry and the other end the bedroom and bathroom area. It was so large, that's what amazed her. Twice the size of the island room, plus it had the massive picture windows on one side.

Susan walked over to stare out the picture windows, all sequenced so that the windows looked like they were next to each other on a wall. They showed an amazing view from atop an extremely tall, snowy mountain, looking down over lush, green valleys below.

Christoph took the picture window remote and walked over to her. "Here is the remote to change the picture windows to whatever you want," he said, as he handed her the remote. She just stared dumbfounded at it.

"I need to get a water bowl for Sam, he's thirsty after the brisk walk," she said.

He could tell she was really exhausted, and he knew she couldn't stay awake much longer. "Of course, here, let me," he said, as he walked into the kitchen area and took out a huge bowl from a cabinet and filled it up with water for the dog. He set it down on the floor, saying, "Come, Sam, here's some water for you." The dog happily trotted over and started messily lapping up the water, before picking a spot on the cool kitchen tile floor to lie down.

Christoph went back to the living room to Susan and said, "Here, come with me." taking her by the hand and guiding her across the room.

He led her over to a mahogany bed, draped with what looked like burnt-red velvet.

The canopy draped down the posts, with side curtains just like the one in the island underground compound. It was open on one side, but already closed on all the others.

"How are you doing?" Christoph asked. He knew that she should be feeling sleepy by now. He'd given her one of the special tablets in her juice before they left the house. She needed it to deal with the shock.

"I'm really sleepy, Christoph. I guess the jet lag is catching up to me," she said, sounding disoriented. "Am I safe here, Christoph? I'm really frightened," she admitted. She felt somewhat drunk. Did she really say that to him? She'd never admit that to him. What is wrong with her? "I really want to sleep," she pleaded.

"Yes, dear, you're safe here. Just like on the island, I promise. Lie down here, and if you need anything, just text me. Here's your phone on the bedside table, and a glass of water." He pulled back the dark-red velvet duvet for her, exposing the soft, white sheets.

"Oh, that looks divine," she said, as she slipped off her shoes and quickly lost her pants and shirt. Getting in the bed in only her skivvies and bra, she smiled up at him and said, "Thank you." She closed her eyes, and she was asleep before Christoph could lean over and kiss her – but he did it anyway.

She was his, and she was safe for now. He needed to meet with his security team, see about interrogating their captive, and determine how they were going to handle the increasing threat of the Grogans.

———————————

Susan woke up alone to the nightmare again. She sat up in bed, sweating. The curtains around the bed blocked out all light from the room, so she pulled it back to look out. She was alone. There was muted lighting around the room in the various areas, but nobody was there. The picture window showed a nighttime scene. She decided to take a shower since she was so wet. She didn't even know what time it was, and didn't really care. Right now, all she could think about was a shower.

When she was finally standing under the water, she felt normal again. For a moment she was able to pretend that she was in her shower at home, getting ready to go to work in the morning. But when she opened her eyes to the opulent, new-wave tile design in the shower room, she knew that her life had changed – and it would never be the same again.

Bundled up with a towel on her head and wrapped up in a thick, full-length bathrobe, she found some slippers and padded to the kitchen. Her stomach was growling and she needed something to eat. A cup of tea would be just the thing, too.

She had a craving for pancakes, so she got all the items out to make pancakes and then decided she wanted scrambled eggs too. Before she was done, she had also heated up some sausage links. She'd made a smorgasbord of wonderful breakfast food. She ate it all, every single bite, except that she'd only eaten three of the pancakes, so the others would be for later. She guessed it had been a while since she'd eaten. Again she wondered what time it was. Where did he say he'd put her cell phone?

She left her mess and dishes in the kitchen for now, went over to the bed and found her cell phone. It looked like it was 10:00 a.m. That sounded right to her, except then she realized the date. Yesterday was the 23rd, but her phone said the 24th. She double-checked to make sure it was on Eastern Time zone. 'Holy cow!' That meant she'd slept more than twenty-four hours. How could that be possible? Was she in that much shock, she wondered?

She decided to text Christoph:

:: Good morning :)

Christoph:

:: Hi, glad you're awake.
:: Want me to come down?

Susan looked at his text for a little bit. She wasn't sure she wanted to deal with him just yet. She wasn't even sure what her questions were anymore. He was an alien, and she wasn't sure what to make of all this right now. The shock of it all was overwhelming, so she tried to breathe and just be in the moment.

Susan:

:: Not necessary, I just want to be alone for a while.
:: When are you planning to come back?

Christoph:

:: Not for a few hours, okay?
:: If you need anything, I can be there in 5 minutes.

Last night, Christoph had told her not to worry about anything, and just relax. His chamber was fully equipped, complete with computer, TV, kitchen, bathroom, library and picture windows.

The window brightness would change in intensity according to the clock, keeping in sync with the outdoor day or night. Argon scientists had found that this, along with ionized air and special ultraviolet bulbs, could give a person the belief and experience that all was well in the world, and that they were actually seeing day and night. But Susan didn't know all these details.

She just knew she wanted daylight. She figured Christoph had put it on a night setting since she was asleep. She really didn't want to face the outside right now. Not after being hunted the way she had been. She had to be honest with herself, she was terrified. And now, ALIENS!

Seeing the couch in his island library, shredded by the blue-lighted bullets, was a critical eye opener for her. She really needed to figure out what she was going to do from here. What about her job at the security firm? Did she really want to go back to her job? She had to make a living doing something. But with the sabbatical he promised her, she wasn't going to think about it now. That did, however, bring to mind their relationship.

What now that she's sleeping with the CEO? She had no idea what to even think of her life, now that it had taken such an unexpected turn. What happened to the simple hookup? She was existing in an unseeing daze. What about her fertility appointment? It had to be in a day or two. It was all too much for her to think about now.

Susan changed the picture window to a bright, cheery spring scene, and tried to do some yoga. Normally, yoga relaxed her, and it helped her move through whatever issues were troubling her. It helped ground her in some strange way. But this morning, after twenty minutes, she was having a hard time doing any pose with thinking about Christoph and the aliens. *He is an alien!*

With all this alien race talk, and all the events of the past month, it was literally too much for her. She got up and went to the kitchen to pour herself a glass of juice. She noticed the pills Christoph had left for her with a note that said:

> *"Take this if you feel overwhelmed, have a headache, or want to relax and/or maybe sleep."* ~ C

Is this the special Argon herb he'd mentioned that would help her to deal with the emotions and events that had traumatized her? When he offered them to her on the plane, he had said it would help her identify and move through the emotional trauma. She'd refused them on the plane, but that was before she'd had yet another attempt on her life and found out that he is an alien. Besides, she did have a slight headache, and she was ready to sleep some more.

'Did he say take one or two of these pills?' Susan couldn't remember exactly, so she read the note over three more times. There were no directions on the label either, so she figured two wouldn't hurt. She took two and went back to bed. She scrolled through the nighttime views available on the picture window program, and searched for one where the soundtrack and temperature setting would be soothing. She flipped to a view of the Himalayas and it suddenly got extremely cold in the room, so she flipped quickly to a beach scene, then struggled with how to turn down the temperature. She couldn't figure out how to change the setting, but she didn't care since it was the beach. It was warm, and she could barely keep her eyes open any longer. All she wanted was to escape. Her headache was becoming a migraine. She made her way back to the divine bed and drifted off to sleep.

Christoph found her lying on the top of the covers with a beach night scene on the window. The room was a little too warm, so he reached for the remote, which had fallen from her hand onto the floor beside the bed. As he changed the temperature, he noticed her starting to toss and turn.

Before he could finish changing the temp setting, she was thrashing more wildly. What could her problem be, he wondered? He shook her shoulder and called her name, but she abruptly swatted at his hands. He looked into the kitchen and saw her juice next to the bottle of pills he'd left her. They were the special pills that allowed the body to process emotions, trauma and information at an accelerated speed. It helped keep a person from being blocked by any physical or emotional trauma. His race had used a version of this formula for centuries.

One pill in a human was enough. It made them sleep, and it gave them what they needed to heal. Taking two would cause enough acceleration to overwhelm humans, as proven in the tests they'd conducted. It caused them to have nightmares, memory loss, and sometimes even heart attacks, if they couldn't be awakened from their dreams.

Susan seemed to be lifeless when Christoph sat on the bed and gently shook her to wake her. She wasn't responding; she was deep in a dream state. Then her body started shaking, and thrashing wildly. Her arms were pushing at him as if he was trying to force himself on her – and she was shaking her head back and forth, saying "No, no, no, no, please stop!"

Christoph went to the laundry, grabbed the first-aid kit and pulled out the adrenaline gun. His kind needed this in emergencies to help them heal faster. It was essential to any Argon first-aid kit. He also knew it was the only way to wake Susan. He loaded the special medicine gun and went back to her, still thrashing about and begging, "Stop! Please!"

Christoph couldn't stand the despair in her voice. He needed to remain calm: one slight wrong move with the medicine gun and he could kill her. He needed to be very careful.

Christoph lifted her shirt and pressed the gun against her stomach, hoping like hell that her stomach was standard size and shape, and he shot it. He hoped it wasn't too much; it was the smallest dose he had. He'd never shot one in a human before and he knew now was no time for doubt; what's done is done. He had no time to fret; he had to get her awake or the consequences would be dire for her.

He put the medicine gun on the nightstand and gently shook her shoulders again. "Susan, wake up... Susan." He held her against him and slowly rocked her, back and forth, trying to get her to wake up from the obvious nightmare she was having.

Susan's mind went from being raped and pushed into a rough rope trampoline to being in the arms of another man. The voice was soothing, and he was rocking her and stroking her back gently, whispering how much he loved her and he would never let anything happen to her. She instantly felt safe.

'OMG... where am I?' she thought. She was so disoriented. 'Who is this man? Where am I?' She raised her head and looked around and didn't recognize anything. It was all strange to her. She lifted herself back from this man's strong arms to look at him and get some space, and he let her, but he still gently held her and caressed her arms.

"Susan, are you okay?" he asked her.

'Who is this guy calling me Susan?' It was startling that this man would think he knew her well enough to call her by that name. She looked at him strangely.

Christoph saw her looking him over as if she'd never seen him before. The next ten minutes would be crucial. He had to get her to remember who he was, or else everything from the time of the nightmare trauma to the present day would be erased. He had no way of knowing what trauma she'd had, and where it was in the timeline of her life. However far back it was in her life would be how much of her memory would vanish. He had to convince her to remember him. He only had ten minutes.

He did the only thing he knew to do, besides calling her name. "Susan, don't you remember me? You work for GTS Company, and there was a code breach. Don't you remember me, darling?" He paused and gently stroked her cheek, hoping she'd remember. "Please say you remember me. Don't leave me. I won't like myself if you have to leave," he said softly as he leaned in and started kissing her.

Susan didn't remember having been kissed like this before. Clearly he didn't think he was a stranger. What is she not remembering? He was kissing her some more, and it was so passionate. She was actually loving his kisses. He moved on and kissed her ears and neck.

She felt safe in his arms, and so far he wasn't doing anything she didn't like. She felt she'd known him forever. He wasn't forcing himself on her, but she wasn't resisting either. But, 'Holy hell, he's a stranger!!' Still, she felt as if she was in the most perfect dream. He was doing all the things she expected, and wanted. It had to be a dream.

Christoph said, "Susan, you have to know how much I love you. Wake up, Susan. We have so much ahead of us… a family… never being alone again," he pleaded. Christoph looked down into Susan's eyes, and they connected. He bent over and kissed her lips again. He slowly opened her robe and bent over to kiss her breasts.

Susan thought she was dreaming the most delicious dream. She was in heaven. This man was touching her in all the right ways, and in all the right places. It was too good not to be a dream, but it could be an ordinary hookup. Maybe she was so drunk she just didn't remember.

Either way, she was going to go with it and enjoy it. Let him pleasure her – he was definitely making it all about her, and she had no problem with that at all. Again, and over again, he touched her with perfection. She encouraged him with her hands, and by moving her body to rub against his. She wanted this dream to keep going, it felt so good.

Christoph didn't want to run out of time. She was participating and not resisting him. He had to continue. Did she think she was dreaming? He hoped she thought she was dreaming now. That meant he was almost there; she's almost awake. He needed to shock her into waking up. He untied her robe and moved it away so that her entire body was exposed to him. He left her for just a moment to pull his shirt over his head, then he kissed her while he tore off the rest of his clothing. When he lay on top of her, she was so soft, and more than willing.

Susan readily opened her legs when she felt him lie down with her. She wanted so badly to feel him inside her. She tried positioning herself so that he could easily enter her. She thought he might be resisting, but when she finally got into the right position, it was natural for him to slide right in. When he entered her as far as he could and pushed against her cervix, she shuddered with her first orgasm.

Susan wasn't sure when it happened, but suddenly she remembered. She remembered who he was, where she was, and almost being killed four times in the last month. She urged Christoph inside her once again. She matched his speed and intensity. It was a wild, quick, and desperate coupling, unlike anything she'd ever experienced. But damn, it was fucking awesome. She liked this hot and heavy side of him, which seemingly had just one intent – to make her come.

Christoph knew she'd already had one orgasm; now he was going to make sure she had another. He reached down in between them and touched her clit with his fingers while he continued to move inside her. That's all it took. She exploded as soon as his fingers touched her. He could feel her moisture increasing; she was so slick. He felt his resistance wearing down, until after only three more strokes, he let himself go as well.

When she screamed out at the end, she screamed, "Christoph!"

Christoph was elated that she'd called his name. He had awakened her. He bent over her and started kissing her again.

Susan gently pushed on his chest, "Christoph, what? What is going on? What happened? My stomach hurts."

He was never so grateful in his life to hear those questions.

She looked at him, pleadingly. "I had this crazy dream. You told me you loved me and wanted us to be a family. Then

I dreamed we were making love, but I woke up and we were making love. I don't understand."

"You took one of the pills I left you?" he asked.

"Yes, I had a terrible headache, so I took two."

"TWO? Yes, well that explains it" he stated flatly. Trying to control his rage. What if she'd taken three, or even four, as humans often do with over-the-counter pain relievers for headaches? He shuddered to think of losing her. He grabbed her and held her tight to him.

Susan was squished against him. "What? What's wrong? Ouch, that's a little too tight, it's hard to breathe."

Christoph released her slightly so that she could lift her head up to look at him. "You are only supposed to take one. Two can cause you permanent memory loss, and three or more will likely kill you. The human system isn't able to handle it yet. We Argons only take up to two ourselves. It's my fault; I should have left you specific directions." He shuddered at his potentially devastating mistake.

"Is that why my stomach aches?" she asked.

"No, that's from the adrenaline shot I had to give you to wake you up," he explained. "I had to wake you from the nightmare, which, while you're on that drug, is a real event that happened, which you're reliving." He paused just long enough for her to process what he'd told her. "I had to wake you before you lost your memory from the time of the tragedy forward. We've found that is often how the brain deals with tragic events and great heartbreak."

Tenderly, he kissed her again, "I'm so sorry. It's my fault for not specifying how much to take. Can you ever forgive me?"

Susan was having trouble processing his apology. She was still thinking about the fact that whatever nightmare she'd been having was a dream of a real event. It made sense; she dreamed of Christoph and making love to him easily enough. It was an event that had happened. But the other, no. 'Did that happen to me?' she wondered.

Susan looked up at Christoph and pushed away from him so she could sit on her own. Immediately she wrapped her arms around herself, hugging herself as she looked him in the eye and said, "So… the nightmare… the one you said I was having when you came in? I remember it now," she said, as she adjusted herself to sit up straighter.

She looked at him, her face almost expressionless. In the most deadpan voice she said, "I do remember. It wasn't a dream." Susan stopped, not looking at him but at some place past him. She kept her arms around herself, "I re…re…mem…ber what happ…happ…ened…" she stuttered. Susan only stuttered when she felt highly agitated. She wasn't sure she could talk about it. She didn't want it to be real. Why did it have to happen to her? Why can't she just forget about it? She doesn't want to talk about it. It is over. O-V-E-R!

"As I explained, the main purpose of the drug is to release you from your traumas. I gave them to you to help with the bombings and the machine gun attack. Wasn't that what you were dreaming about?" he asked.

Tears welled up in her eyes as she looked at him. She couldn't control them, and she tried to talk, but she couldn't. She could only shake her head, "No," then the sobs started.

"Ah, darling, don't worry. It's in the past. What was it about? What can I do to help?" he pleaded. He moved forward to gently let her rest in his arms as he rubbed her shoulders and let her just cry. He didn't know what to do for emotional females.

Christoph is strangely a little thrilled at his quandary. She is making life interesting for him. She has feelings just like he does – although it seems now that the human female might have more than the Argon male.

It was a challenge for him to know that he needs to consider her feelings. She's probably scared. Scared it will happen again. His automatic defenses begin to get riled up as he holds her to him and rocks her back and forth while rubbing her back.

He didn't know what to do or say. He learned long ago with humans that when in doubt, silence is the best policy. After all, the sobs sounded as if they were slowing down.

"I.. uh... I..." she tried to say.

"Easy baby, take some deep breaths. It'll be okay. Just breathe. It's over, and I'll never let whatever it is happen to you again," he promised.

She took some deep breaths and the uncontrollable sobbing stopped. Her eyes were swollen by this time, but still leaking. She tried again, "I was on a boat. I had gone sailing."

"It's okay baby, that's good, keep going, but only if you want. You don't have to tell me," he reassured her.

"It was beautiful... the sail. I'd never been sailing on the ocean before. It was my first time." Susan stopped and watched a spot on the wall, clearly reliving the memories. "It was hot, and I remember I drank a lot of beer that day." She stopped. She was going over it in her mind. It had been over ten years ago. She had never remembered it until now, until this moment. "It was night, and I had another beer after eating. I got sleepy really fast and needed to lie down. I remember not wanting to lie down in the suffocating cabin, and I didn't want to be near him. So I lay down on the rope trampoline that connected the pontoon and the main part of the boat," she said.

He remained silent but continued to hold her and rub her back.

She sniffled and reached for a tissue next to the bed so she could blow her nose. When she was finished, she automatically went back to his arms where she knew she was safe. Her dream seemed like a movie that hadn't really happened to her. She felt numb now, and sounded like a robot as she told him what happened next.

"I was lying there trying to get comfortable, but the knots from the ropes were pressing into my back. I tried moving around, but somehow I couldn't manage it and gave up. I was so sleepy. Then he came down next to me and started touching me. I tried to stop him, but I couldn't move my arms. He started kissing me on the mouth, and I tried moving my head from side to side to tell him no, but he had my head pinned down and I couldn't move it. I couldn't speak. No matter how hard I tried, I couldn't move my arms. I felt him taking off my swimsuit by untying the strings. He kept touching me and I couldn't stop him. I couldn't move. Before I could think of what to do, he was inside me, completely having his way with me. He pressed me hard into the trampoline, and the ropes felt like they were cutting into my back. Just when I thought I couldn't take it anymore, he was done and he rolled off me. I closed my eyes and hoped it would go away. I woke up the next morning, naked, lying on the trampoline with the rope knots still digging into my back. My back felt raw from being pushed into them."

"I got up, found the pieces of my swimsuit, put them on and tried to pretend nothing had happened. I didn't want him to know I remembered. I only wanted to get away from him as quickly as possible. I thought the best way was to play nice until my opportunity presented itself. After all, I was trapped on a boat with him, in the ocean, next to an uninhabited island." She stopped talking, too stunned by what had come out of her mouth. Too shocked by her own self-realization that this hadn't been a mere nightmare all these years, but something that had actually happened to her. She'd been drugged and raped. It wasn't a violent rape, but she couldn't move, and it was rape nonetheless.

"Sweetheart, I promise that nothing like that will ever happen to you again," Christoph said fiercely. He was furious, and if he ever found out who the man was, he would murder him with his bare hands. No man should take a woman's choice away.

"No, it's okay, I know it won't ever happen again. I'll never let myself get into that position again. It was my fault. I should never have gone sailing with him alone. It was my fault. I was careless and stupid. It never occurred to me that anyone would drug me to have sex with me," she finished. She pulled away from him and shook her head. "I was so naive and trusting."

Her long-buried secret was the reason she hadn't trusted him when they first met. It was why she didn't trust any man.

He thought back and remembered how hard it had been for him to gain her trust and get her to open up to him. Night after night, he would spend time playing cards with her, trying to get her to be comfortable with him. He had looked for every opportunity: lunch, breaks, anything where he could be close to her.

He wanted her to feel his frequency and feel his energy so she would become used to it and crave it, the way he craved being with her. It had taken him a while, and now he felt the guilt coming on for kissing her and taking her to his bed after she'd had a few glasses of wine. But he didn't force her – he would never force her to do anything she didn't want.

Christoph couldn't feel guilty because he had manipulated their energies and frequencies to match more easily. Argons knew more about energy, and how all life forms, made of light, communicate with frequencies. These frequencies can stimulate all five senses, or only one or two senses, depending upon the life form. For example, a flower may emit its frequency on smell and sight.

For the Argons, manipulating frequencies was very similar to a human wooing another human – and the results are often the same. It was more difficult for humans to keep their frequencies because the emotional factors in each gender could cause them to mis-identify their respective mate. Christoph was confident that Susan was the mate for him. He needed to make sure she was unharmed.

"Susan, are you sure you're okay? I can call a counselor in if you want to talk to somebody..." he said, before she interrupted.

"No, please, I don't want anyone else to know how stupid I was," she pleaded. "I finally know it's not just a dream. I don't even feel anything about it anymore except shame and guilt for being so stupid."

"Darling, it wasn't your fault," he restated. "You have nothing to feel guilty or shameful about. Another being has no right to take your freedom of choice away from you," he said. But then he was thinking of what he needed to tell her.

'I am a damn hypocrite,' he thought to himself. Was he himself leaving her without a choice? It was the Argon law. He prompted it. 'I just took a chance; humans do it every time they ejaculate,' he reasoned to himself. He had no way of knowing she would get pregnant so soon, but the probability was high.

Was she going to be subjected to the same laws as the Argons? He couldn't take her choice away from her again. Not this way, and not so soon after she remembered this trauma. It would take time for her to move through the memories. Even though she said she was okay, she looked raw and exposed. Challenged though he was because she had so much emotion, he didn't want to push her into a corner. The fear she would feel might cause her harm. No, he had to give her a choice.

But it was time now for him to explain and confess: he had conceived with her, intentionally. It didn't change the fact that he wanted to bind her to him for life through the child she was carrying. Why else would she need to sleep so much these past days? Sure, he let her think she was dealing with the stress of the new information about his race, and also the stress of almost being killed, several times.

She needed to know, and he needed to tell her. With this new information, he was going to leave out some of the details, if he could, about his intention to impregnate her and the Argon law. Perhaps he could convince her to stay because they loved each other. He had to try.

"There's something I need to tell you. I think you should know," he started.

"Oh God, you sound so ominous. How bad could it be? I already know you're an alien. After remembering what happened to me all those years ago, and almost being killed multiple times, I think I can handle whatever it is," she said, as she pulled away enough to be able to look him in the face. She was starting to get apprehensive, he was so serious.

"You're pregnant," he said gently.

For a few moments, she couldn't comprehend what he was saying. She couldn't get pregnant – well, technically she could, but her partner had to take special prescription supplements for pregnancy to occur, and she didn't have a willing partner.

She turned and looked at Christoph with incredulous wonder in her eyes, and she laughed at him. She laughed hysterically at him for at least a minute; then she had to stop herself. He wasn't laughing. "Oh, I'm so sorry," she said, as she wiped the tears from her eyes, still giggling, trying to stop. "Please forgive me, but thank you for giving me something to laugh about."

Christoph just looked at her. She didn't believe him. Well, and why would she? "I know you don't believe me," he stated, matter-of-factly, "but you're pregnant."

"How?" she asked, sarcastically. "Look, it's not possible for me. I have a fertility problem and you would have to be taking a special drug, because my womb is too acidic for the sperm to survive." She stopped herself. Hadn't he said something about his species having more acidic body fluids? But no, it can't be. "If I can't get pregnant with an Earth human without the drug, I definitely can't with you!"

He just looked at her. He didn't say a word. Again, he didn't want to trample on her emotions, she was so confident. He had to find a way to gently let her realize that her confidence was misplaced. Lucky for him, he didn't have to wait long before she continued.

Her mind made note of all she'd slept and how hungry she'd been. With nervous anticipation, she asked him, "The only way is if... well... did you take adropophein? It's the only way. I have a special blood condition. I can't get pregnant unless my partner takes adropophein," she explained. She knew she'd already been taking the supplements she needed to take, because the fertility clinic was preparing her for her artificial insemination treatments.

He smiled into her eyes and answered, "Yes. Argonians take adropophein to make our bodily fluids more compatible with those of humans and not cause any problems with human acidic levels. Argonians' blood acidity levels are the only major difference between our races. Is this a problem?" he asked.

"No, it's just that... Oh My God... wait," she paused and started counting on her fingers. "Well, no, never mind, I'm only two days late, so it's not a big deal," she said. She felt the need to explain her situation, "Taking this drug supplement is the only way I can get pregnant. It's not a normal thing for a human to even know about unless he is part of a fertility treatment plan, actively pursuing pregnancy with a partner," she finished.

Christoph didn't reply. He allowed her to think and continue.

"Are you sure? I mean really? How in the world do you think you know, anyway?" she asked, still disbelieving his facts.

"After the attack on the island, we were examined to make sure we didn't have any island bug, or had been exposed to any chemical-warfare component the Grogans are notorious for. My physician team did a full analysis on us," he explained. He knew she was wondering how he knew her results.

"Wait, how did you know my results? Don't you Argemmions, or whatever, believe in patient confidentiality?" She was starting to get pissed off. She stopped for a minute. She's pregnant. But how dare he intrude on her personal medical records? Not that she wouldn't willingly tell him; all he'd have to do was ask. Presuming was what made her mad.

"Argonians," he stated flatly before continuing. "In my society, we don't have any patient confidentiality between partners. You're considered my partner," he briefly explained.

"Your partner?" she queried. "I don't understand. We're not married. How can I be your partner? I've barely known you for two weeks now, although it does feel like years," she conceded.

"In Argon we don't have the same concept of marriage that humans do. We have partners, and then we, hopefully, have mates. Our mates are for life. We will be considered mates once you give birth to our child," he gently explained.

She looked at him in amazement. She wasn't sure she was comprehending this. He wanted to be with her forever. He wanted to be her mate – or was this an accident? "Does that mean you want to be with me and you want to be with me forever, or was this an accident?"

It was time. She had asked, and he couldn't avoid telling her the truth any longer. He had to confess to her. "It was no accident. I want you. I've told you that I love you," he said, as he leaned over and kissed her again.

Her brain was screaming at her. She should have gotten out when he was spewing all that mumbo jumbo about her being his. 'Oh my God,' she thought. She thought he was just saying romantic B.S.; it's what all hookups do. Weave a little fantasy for one night, but leave before morning and it's like it was never said. It was just pretend. But he doesn't sound like he's pretending.

"Ever since I met you, I wanted to act and be like a human with you," he started explaining. "I wanted to treat you in a way you were familiar with. I wanted to charm you, and get to know you more. The more I got to know, the more I wanted. My instinct for protecting you grew until I realized, on that first day, that I wanted you as my mate."

"You knew even then? Before we ever went to the island?" she asked in wonder.

"Yes, even then," he confirmed. "I assumed all the human customs, the dinner, the escorts, the card games. Lunches and all the things that one should enjoy with another on a daily basis without talk of aliens or the danger the world is in right now." He paused, knowing what he had to tell her next, and not sure how to say it.

"I studied all the dating guides and social materials we have on humans over the years. My goal of having you as a mate is the main difference from what your society is today," he explained.

"I even assumed the unspoken rule of consensual sex between humans… if nobody talks about pregnancy prevention, then they are generally willing to take their chances, knowing it might result in a pregnancy," he tried to explain. He was worried it didn't sound right. He wasn't sure how else to explain it.

"But I thought I was *safe* from pregnancy!" she yelled at him. "It's as if I was taking the birth control pill or using some other contraceptive. I was in control, and I *knew* I could not get pregnant," she started defending herself. It was okay for him to be accepting of it. It seemed as if he was willing all along. What bothered her is that her control was taken away from her, and neither of them knew it. She couldn't blame him. He didn't know about her condition.

Christoph felt he needed to tell her the whole story now. "My race… we have the ability to know and control when we release reproductive sperm. It gives us the opportunity to choose – and I chose you." He paused before touching her face and telling her, "I love you, Susan. You are amazing, and I'm drawn to you like no other. I want you in my life forever."

At first, the excitement coursed rapidly through her because as a girl, this was what fairytales were made of. Except, '*WAIT*,' her subconscious insisted. 'Just take a minute here.' Had he even given her a choice in the matter? What if she didn't like him? What if he was awful to her? She didn't know if she wanted to have children with him – and definitely not without talking about it first. 'What the fuck?' She started getting pissed off, seriously pissed. "You asshole!" she yelled, before she slapped him across the face and pushed away from him. She walked into the living room and began pacing back and forth.

He was silent as he watched her, glorious and magnificent in her nakedness. Again, his lack of experience with female emotions showed as he hoped his silence would give him clues as to what to do and say next. Clearly, the truth wasn't doing him much good. He didn't want to interrupt her thoughts, but he had to think of a way to get his feelings across to her. He'd simply taken a calculated risk. Humans do it all the time, he thought. He had no idea her situation was different. 'Is that any excuse?' he asked himself.

"Such arrogance!" she spat at him vehemently. "You think you can just take what you want without consent." 'Sure, I had sex with him,' she said to herself, 'but I took precautions – well, the precaution that I knew I couldn't get pregnant! There was no way unless my partner was taking adropophein. Shit, shit, shit!' she thought, and stamped her foot.

Adropophein is a well-known fertility drug supplement, *only* used in fertility treatments, at least on Earth by the humans. But how do you think the humans learned about it in the first place? Her pregnancy risk was zero unless, just her luck, her partner was a damn alien and takes it to regulate the acidity level of his bodily fluids so as not kill a human!!!

'Oh. My. Fucking. God! Do I even hear myself?' She is shaking her head, 'Alien. That can *not* be an excuse,' she thought, 'No, he still took my choice. How was I to know there was even an option of being intimate with an alien? How can I be responsible for not knowing that I don't know what I don't know?'

'MOTHER-FUCK-ER!!!' she screamed, inside her head.

Susan's mind started replaying their entire relationship.... Here was the most handsome man she'd ever seen or ever kissed, and he wanted to be with her. More than anything, enjoying his friendship, laughing with him over games, simply watching the island sunsets; they had a connection and they understood each other. At least she thought they had. He said he loved her. He said he wanted to be with her forever. He was painting a fairytale picture. She thought it was just the hookup game.

Fucking asshole, just like human men! She had to get away from him. How could he have done this to her? She had trusted him.

He purposely tried to get her pregnant because he "chose her as his mate." He didn't even ask her? She was outraged. How could he even compare it to regular human sex? Regular humans don't take adropophein. How could she hold him responsible for that? Besides, it's not that she would have said no, exactly, but that's when she thought he was human. She couldn't kid herself – HE IS AN ALIEN!

Again, she was stunned at her quandary. He loved her. He's a fucking asshole for taking away her choice. Suddenly, the reality of the situation hit her. 'Oh! My! God! I'm pregnant with an alien's child!!!' And for the second time in her life, she fainted.

Heather Harlow

Heather graduated from University of Memphis (BBA) and Tennessee Technological University (MBA). She currently resides in Atlanta, Georgia with Mickey, her Golden Retriever, and two cats, Smokey and Cali. Visit her website at:

www.TheRealHeatherHarlow.com